CONTENTS

ELIZABETH LANE

'This tender and loving story, spinning off
from Lane's previous Western, showcases her talent
for drawing three-dimensional characters
and placing them in an exciting time and place.'
—*RT Book Reviews* on HIS SUBSTITUTE BRIDE

'Lane uses her turn-of-the-century backdrop
and her knowledge of aviation to her advantage
in a lively story featuring strong-willed characters.'
—*RT Book Reviews* on ON THE WINGS OF LOVE

KATE WELSH

'Welsh writes of a time in history
that's rarely featured in romance novels—
the beginnings of unionisation in the coalmines of
the United States. The plot is compelling, with
several subplots that add complexity to the story.'
—*RT Book Reviews* on QUESTIONS OF HONOUR

'A mistaken identity and a deathbed promise
throw two strangers into marriage and mayhem.
Welsh's latest is a heartwarming novel
about greed, revenge, love and desire.'
—*RT Book Reviews* on
HIS CALIFORNIAN COUNTESS

LISA PLUMLEY

'There's plenty of gun-slinging, bloodshed and
lovemaking going on from start to finish, which will
keep readers turning pages until the very end.'
—*RT Book Reviews* on MAIL-ORDER GROOM

'How does one spell romance? P-L-U-M-L-E-Y.
Readers are in for a treat with her latest tale, a funny,
lively and often outrageous battle of wills that will
keep readers riveted until the last page.'
—*RT Book Reviews* on THE SCOUNDREL

Elizabeth Lane has lived and travelled in many parts of the world, including Europe, Latin America and the Far East, but her heart remains in the American West, where she was born and raised. Her idea of heaven is hiking a mountain trail on a clear autumn day. She also enjoys music, animals and dancing. You can learn more about Elizabeth by visiting her website at www.elizabethlaneauthor.com

As a child, **Kate Welsh** often lost herself in creating make-believe worlds and happily-ever-after tales. Many years later she turned back to creating happy endings when her husband challenged her to write down the stories in her head. A lover of all things romantic, Kate has been writing romance for over twenty years now. Kate loves hearing from readers, who can reach her on the internet at kate_welsh@verizon.net

When she's not writing, **Lisa Plumley** loves to spend time with her husband and two children, travelling, hiking, watching classic movies, reading and defending her trivia-game championship. She enjoys hearing from readers, and invites you to contact her via e-mail at lisa@lisaplumley.com, or visit her website at www.lisaplumley.com

WEDDINGS UNDER A WESTERN SKY

BY

ELIZABETH LANE
KATE WELSH
LISA PLUMLEY

First published in Great Britain 2012
by Mills & Boon, an imprint of Harlequin (UK) Limited.
Large Print edition 2013
Harlequin (UK) Limited, Eton House,
18-24 Paradise Road, Richmond, Surrey TW9 1SR

© Harlequin Books S.A. 2012

ISBN: 978 0 263 23838 9

The publisher acknowledges the copyright holders of the individual works as follows:

THE HAND-ME-DOWN BRIDE © Elizabeth Lane 2012
THE BRIDE WORE BRITCHES © Kate Welsh 2012
SOMETHING BORROWED, SOMETHING TRUE
  © Lisa G. Plumley 2012

Harlequin (UK) policy is to use papers that are natural, renewable and recyclable products and made from wood grown in sustainable forests. The logging and manufacturing process conform to the legal environmental regulations of the country of origin.

Printed and bound in Great Britain
by CPI Antony Rowe, Chippenham, Wiltshire

THE HAND-ME-DOWN BRIDE

Elizabeth Lane

To the Fillies

Chapter One

Buffalo Bend, Montana
April 29, 1876

Arabella Spencer huddled under the dripping eave of Brophy's Feed and Mercantile where the stage had let her off with her trunk. Rain had churned the deserted street into a quagmire of mud and manure. The muck had ruined her new kidskin shoes and wasn't doing much for her disposition. After more than twenty minutes of waiting, she was wet, worried and getting madder by the second.

Charles, her fiancé, had certainly known she was coming. He'd mailed her the tickets three months ago, with a promise to meet the stage and drive her to his new ranch. Only the thought of their wedding, and the fine home he'd refurbished especially for her, had sustained her on the grueling journey by train and stagecoach, all the way from Boston to Buffalo Bend. Now she was here at last, bruised, chilled and bone-weary, with Grandma Peabody's wedding dress packed into her trunk.

The bride had arrived. So where was her groom?

True, the stage had been delayed two hours by a broken wheel. But that was no excuse for Charles not to be here—especially given that she had no place to get out of the rain. Brophy's Feed and Mercantile, which appeared to be the only store in this ramshackle excuse for a town, had long since closed for the night. There wasn't a hotel in sight, or even a restaurant; and the church at the street's far end looked as dark as a tomb.

Only the saloon across the street showed any sign of life. Lamplight filtered through gray sheets of rain. Occasional bursts of laughter and the wheeze of a concertina drifted over the drone of the storm.

Arabella shivered beneath her damp woolen traveling cloak. The thought of shelter was tempting. But she'd have to leave her precious trunk behind and wade through ankle-deep mud to cross the street. In any case, well-bred young ladies simply did not venture into saloons—not even in a deluge fit to float Noah's ark.

A flicker of movement across the street caught her eye. Someone had just come out of the saloon. Was it Charles? Had he been waiting for her in that disreputable place?

But the man who stepped into the street was

too tall and too broad-shouldered to be her fiancé. Charles was of average stature. The figure striding toward her, wearing a bulky sheepskin coat, loomed like a giant against the roiling sky.

Arabella shrank into the doorway. If the man meant her harm, she'd have no place to run. But she could kick and bite and scream for all she was worth. If it came to that, she vowed, she wouldn't go down without a fight.

He stopped a pace away from her. Close up, he wasn't as huge as she'd first thought. But he was big enough—six foot four, by her reckoning. His face was obscured by rain streaming off the broad brim of his hat.

"Miss Arabella Spencer?" His voice was like the rumble of an iron wheel over a graveled road. "I was told to look for a redhead, so I'm guessing you're the one."

Staring up at him, she nodded.

"McIntyre's the name. I've come to fetch you to the ranch. Wait here, and I'll bring the buckboard around."

He thrust something toward her. Realizing it was an oilskin, Arabella seized it eagerly and wrapped it over her damp cloak. Before she could utter a proper thank-you, the man had melted into the rain.

Moments later he reappeared from behind the store, driving an open rig behind a team of sturdy bays. The back was filled with some kind of bulky cargo covered by a canvas tarpaulin. There was one bench seat in front, with nothing to shelter its occupants from the rain.

For heaven's sake, if Charles couldn't come himself, why couldn't he at least have sent a covered buggy?

McIntyre halted the horses, climbed to the ground and came around the rig—a buckboard, he'd called it, though it was more like a wagon, drawn by two horses instead of one. Hefting Arabella's trunk as if it weighed nothing, he slid it under the canvas in back.

"Where's my fiancé, Charles Middleton?" Arabella demanded. "Is he all right?"

"Far as I know, he's fine." McIntyre's big hands caught her waist and boosted her onto the bench as if she were no bigger than a child.

"Then why didn't he come to meet me?"

"Spring's a busy time for ranchers. I had to drive to town for feed and salt, so he asked me to pick you up." He climbed onto the bench beside her. "It's a long ride. Too bad I hadn't counted on the rain, or on the stage being late."

As if that had been *her* fault! "Well, at least you got to spend a couple of hours in the saloon," she sniffed.

"Uh-huh. Had a drink and won fifty dollars in a

game of five-card stud." His hands flicked the reins. The wagon plowed forward through the sticky mud.

Struck by a sudden realization, she stared at him. "Wait—you were in the saloon when the stage arrived. You must've heard it stop, and you knew I'd be getting off. Why on earth did you leave me standing outside in the rain?"

He shrugged. "I was holding a royal flush."

"Of all the oafish, inconsiderate—" Arabella squelched the rest of her tirade. McIntyre didn't strike her as any kind of gentleman. If a woman got on his nerves, there was no telling what he might do. She could find herself standing alone in the mud.

She resolved to hold her tongue for now. But she planned to have a word with Charles about McIntyre's behavior. Such insolence! The man should be dismissed from service at once.

They left the town behind. There appeared to be a road of sorts, but it was even rougher than the stage route from Laramie which, after five days of constant jouncing, had left her black-and-blue. The wagon swayed and groaned, its wheels lurching over rocks and sagging through puddles of mud. Rain poured down in a steady deluge. Peering out from under the oilskin, Arabella could see clumps of sagebrush on either side, but whatever lay beyond that was obscured by darkness.

At least the horses seemed to know where they

were going. They plodded along at a calm pace, ignoring the rain that sheeted down their sides. McIntyre sat hunched over the reins, water drizzling off his hat and streaming down his sheepskin coat. His very silence was an affront, as if he didn't consider her worth the bother of polite conversation. Clearly, for whatever reason, the man didn't like her.

At least she could try to discover why.

"How long have you been working for Charles?" she asked.

"I don't." He didn't bother to look at her.

"You don't work for him?"

"No."

So much for asking Charles to fire the man. "You're a friend of his, then?"

McIntyre didn't reply.

"A neighbor?"

"You could say that."

"Then you'll be my neighbor, too! I suppose Charles told you we were going to be married."

Did McIntyre flinch beneath his coat? Maybe she'd just imagined it, Arabella thought as she waited for the response that never came. Where were his manners?

"Did you hear me?" she demanded. "I said Charles and I were going to be—"

"I heard you." His voice was a growl. What was eating at the man? Arabella was tempted to give him a lecture in courtesy. But that, she sensed, would be a waste of breath.

She'd done her best to make pleasant conversation. But if her driver wanted to be rude, she wouldn't trouble him further. Instead she would pass the time as she had on the train and inside the dusty, rattling stagecoach—thinking about Charles, their wedding and their future.

She had known Charles Middleton all her life. They'd grown up next door to each other in Boston. Everyone who knew them had assumed they'd marry one day. When Charles's aging father had died last year, his older brother, Frank, had inherited the family estate and ship-building business. Charles had used his own generous inheritance to buy a Montana cattle ranch complete with a two-story house, corrals and outbuildings, and a herd of five thousand cattle.

"I'll send for you next spring, dearest," he'd promised her at the railway station. "While we're apart I'll have a crew remodeling the house into a home to make you proud—a home where we can raise our children and live happily for the rest of our days."

Charles wasn't the most reliable of men—his enthusiasm often overran his better instincts. But in this case, he had kept his word. After the tickets arrived, Arabella had passed the long winter days sewing her trousseau and planning her wedding. She wasn't sure what life would be like on a Montana ranch. But as long as Charles was there, she knew she'd be happy.

She imagined standing before the preacher, wearing Grandma Peabody's wedding dress and gazing up into Charles's tender blue eyes as she spoke her vows. *I, Arabella, take thee, Charles—*

"Damnation!" McIntyre's curse shattered her reverie. The wagon had halted, the way broken by a four-foot drop-off above a flowing torrent of muddy water.

McIntyre purpled the air with half-mouthed curses. "Damn, blasted bridge is washed out. If we can't ford the creek we'll be stuck here waiting." Turning, he thrust the reins into Arabella's hands. "Can you handle a team?"

"I've driven a chaise."

"That'll have to do. Hold the horses steady till I get back." He vaulted to the ground and strode off into the storm.

Arabella peered through the murk. Fear uncoiled in her stomach and crawled up into her throat. McIntyre was probably looking for a shallow place to cross. But the water looked fast and deep, and so wide she couldn't see the far side of it. What if he lost his footing and was swept away? What would she do out here alone if he didn't come back?

Minutes crawled past. The horses danced and snorted. She gripped the reins hard, praying the skittish beasts wouldn't bolt. She didn't want to die out here in the cold, dark rain. She wanted to make it to the ranch, marry Charles and spend happy years raising his children.

The sound of the water was a dull roar. Was it deep enough to drown a man? Panic ran an icy finger up her spine. "McIntyre!" Her shout was lost in the storm. "Where are you?"

"Right here." He appeared on the far side of the wagon, tossed the branch he was holding into the back and climbed onto the seat. His trousers and boots were coated with mud.

"Did you find a way across?" she asked.

"Nothing sure. The smart thing would be to wait here till morning. We'll have daylight then, and the water should be down."

"Oh, no!" Arabella responded with a horrified gasp. "We can't possibly do that! Think of my reputation! Think how Charles will worry! We simply must go on!"

McIntyre exhaled raggedly, shaking his head. "I had a feeling you'd say that. There's a place upstream that might do for a ford. But if you get a soaking, don't say I didn't warn you."

"I'm soaked now!" she huffed.

Without another word he took the reins, backed up and swung the team to the left. The wagon lurched over rocks and crashed through clumps of sagebrush, stopping fifty yards upstream at the crest of a sandy incline that sloped down to the swollen creek.

McIntyre studied the roiling current. "We'd still be better off waiting for daylight. I know what you're thinking, but this is Montana, not Boston. Nobody here's going to give a damn about your precious reputation. As for your virtue…" His eyes flickered toward her, and when he spoke again his voice was dry and cold. "Lady, you've got nothing to worry about there."

Arabella's chin went up. "Believe me, if you did give me any cause for concern, my fiancé would have you shot."

Something between a snarl and a curse rumbled in his throat. "What the hell," he snapped, "let's go."

His big hands urged the horses down the bank. Stopping them at the water's edge, he handed her the reins. "I'll be going ahead to test the bottom and lead the team," he said. "All you'll need to do is hold on and keep them from moving too fast. All right?"

Arabella nodded, feeling a vague chill of fear. The water looked swift and deep. Maybe she should tell McIntyre she'd changed her mind. But the idea of admitting he was right stuck in her craw. And the thought of Charles, waiting with open arms, sealed her resolve. She held her tongue as he stripped off his coat, lifted the branch from the bed of the wagon and swung to the ground.

Without a backward glance, he walked to the head of the team and placed himself between the two husky bays. Even next to his horses, McIntyre looked powerful. He glanced from one animal to the other, as if reassuring them. Then with a voiced command Arabella could barely hear, he urged them into the flooded creek.

Knee-deep, then hip-deep, he eased forward. One hand held the branch, which he used to probe the depth of the creek bed in front of him. The other hand controlled the horses, moving from one to the other. Arabella gripped the reins as the wagon swayed into the current. McIntyre was trusting her with his life, she realized. If she let the horses bolt they could drag him under and trample or drown him.

The water was over the wheel hubs, but the spring-mounted bed of the buckboard wagon remained dry. Arabella thought of Grandma Peabody's silk wedding dress. She had wrapped the precious garment in oilcloth, but little good that would do if the trunk slipped into the creek and washed away. She willed herself to focus on holding the horses. They were making slow but steady progress. Now, through the rainy darkness, she could make out a stand of willows on the far side. They were almost there.

"Whoa!" McIntyre's shout rang out above the rush of the current. Arabella jerked back on the reins, but not fast enough. As the wheels rolled forward, the rig sagged toward the right front corner and groaned to a halt.

McIntyre was cursing. "Damned hole. We're stuck."

"Can we get loose?"

"Not likely. All we can do is try. Hold the horses steady." He left his place at the head of the team and made his way around to the sagging side of the wagon. Taking the branch he'd used to test the creek bottom, he wedged it behind the stuck wheel. Keeping the reins taut, Arabella watched him.

"As long as you're using a lever, it would help to have a fulcrum," she said.

He glared up at her with murder in his eyes. "It would help to have a lot of things. But right now I'm up to my ass in muddy water and it's all I can do to push on this damned wheel. So I'll thank you to just keep your pretty mouth shut and do what I tell you. All right?"

"All right," Arabella snapped. She'd only meant to help. But clearly McIntyre wasn't the sort to take advice from a mere woman.

"When I push, you ease the team forward. But not too hard, mind you, or the wheel will break and spill everything overboard, including you. Understand?"

"Go ahead. I'm ready." She gripped the reins, pretending they were wrapped around his neck.

He braced against the limb, water rippling around

his lean hips. "Now!" he grunted, pushing with his full weight.

Arabella flicked the reins, keeping them tight. The horses leaned forward in their traces, their massive shoulders bulging. The wagon creaked fearfully with the strain but the wheels didn't move.

"Whoa!" McIntyre straightened, breathing hard. "Give me a minute, and we'll try it again."

Arabella risked a furtive look past her shoulder. He was soaked with muddy water, his denim work shirt clinging to his muscular frame. His hat was gone, his hair wet and flat against his head. His craggy features looked as if they'd been chiseled from living rock.

McIntyre could never be called handsome. The raw, masculine aura that hung about him was more frightening than appealing. He was like an untamed beast. Yes, that was the word for him. Untamed.

He took a deep breath. "Ready?"

"Ready." As he shoved his weight against the branch, she coaxed the team forward. The wagon strained and quivered like a living thing. Just when she thought it might shift free, Arabella heard a snap and a curse. She stopped the horses. McIntyre was standing next to the mired wheel, the broken branch in his hand.

"That's it," he growled. "This damned rig's not going anywhere till morning."

Her heart sank. "You mean we're just going to sit here all night in the middle of the creek?"

He tossed the broken branch into the flood. "Horses can't stand in the water that long. I'll have to unhitch them and lead them to the bank. We can ride the team the rest of the way home. At first light I'll come back with some men and haul the rig out."

"Fine. But I can't leave my trunk."

"Your blasted trunk weighs sixty pounds. I'll get it tomorrow and drop it off for you."

"My grandmother's wedding dress is in that trunk. I'm not leaving without it."

His eyes narrowed to wolfish slits. "Fine, woman. I'll take the horses home and you can sit here all night with your trunk. If any Blackfeet come by you can pour them a cup of tea!"

"Blackfeet?" Arabella's heart lurched into her throat. "You mean *Indians*?"

"They've been known to wander this way. Most likely they'd have enough sense to stay home on a night like this, but you never know…" Letting the words hang, he sloshed forward through the water and began unbuckling the first horse from the traces.

Without a second glance at Arabella, he led the horse to the far bank, tied it in the willows and started back. The current was strong enough to carry a man away. Without support, it was all McIntyre could do to keep his footing. Watching him struggle,

Arabella knew she'd never make it to shore without his help.

Would he really leave her? She wouldn't put it past him. McIntyre was, without doubt, the most exasperating man she'd ever met. But he was right about one thing—there was no way to get her heavy trunk ashore or carry it on a horse. For now, it would have to stay on the wagon. The only question was whether or not she would stay with it.

What if the flood rose and swept the trunk into the water; or what if someone came by and took it? She couldn't imagine what an Indian would do with Grandma Peabody's wedding gown, but the thought did give her a sudden idea.

Looping the reins over the seat, she scrambled into the back of the wagon, found the trunk under the canvas and opened it with the key she wore on a ribbon around her neck. Rummaging through the tightly packed layers of clothing, she lifted out the precious bundle—the one thing in the trunk that couldn't be replaced.

"Change your mind?" McIntyre had made it back to the wagon and had started unbuckling the second horse.

"You knew I would! Indians, indeed! Why not man-eating tigers?" Arabella locked the trunk and shoved it back under the sheltering canvas. "My grandmother's wedding dress is coming with me. Rain or shine, I mean to be married in it!"

She'd expected a sharp retort, but McIntyre had turned away. He didn't look up until she'd returned to the front of the wagon. "I'll have to carry you to the horse." He moved to stand below her. "Let's go."

Arabella stood on the edge of the wagon, clutching her precious bundle. Seized by hesitation, she stared down at the rushing water.

"Stop wasting time. I'll catch you. Trust me."

Trust was the last thing Arabella felt. Few things, she suspected, would give the man more pleasure than dropping her in the creek. But she had little choice. Gulping back her fear, she leaned over the water and willed herself to let go.

He caught her handily, one arm supporting her back, the other cradling her legs. Through his wet clothes, his chest was as solid as a granite wall. She could feel the strong, steady pulsing of his heart.

Gazing up at his face she noticed, for the first time, a slashing white scar running from his cheekbone to the corner of his mouth. Had he been in the war—or maybe fought Indians? He was an intriguing man, and she couldn't deny the curiosity she felt. But something told her he wouldn't welcome personal questions.

McIntyre held her as if she were covered in poison ivy. Arabella could sense the resistance in him. He strode toward the horse, pushing through the current as if he couldn't wait to get rid of her. Clearly she made him uncomfortable. But why? What had she ever done to him? Maybe he had something against women—or against redheads.

The second horse was still harnessed to the wagon. Clutching the bundled wedding dress, Arabella clambered from McIntyre's arms onto its back. She'd never ridden astride, but this was no time to be fussy. Rucking her skirts above her knees, she straddled the slippery barrel of its body. Her free hand kept a death grip on the harness. All she wanted was to be on solid ground again.

"Hang on." McIntyre climbed back into the wagon. He found his sheepskin coat, rolled it tightly and slung it over his shoulder. Then he reached under the bench and lifted a rifle from its hiding place. Maybe he hadn't been fooling about Indians after all.

He was still in the wagon when it happened. A twisted piece of broken limb came washing down the flooded creek. The limb wasn't large enough to do much damage, but it was headed straight toward the horse.

The nervous animal screamed and bucked. Grabbing the harness with both hands, Arabella managed to stay mounted, but her precious bundle flew out of her grasp and into the fast-flowing water.

"No!" Ignoring safety and common sense, she

flung herself off the horse and into the flood after it. Here at the ford, the water wasn't much higher than her waist, but the current was rough and shockingly cold. A dozen yards ahead she could see the yellow oilcloth bundle, bobbing along the stream.

McIntyre was shouting at her, probably swearing a blue streak. Ignoring him, she plunged after her treasure. Not far ahead, a dead alder had washed free of the bank and fallen across the stream. The current had formed an eddy there. She caught glimpses of the bundle as it swirled round and round. Could she reach it before the eddy pulled it under?

She pushed ahead. The water was deeper here, almost up to her armpits. Arabella was no swimmer, but as long as her feet could touch bottom she felt safe enough; and she had almost reached the eddy. The bundle was circling toward her now. She lunged for it. Her fingers touched the slippery oilcloth. Another lunge and she had it. She clasped it close to her chest.

Only then did she realize her feet could no longer feel bottom. She'd been swept into the eddy's powerful current. It was pulling her down. She groped for the fallen tree with her free hand. The twig she managed to catch snapped off in her fingers.

"Help!" she shouted, but her cry was lost in the muddy water that filled her mouth and blinded her eyes. Her feet thrashed helplessly. She was drowning. This was the end.

Strong arms jerked her out of the current. Her head broke water. She gulped life-giving air.

McIntyre's arm was hooked around her waist. He didn't speak, but she could feel the anger in his taut body as he dragged her back upstream, toward the bank. Incredibly her grandmother's wedding dress was still clasped tightly under her arm. She had saved it after all.

He hauled her ashore and dropped her, none too gently, on the wet grass. From under his dark brows, his deep-set eyes blazed lightning fury. "Not a word, woman!" he snapped. "Not till I get you to where you're going!" He swung back toward the creek where the second horse waited, still harnessed to the wagon. At the water's edge he paused and turned. His expression made Arabella shrivel.

"Damn that wedding dress!" he growled. "I should've let you drown for it!"

By the time they were underway again, the rain had let up. Wrapped in her dripping cloak, Arabella clung to the harness in shivering silence. The horse's broad frame stretched her thighs and chafed her legs to the point of misery. She'd be doing well to get out of bed tomorrow.

McIntyre rode beside her. He'd lost his coat in the

plunge to rescue her, but he'd saved the rifle. It lay across his knees, ready if needed. For all Arabella knew, he was thinking of shooting her with it.

She couldn't blame the man for being annoyed. If not for her, he could've left town ahead of the storm and crossed the creek before the bridge washed out. If she hadn't insisted on fording the creek, the wagon wouldn't have become stuck, and she wouldn't have risked drowning to save her grandmother's wedding dress.

Any man short of sainthood would have been angry. But McIntyre's resentment appeared to go deeper. It was almost as if he'd hated her on sight.

Could he have something against Charles? But if that were so, why had he agreed to pick her up in town?

Never mind the questions, Arabella told herself. When she was safe with Charles, the answers would be made clear enough. She could wait that long.

The moon had come out, painting the rain-washed prairie with silver. It was eerily beautiful. But the most beautiful sight of all was the distant barn, surrounded by sheds and corrals and, on a little knoll, a two-level white frame house with a broad porch, commanding a view of the countryside.

Her heart skipped as they rode closer. She clutched the bundled wedding gown against her chest. The place was just as Charles had described it in his letters. At last she was home.

The hour was late, but lamps lit the porch and the curtained front window. McIntyre stopped the horses at the gate, where a walkway led up to the front steps. Dismounting, he came around to help Arabella to the ground. She was so chilled and sore she could barely stand, but he made no move to assist her the rest of the way to the house.

She did owe him, at least, a token of politeness. "You're welcome to come in," she said. "There's bound to be something to eat, and I'm sure Charles will want to thank you for bringing me home."

He stepped back. For a moment his gaze held hers. In his shadowed eyes she glimpsed impatience, frustration and something else—something unreadable. With a shake of his head, he turned back to the horses, mounted and rode off into the night.

"Arabella!" The front door had opened. Charles stood in the rectangle of light that spilled onto the porch. He hurried down the walk. Numb-footed she stumbled toward him and fell into his arms. For a moment he held her close, then shifted her away, so he could look at her.

"My word, Arabella, what happened?" he gasped. "We were worried about you."

"It's a very long story. Get me warm and I'll tell you." She leaned on him going up the walk. It struck her as odd that he hadn't kissed her, but she could hardly blame him. She must look a fright.

Another figure had appeared in the doorway. Half silhouetted by the lamplight was a tall young woman wearing a man's robe over her nightgown. As she stepped out onto the porch, the light revealed a fresh, pretty face and flaxen braids that hung over her ample breasts.

How thoughtful of Charles, Arabella thought, to hire a female near her own age to be her maid and companion. She mustn't forget to thank him.

Charles paused for a moment, nervously licking his lips. "I sent you a letter," he said. "But I couldn't be sure it would arrive in time to keep you in Boston. That's why I asked McIntyre to wait till the stage showed up."

She stared up at him. "A letter? To *keep* me in Boston after you sent me the stage ticket to come here? Why, Charles, what on earth are you talking about?"

The young blonde woman had come down the steps to stand beside him. She smiled timidly. Charles cleared his throat. "Arabella, dearest," he said, "this is Sally—my wife."

Chapter Two

It was as if the earth had turned to quicksand under Arabella's feet. She stared at the woman who'd stolen her rightful future—her husband, her unborn children and her home. Her eyes took in the sweetly wholesome face, the flaxen hair and the figure that tapered from voluptuous bosom to...

Oh, merciful heaven...

Sally's robe was tied several inches above her waist. Below the knot, the bulge of her pregnant belly was slight but unmistakable.

It was too much. Chilled, exhausted and shocked beyond her capacity to cope, Arabella felt her world crumbling like a plaster wall in an earthquake. She wanted to run back outside, track down McIntyre and demand that he take her...somewhere. Anywhere but here. And yet when she tried to turn away, her legs refused to cooperate. Sally's face blurred before her eyes. Charles's hands reached out to steady her as she reeled. Then her legs buckled beneath her, and everything went black.

McIntyre stabled the horses, fed them some hay and toweled their wet coats before leaving the barn and stumbling up the steps of his rambling log and stone house. He felt like the raw edge of hell; but he'd be lucky to get much sleep before dawn, when he'd have to round up some help and go after the mired buckboard.

Blast the woman! Why couldn't she have gotten Charlie Middleton's damned letter and stayed in Boston where she belonged? He'd known how things stood when he'd picked her up in town. But it hadn't been his place to tell her. That, as he'd made clear, was Middleton's job.

He'd been hard on her, letting her wait in the rain, then telling her that story about the royal flush. When the stage pulled in, he'd been settling a quarrel between two friends. He could've dropped everything and rushed outside. But his friends had needed him. And given what he knew, he'd been none too eager to face Charlie Middleton's jilted fiancée.

By now Arabella would have learned the truth about the man she'd loved and trusted. McIntyre could imagine how she'd take the news after coming all this way. It might have been kinder to tell her in town. But then what? She'd have been stuck in the rain in Buffalo Bend with no place to stay and no easy way to leave. For all he knew, she might've tried to jump out of the wagon and drown herself.

Hellfire, she'd nearly done just that, going after her damnfool wedding dress in the flood. The woman was a willful brat. Middleton would have an easier life with sweet, patient Sally. But McIntyre couldn't help admiring the little redhead's spunk. Even half drowned and spitting fury, he had to concede she was uncommonly pretty.

That made him even more eager to see her leave. Charles had been reluctant enough to do his duty by Sally. Throwing the woman he'd *wanted* to marry into the mix wouldn't do the newlyweds any favors as they settled into married life. And the last thing McIntyre wanted was to see Sally hurt again.

Yes, it would be better for all of them if Arabella Spencer left—and left soon. If he never saw the little snip again, it would suit him just fine.

A glance at the clock next to the massive stone fireplace told him it was nearly 3:00 a.m. Since he would need to rescue the buckboard at first light or risk losing the cargo to thieves, it was scarcely worth going to bed. But he was chilled to the bone, and the old hip wound, a souvenir of Gettysburg, was throbbing. Even a couple of hours of sleep would be better than nothing.

Dragging himself into the bedroom, he peeled off

his wet clothes and left them in a heap on the rug. Naked and shivering, he crawled between the worn flannel sheets and closed his eyes. Morning would be here all too soon.

Arabella stirred and woke. A streak of sunlight, falling between the drawn drapes, stabbed her eyes. She turned over with a moan. Her sleep-blurred eyes glimpsed yellow flowered wallpaper, a quilted coverlet and a tall mahogany bedpost. Where was she, and how did she get here?

She stretched cautiously, wincing in pain. Her body felt as if every muscle had been pounded like a slab of beef. And last night she'd had the most horrible dream about Charles…

"Arabella?"

The voice jarred her to full awareness. She raised her head to see Charles standing in the doorway, dressed in a white shirt and a leather vest. His once-pale skin had acquired a healthy tan, but the gentle blue eyes and light brown curls were just as she'd remembered. Talons of pain clenched around her heart.

"Last night wasn't a dream, was it?" she whispered.

He shook his head. "Arabella, dearest—"

"How could you?" Jerking upright in the bed, she

flung the words at him. "How could you do this to me? To *us*?"

"I wrote you a letter."

"*You wrote me a letter!* A letter I never received! Is that all you've got to say for yourself?"

He sighed. "I suppose I do owe you an explanation. May I sit down?"

She nodded toward a bedside chair, then took a moment to adjust the pillow behind her back. The faded flannel nightgown she was wearing felt several sizes too big. How she came to have it on was something Arabella didn't even want to know.

She glared at her ex-fiancé, now another woman's husband. "No more surprises, Charles. Tell me the truth—the whole sordid little story."

He fiddled with his thumbs, avoiding her gaze. After a long moment he cleared his throat. "Sally kept house for her brother on the next spread north of here. When I moved to the ranch last summer, she came over with an apple pie, expecting to find a family. Instead she found me. She was shy at first, but over time we became…friends."

"*Friends.*" Arabella cast him a withering look. "Did you tell her you were engaged to be married?"

"Of course I did. I even showed her your picture. But she was lonely and so was I. Her brother was out on the range for days on end, so it wasn't hard to find time together. Mostly we just talked or went for rides. She even taught me how to fish. We behaved ourselves pretty well until the big January blizzard. She happened to be here the day the storm blew in. There was no way she could leave. One thing led to another…" He stared down at his thumbs.

"Oh, Charles!" Arabella felt as if she were scolding a wayward child. It was a feeling she'd had many times before with him, dating back to when he actually *was* a child, and could never seem to keep himself out of mischief. He was always genuinely sorry afterward, and faithfully promised to mend his ways…until the next time temptation got the better of him.

Everyone had said his character would become steadier as he grew to manhood, but if recent events were any indication, he still had quite a bit of maturing to do.

"Why didn't you tell me then?" she asked.

He shook his head. "Afterward, Sally was upset. She said she'd done a bad thing, sinning with a man who was already promised. When she left here, she told me she never wanted to see me again."

"And what about you? Were you even sorry?"

"Sorry?" He made a little choked sound. "I'd betrayed you and taken advantage of an innocent girl. I despised myself for what I'd done. But the one thing I knew for sure was that I didn't want to lose you. When I didn't hear from Sally, I sent you the tickets and put the finishing touches on the house. Everything was going as planned until three weeks ago."

"I can just imagine." Arabella masked her pain with icy calm. "Go on."

"I heard a knock at the door. When I opened it, there was Sally on the porch, crying her eyes out. Her brother was with her, looking as mean as a grizzly bear. He'd brought along a preacher and the biggest shotgun I'd ever seen." His voice choked with tears. "If I'd refused to marry her, I've no doubt the man would have killed me. Oh, Lord, don't hate me, Arabella! I didn't mean for this to happen!"

He looked like a little boy who'd been caught with his hand in the cookie jar. Arabella felt frozen inside. "You're not worth hating, Charles Middleton. All I can do is wish you and your bride the best and get out of your life."

Charles reached for her hand, catching it tight. "You've got to understand. Sally's a sweet girl, a fine girl. I care for her. But, so help me, it's you I love, Arabella. If there's a way, any way at all…"

Disgust thawed Arabella's composure. She jerked her hand away. "I can't believe you'd suggest such a thing! Shame on you, Charles! You've made your bed, so lie in it with that poor girl and try to be a decent husband! As for me, I'm well out of this mess. As soon as my trunk arrives, one of your hired hands can drive me back to Buffalo Bend."

He rose, his mouth set. "Your trunk was on the front porch this morning. But you can't leave yet. The bridge is washed out. Even if you could get to town there's no place to stay, and the stage only comes through every ten days—less often if the weather's bad. For now, I'm afraid you're stuck here."

"Stuck here. In this house, with you and your bride." Arabella felt as if she'd just pronounced her own prison sentence. This was unthinkable—a nightmare with no escape. She thrust out her chin, fighting tears. "Very well, I'll stay if I must. But the less I see of your lying face, the better!"

He flinched as if she'd slapped him. Good. The cheating bastard deserved that and more. But her own self-control was cracking around the edges. "Get out," she muttered. "Just go."

"Your trunk will be in the hall. I'll have some breakfast sent up."

When she didn't reply he walked out, closing the door behind him. As his footsteps faded, Arabella gave in to fury. She had loved Charles, trusted him completely. But he was weak and deceitful. While she'd been dreaming about him and planning their future, he'd been sleeping with another woman—*sleeping* being the polite word for an act so intimate that Arabella could scarcely imagine it. Then, as if nothing had happened, *he'd sent her the blasted tickets!*

If he hadn't gotten the wretched creature with child, Arabella would have married him and never been the wiser—until the next time he strayed. Oh, there would always be a next time. A man didn't change that much.

How could she have been such a fool?

Turning over, she punched her pillow—once, then again and again. Was it Charles or herself she was pretending to beat? It didn't make much difference. The release felt like something she needed.

A solid blow split the stitching of the pillowcase. Feathers exploded in a blizzard of white, falling around her like the fragments of a shattered dream.

All her hopes, all her plans—her wedding, her home, her future family—everything was gone because of a scheming little Montana prairie flower with an apple pie and a man too weak-willed to keep his word. What had she done to deserve this? And what was she going to do now?

Clutching her ribs with her arms, she doubled over in the bed. As the feathers settled around her, Arabella's body shook with hard, dry sobs.

A light rap at the door riveted her attention. Swiftly composing her features, she sat up. "Who is it?"

"Breakfast." The voice was a woman's, the word so faintly spoken that it barely penetrated the wood.

Arabella sat up, adjusting herself in the bed and smoothing back her unruly red curls. At least the hired help wouldn't be expecting her to answer any questions. "Bring it in," she said.

The door opened slowly. The young woman who stepped over the threshold with a tray was uncommonly tall and dressed in faded calico. Her hair fell over one shoulder in a thick flaxen braid. Arabella's spirits sank to a new low. The last person she wanted to see this morning was Charles's wife, Sally.

"I hope you like ham and eggs," she said. "I brought fresh biscuits, too, and—" Her dove-gray eyes shot open as she noticed the feathers. "My stars! What happened?"

Arabella bit back a stinging retort. She was starved, and that breakfast did smell good. Her stomach growled. "Excuse me." Her politeness was brittle. "I'm afraid I took out my frustrations on that pillow. I'll be happy to pay for a new one."

"No, no!" Sally set the tray across Arabella's knees and began scooping up the feathers. "I can mend it. No trouble at all. Oh, and I washed your muddy clothes and hung them to dry. Your beautiful silk gown had some mud stains, but I managed to get the worst of them out. Maybe you can add a row of lace to cover what's left of them, along with the watermarks."

"Thank you. That gown was my grandmother's."

Arabella nibbled a piece of flaky biscuit. Strange, how the dress she'd saved for her wedding had been salvaged by the very woman who'd laid ruin to her plans. It was as if she'd stepped into a world of smoke and mirrors, where nothing was as it seemed—including Sally's friendly manner. What schemes and plans lay behind that sweetly smiling face?

"My grandmother was married in that gown," Arabella added. "She and my grandfather were happy together for almost fifty years. I thought it might give me luck to wear it." She shrugged. "So much for luck."

"You're so pretty, Arabella. Even prettier than your picture. Surely you'll get other chances."

Other chances. Arabella's spirits sank a notch deeper. True, there were men standing in line back home. But none she wanted to spend her life with. Her heart had always been set on Charles.

Cheating, lying, two-faced Charles, who'd fathered another woman's child and married her only because he was forced to.

Assuming a mask of politeness, Arabella changed the subject. "This breakfast is delicious. My compliments to your cook."

Sally flushed. She had skin like a ripe peach, with the lightest dusting of freckles across her classic nose. There was a part of Arabella that wanted to fly at her and yank that long golden braid until she screamed. But what purpose would that serve now?

"I'm the cook," Sally said. "There's a Chinese man who does the heavy work and washes up in the kitchen, but I enjoy cooking and cleaning—and it does save Charlie a bit of money."

Arabella choked on a bite of airy scrambled egg. She'd assumed that Sally had set out to snare herself a rich husband. But Charles's wife seemed as guileless as she was pretty.

That, or she was putting on one humdinger of an act.

"Charles has plenty of money, Sally," Arabella said. "In fact he's quite wealthy. He can certainly afford to hire more help for you."

"Oh, but I don't mind." Sally was stuffing handfuls of feathers back into the pillowcase. "I've worked hard all my life. I'm used to it."

"But you're expecting a baby. You're certainly going to need a woman's help soon."

"My mother raised seven children in a log cabin without any help at all. I'm strong, just like she was. I'll manage fine."

Putting the pillowcase aside, she sat down on the foot of the bed. "I know you'll be needing some time to yourself. I'll have Chung bring in your trunk and fill the bath. But before I go, there's something I want to say."

Her work-worn hands clasped and unclasped in her lap. She wore no wedding ring—evidently that hadn't been included in the shotgun ceremony. Someone should tell Charles to buy her one.

"I know you have every reason to hate me, Arabella," she said. "You came here expecting to be married. Instead you found…me." Her hand brushed the curve of her growing belly. "I never meant for you to be hurt. When I found out about the baby, I planned to raise it on my own. I kept the secret from my brother for as long as I could, but he finally noticed. He was the one who forced Charlie to marry me." She shook her head. "I can't blame Stewart. He was only trying to do the right thing."

"Do you love Charles?" Arabella was startled by her own question.

She nodded, blinking back tears. "If I didn't love him, this—" Her hand stroked her belly again. "This never would have happened. But he was yours. I never meant to take him away from you."

Arabella's emotions caromed between anger and pity. Sally had Charles. She had his house, his child and the status of being his wife. But how much was that worth if her husband claimed to love another woman?

What a mess! Arabella could hardly wait to be on that train back to Boston.

"I was thinking this morning," Sally continued.

"You've traveled all this way. Maybe there's still some good that can come of it. My brother, Stewart, is a good man. He's kind and responsible, and he has his own ranch, bigger even than this one. Now that I've married Charlie, he's all alone. What if you and he—"

Arabella's fork clattered to the tray. "Your brother?" she gasped. "What makes you think I'd be interested in the man who forced you and Charles to marry?"

Sally's face fell. "You could give him a chance while you're here. Stewart's a quiet man, but he can be pleasant once you get to know him. He's even a war hero. He won a medal for bravery at Gettysburg."

A war hero? No wonder he was able to scare Charles into the wedding ceremony. Mean-as-a-grizzly, shotgun-toting Stewart, Charles had described him. He'd probably scared the Rebels to death.

"We invite him over for dinner every Sunday," Sally said. "He's coming this evening. You might enjoy spending some time with him. What have you got to lose?"

Arabella chose not to answer the question. But it did start her thinking. Paying a little harmless attention to another man might show Charles that she was capable of moving on. And Sally was right about one thing—even if Stewart proved to be a troll, what did she have to lose? She'd be leaving on the next stage out of Buffalo Bend.

Arabella drained her tea and set down her fork. "All right, Sally. No promises, mind you, but I'm willing to meet your brother."

"Oh, but you've already met him. Didn't he tell you who he was?"

Arabella's jaw went slack. She groaned as the truth sank home. How could she not have seen the resemblance—the height, the strong features, the deep-set gray eyes.

"Stewart McIntyre." Sally's smile confirmed her worst fears. "My brother's the man who brought you here."

Stewart surveyed the banquet laid out on the white linen tablecloth. Sally had outdone herself tonight, with roast chicken, braised potatoes and carrots, hot buttered rolls and a fresh apple cobbler with cream for dessert. Much as he relished a good meal, he worried that his sister was working too hard. Maybe it was time her husband took a firm hand and hired more help.

Not that Charlie Middleton took a firm hand in much of anything. Stewart didn't have a high opinion of any rancher who wouldn't get his fingernails dirty. And after what Charlie had done to his sister, he could scarcely abide the man's company. But he accepted these weekly invitations to keep in touch with Sally and make sure she was well taken care of.

He'd been of a mind to make his excuses tonight. With Arabella Spencer in the house, tensions were bound to be running as high as the Missouri in flood. But early that morning, when he'd delivered Arabella's trunk, Sally had met him on the porch and begged him to come. Sensing that she needed his support, he'd said yes.

They sat around one end of the long table, Sally on her husband's right and Arabella on his left, directly across from Stewart. From where he sat, there was no way to keep his eyes off her.

She'd cleaned up right fine since he'd left her, shivering like a wet pup at Charlie's gate. Her pale yellow gown was simple but elegant, with a pert little ribbon at the throat. Her fiery locks were twisted up and pinned at the crown of her head, leaving a few loose curls to tumble around her heart-shaped face. He noticed for the first time that her eyes were the color of fresh spring grass.

She looked like a little porcelain doll. And the sidelong glances Charlie Middleton was giving her made Stewart want to stand up and punch the bastard.

It had been his worry all along—that the presence of Charlie's former fiancée would put a strain on his sister's marriage. Seeing Arabella for the first time had doubled his worries. Sally was a beautiful girl with a true and tender heart. Given time, Charlie might see her fine qualities and grow to love her. But Arabella Spencer was a dazzler—lively, spirited and confident of her charms. If she made up her mind to get Charlie back, poor Sally wouldn't stand a chance.

Maybe he should've left the damned woman back in town!

"Sally tells me you're a war hero, Mr. McIntyre." Arabella had turned her wiles on Stewart now. She was clearly trying to make Charlie jealous. Stewart fought the urge to get up from the table and walk out, away from all of this nonsense. Only Sally's pleading eyes kept him in his seat.

"Oh, call him Stewart, Arabella. We don't hold with formality in these parts." Sally's gaiety was as brittle as glass.

"Very well, Stewart." She smiled and batted her impossibly long eyelashes. "I was told you won a medal at Gettysburg. There must be a good story behind that, if you'd care to entertain us."

Stewart took the time to spear a drumstick from the white china platter. "It was a long time ago, and it's hardly fit for entertainment. If I told you what Gettysburg was really like, you wouldn't be able to finish your dinner."

Her delicate brows shot up. "I'm sorry, I was only—"

"I was nineteen years old and scared spitless. What I did involved killing boys as young and scared as myself. I threw away the medal, and I've since done my best to forget the whole miserable experience. Is that entertaining enough for you, Arabella?"

Charlie had gone pale around the mouth. "Really, Stewart, Arabella was only trying to make polite conversation."

"Fine. But let's make polite conversation about something else." He knew he'd been harsh, but of all subjects for Arabella to fix upon, that was the worst choice. Remembering the war was the last thing he wanted to do.

Stewart drizzled gravy onto his mashed potatoes. Without looking up, he could feel three pairs of eyes—Charlie's blazing with proper outrage, Sally's overflowing with dismay. And Arabella's, most likely shooting daggers from their emerald depths.

"Since you had to go back to get your wagon, maybe you can tell us about the road," she said. "As soon as it's fit to travel, I mean to be gone from here."

"Then you'll have to wait for a while," Stewart replied. "What I saw of that road's not much better than a hog wallow. So you might as well settle in and enjoy your stay. Montana can be a pretty place in the spring when the wildflowers are in bloom. Have you had a chance to look around?"

"I'm still recovering from last night. So far all I've managed to do is sleep, bathe and dress."

"I'm sure Stewart would be happy to show you around, Arabella." Sally's voice quivered with hope. Good Lord, was this his sister's attempt at match-making?

Arabella's silence expressed how she felt about Sally's suggestion. Stewart breathed a sigh of relief. He'd already had enough of Miss Arabella Spencer.

"I'll be busy rounding up spring calves," he said. "If I took time off to play guide, I could lose a few of them."

"I'd be happy to take you out for a ride." It was Charlie who spoke up. "The sidesaddle I ordered is waiting in the barn. We could go first thing tomorrow morning."

Stewart saw the hurt that flashed across his sister's pretty face. At that moment he could have lunged across the table, grabbed his brother-in-law by the collar and shaken him until his teeth fell out.

Flashing Stewart a look of dismay, Arabella shook her head. "After last night, I'm so sore, I couldn't ride a hobby horse. Don't trouble yourself, Charles. I'll see the country in my own good time."

"You're sure?"

"Quite." As if to punctuate the word, she jabbed

a carrot slice with her fork. "And now, if you don't mind, this delicious dinner is getting cold."

She lowered her gaze and attacked her plate with the ferocity of a small red fox. The meal was finished in snatches of awkward small talk. Stewart was relieved when the last bite was eaten and the chairs were pulled away from the table.

He was about to take his leave of his sister and go when Arabella stepped in front of him. "I'm in need of some fresh air, Stewart," she said. "Would you be so kind as to walk me around the yard? It's dark out, and I don't want to risk a misstep."

"Certainly." Stewart offered his arm and allowed himself to be led out onto the porch. He knew better than to expect a pleasant evening stroll. Arabella's request had been more like a summons from the Spanish Inquisition. The little redhead wanted answers and would stop at nothing to get them.

Any way it went down, this was not going to be pretty.

Chapter Three

The night sky was a sea of stars. Arabella's eyes traced the arc of the Milky Way, like a spill of crystal sand across the vast, dark bowl of the heavens. Boston's misty nights were lovely in their way. But Montana's dry, clear air sharpened the senses to razor keenness. In the chirr of tiny grass-dwellers she could make out individual voices. The wings of a nighthawk sliced the air above her head. Stewart's horse, tethered by the gate, snorted in the darkness. Arabella could hear the sound of its teeth cropping the fresh spring grass.

Beneath her light touch, Stewart's arm was as taut as steel cable. He was silent, waiting for her to speak.

She cleared her throat. "You might have told me," she said in her sternest voice.

"It wasn't my place to tell you. I agreed to meet the stage, in case you were on it, and give you a ride to the ranch, but after that, you were Charlie's problem. It was up to him to break the news."

"So you let me blather on about getting married, when all the time you knew!"

"What would you have done if I'd told you?"

"I don't know. But at least I'd have been prepared." She gazed past the fence, toward the hulking silhouette of the barn. "At least I know why you've been so hateful toward me."

She caught the sharp intake of his breath. "Hate is too strong a word, Arabella. I don't hate you. But I'm protective of my sister. Sally's happiness means the world to me."

"And you see me as a threat to her."

"Aren't you?"

The question brushed the hair trigger of Arabella's temper. "What exactly are you implying?" she snapped.

"That you're a beautiful woman who knows how to use her charms, and that you have everything to gain by doing so. I saw the moon-calf way Charlie was looking at you tonight. All you'd have to do is crook your pretty little finger, and—"

Arabella's palm struck his face with a slap that sent a jolt of pain up her arm. It was like striking granite. "How dare you?" she gasped. "The very idea that I'd want Charles back, or that I'd plot to take him away from the mother of his child—"

His frigid expression silenced her. "That's enough, Arabella. I'll go now. You've made your point—but don't forget mine. Hurt my sister and you'll answer to me."

He strode to his horse, untied the reins and swung into the saddle without looking back.

"Go, then!" Arabella hurled the words after him. "See if I care! I never want to see you again, Stewart McIntyre!"

Her words were lost amid the clatter of departing hooves.

Stewart took the tall buckskin at a lope, thundering over the two-mile trail that linked his ranch to Charlie Middleton's. Arabella's palm print burned like a brand on his face. Damn fool, that's what he was. He should've been man enough to stay and smooth things over with her. At least her outrage showed she had no intention of getting in the way of Sally's marriage. Maybe he should have apologized for offending her. Instead he'd bolted. But wasn't that what he'd always done at the first tingle of attraction to a woman—thrown up a barrier and run like a scared jackrabbit?

Pretty little dolls like Arabella Spencer had always made him feel awkward and ugly. But Arabella wasn't just pretty. She was smart, spirited and damned sexy in her ladylike way. Everything Charlie might see in her in her, Stewart saw, too. A man, even a married one, would have to be crazy not to want her in his bed.

Charlie hadn't been able to keep his eyes off her all evening—it was clear to Stewart that his brother-in-law had every intention of winning back Arabella's affection. And Arabella *had* loved Charlie—since they were children, if he remembered correctly. If Charlie used the days before the stage returned to woo her in earnest, would she be able to resist returning to his arms? *Sally* had certainly found those arms all too tempting.

The comparison brought him back to thoughts of his sister. Growing up, she'd been the baby of the family. As the firstborn, Stewart had always looked after her. She'd been fifteen when their mother died. By then Stewart had acquired his ranch, and he'd taken her in. He'd hoped one day to see her married to a good man. But he'd been unable to protect her innocence from the likes of Charlie Middleton.

Had he been wrong to force the marriage? At the time he'd thought it the only thing to do. Middleton had been responsible for Sally's pregnancy. He had ample means to take care of her and the baby. And Sally had said she loved him.

Lord help him, had he ruined his sister's life?

He'd honestly believed they had a chance to be happy. Then Arabella had shown up, with her delicate beauty, fine clothes and lively manner, to set everything topsy-turvy.

Arabella had insisted she didn't want Charlie back. Stewart believed her. She'd been cruelly betrayed by the man and had every reason to hate him. But she could still be swayed by sentiment, and long-held feelings. It didn't matter that she didn't *plan* to steal Charlie away. After all, Sally hadn't *planned* to fall into an engaged man's bed. Things didn't always go according to plan.

As he rode, the night breeze cooled his burning face. But lower down the heat smoldered, fueled by his imagination. Now he knew why Charlie had struggled so hard against the idea of wedding Sally. What man wouldn't fight against losing the chance to see those russet curls tumbling over his pillow, those mischievous absinthe eyes, challenging a man to take her and ravish her ripe little body until she yowled like a cat in heat…

Damn!

The truth of it was, he wanted her. How could any man with fire in his belly *not* want her? But he couldn't let desire cloud his judgment. He'd be better off without her around. They all would. When the next stage pulled out of Buffalo Bend, it would be his sworn duty to make sure Arabella Spencer was on it.

Any way you looked at her, the woman was trouble.

* * *

Arabella lay awake in the darkness, staring up at the ceiling. The memory of Stewart's words and the scorn in his voice stung like lye. It was bad enough that he viewed her as evil and conniving. But what galled the most was his notion that she'd be stupid enough to want Charles back.

She should have hit him even harder.

From the other side of the wall came the rhythmic creak and thump of shifting metal bedsprings. Merciful heaven, couldn't Charles and Sally have put her in a different room? Arabella knew little more about marriage than what she'd read in her aunt Pearl's doctor book. But she could guess what was going on.

Charles had said he still loved her. But that didn't stop him from taking his pleasure with his wife. Surely he would know that Arabella could hear them. But maybe he didn't care. Maybe he was even trying to make her jealous.

She should get down on her knees and thank the good Lord she hadn't married the jackass. Poor, sweet Sally had done her a favor.

Hurt my sister and you'll answer to me.

Stewart's threat came back to her as she slipped out of bed, pulled on her light woolen robe and pattered down the stairs. For a moment, she envied Sally. As an orphan and an only child, Arabella had always felt that she was largely on her own. Yes, she'd had the doting aunts who'd raised her, and plenty of friends, but she'd never had a protector, a hero willing to go to battle to defend her from harm. Yet her brother's protection wouldn't be enough to shield Sally in this case. Unless something changed, Sally was liable to get her heart broken.

She was a lovely young woman in her own way. But she'd grown up on the frontier in a log cabin, and it showed. She needed someone to take her in hand, someone to help her be more of a lady.

Sally needed a friend.

Opening the front door, she tiptoed across the porch and sank onto the top step. The air was cool and fresh. A sliver of crescent moon hung above the distant hills.

Don't get involved, her sensible side argued. *Mind your own business and leave as soon as you're able.*

Sound advice. Charles and Sally had created their unhappy situation. Her meddling could make it even worse, especially if Stewart saw it as an attempt to break up his sister's marriage.

Blast Stewart!

He'd deserved that slap for judging her so harshly. Arabella wasn't accustomed to being judged. After the death of her parents in a tragic accident, when she was little more than a baby, two maiden aunts had taken her in and raised her with all the tender pampering a girl could want. She'd had friends, clothes, parties, dancing and riding lessons. Everyone had loved her—especially Charles Middleton. True, she might have been spoiled, but not in a bad way. What had happened to make her the villainess in this melodrama?

She felt so utterly alone. Coming to Montana was supposed to open a new chapter in her life—a chapter that would be filled with the family she'd always longed for. Instead she was left with nothing.

A touch against her arm triggered a start. Her muscles tensed for a sprint to the door. But it was only a dog, a shaggy mutt that looked to be part collie, working its damp nose beneath her hand. Arabella liked dogs. This one smelled of wet grass and probably had ticks, but at least it was friendly. She scratched its ears and was rewarded by the vigorous thump of its tail. Even a scruffy dog was better than no friend at all.

"Where did you come from, boy?" Her fingers found a worn leather collar, its strap molded to its rusty buckle. The dog appeared well fed. Most likely it belonged here.

Stretching out at her side, the dog laid its head on its muddy paws. Lost in thought, Arabella gazed up at the vast expanse of stars. Her aunt Phoebe had always said that everything happened for a reason. Could that be true? Arabella thought she'd come to

Montana to marry Charles. But maybe she'd been brought here for an entirely different purpose.

It was a deep thought—too deep for tonight. She yawned, suddenly tired. Surely by now Charles and Sally would be asleep.

The dog had begun to snore. Easing to her feet, Arabella crept back into the silent house and closed the door behind her.

She woke at first light the next morning. A quick glance from between the drapes showed mauve ribbons of cloud above the distant hills. The crystalline warble of meadowlarks greeted the prairie dawn. It was going to be a beautiful day. But the prospect of dealing with Charles and his marriage was enough to curdle Arabella's mood like vinegar in milk. She felt like a prisoner. If only she could escape, even for a few hours...

The notion came in a flash. Charles had mentioned the sidesaddle in the barn. Where there was a saddle, there was bound to be a bridle and a spare horse. She would slip out of the house and go for a morning ride.

Her spirits rose as she turned up the bed, splashed her face and dressed in her smart new riding habit and boots. Secrecy was vital. If Charles knew where she was going, he'd insist on going with her. Since

Sally's pregnancy made riding a risk, she would be alone with him. That was the last thing she wanted.

Twisting up her hair, she pinned it in place and topped it with a rakish straw hat. The hat was new, with a long, curling feather tucked into the brim. Arabella had bought it especially for riding on the ranch. With a final, satisfied glance in the mirror, she closed the door behind her, stole down the stairs and crossed the porch. The dog was still there. It raised its head, shook its tangled coat and followed her toward the barn.

The only other sign of life was a thin curl of smoke from the bunkhouse chimney. Charles had mentioned last night that most of his hands were out on the range rounding up calves for branding. Only two men remained here to take care of the chores. Neither of them was in sight to help her.

The saddle and bridle were easy to find, and the dappled gelding in the second stall seemed docile enough to ride. Straining with effort, Arabella hefted the new saddle onto its back and tightened the cinch. Minutes later she was stealing out the back door of the barn.

The horse seemed nervous, snorting and dancing as if to rid itself of an unaccustomed weight. Maybe the animal wasn't used to a sidesaddle. But never mind, it would settle down before long. Arabella urged the gelding to a trot, putting distance between herself and the ranch. The dog loped along behind, ignoring her attempts to send it home.

At the top of a rise, she reined in to get her bearings. By now the sun was up. Rolling plains, carpeted with wildflowers and glistening with morning dew, spread around her in all directions. To the far west, snowy peaks jutted above the horizon. The vastness boggled Arabella's imagination. She had never seen so much land or so much sky. The beauty of it almost brought her to tears.

Looking back the way she'd come she could still see the ranch, but from this distance the buildings looked like toys. She willed herself to memorize the lay of the land and note the position of the sun. It wouldn't do to get lost in this wild country where so many places looked the same. Maybe it was a good thing the dog had come with her. At least the shaggy mutt seemed to know its way around.

Nudging the horse to a trot again, she headed west, with her face toward the mountains. Damp earth, fresh grass and wildflowers perfumed the air. The sun climbed the sky as she rode. A herd of pronghorn antelope raced over a hill and out of sight. High overhead, a golden eagle circled on outstretched wings. What glorious country this was. It was almost a shame she'd soon be going back to Boston.

Her aunts and her friends would wonder what had happened. Arabella detested lies and liars, but the truth was so humiliating. Maybe she could just say that Charles had changed and was no longer the man she'd fancied herself in love with. That was close enough to the truth, wasn't it?

Glancing back, she could no longer see the ranch. Never mind, she was sure she could find it again. All she had to do was turn around and ride with her back to the distant peaks.

But which way were the mountains? She turned the horse one way, then another. Rolling hills blocked her view in every direction. And the sun was at the peak of the sky.

Could she be lost? Certainly not, Arabella told herself. She was just…disoriented. She would find her way again in no time. All she needed to do was head for higher ground.

Mounting a ridge, she gasped in wonder at the sight below. Buffalo—hundreds, perhaps thousands of them—were pouring out of a hollow and spreading onto the plain. She'd glimpsed the huge animals from the train and from the stage, but never so close or so many. There were great lumbering bulls, and cows trailed by gangly brown calves. The earth rumbled beneath their pounding hooves.

Mesmerized, Arabella urged the horse closer. Almost under the gelding's belly, a flock of prairie chickens whirred out of the grass. The nervous horse screamed, reared and bucked. Arabella flew off the sidesaddle, her boot catching in the single stirrup. Hot pain shot up her leg as her foot pulled loose. She lay on the ground, writhing as the horse bolted over the hill and vanished from sight.

The dog circled her, uttering agitated little barks, almost as if it wanted to play. Arabella's hat lay nearby, where it had fallen. Seizing the hat in its jaws, the big mutt bounded off through the grass.

"Come back here!" Arabella shouted. But her cry was lost in the great silence of the prairie.

Stewart peered through his binoculars, scanning the hills for any sign of stray calves. The smaller ones, even with their mothers standing guard, were easy prey for wolves and coyotes. It was vital that he bring them in to the safety of the pasture. This afternoon he saw none. But as he lowered the glass, he noticed a low, brown shape moving through the distant grass. A solitary wolf? He raised the binoculars and sharpened the focus.

Blasted dog. He'd always been a roamer, but what was he doing clear out here? Swinging out of the saddle he gave a sharp whistle. Tail flying, the dog bounded toward him. Stewart dropped to one knee as sixty pounds of burr-tangled canine hurled itself joyfully at his chest. Although Slocum was Stewart's dog, he was equally attached to Sally and made regular visits to her new home. But he didn't usually venture this far out alone.

"You old rascal, what're you— What the hell is this? Did you bring me a present?" Stewart worked the crumpled hat free of the dog's dripping jaws. It was like no hat or bonnet he'd ever seen, woven of fine dark straw that was almost as soft as linen. The ridiculous feather sewn into the grosgrain band had suffered from Slocum's drooling grip, but it was clearly meant to be something special.

Stewart swore out loud. Only one person he knew within fifty miles would wear a hat as silly as this one. Still muttering he swung back into the saddle.

"Come on, boy. Show me where you found this."

Arabella dragged herself forward through the long, prickly grass. She'd tried walking in the direction the horse had gone, but between her missing boot and her throbbing ankle, she could barely take a step. Given the choice between lying where she'd fallen and crawling as far as she could make it, she'd chosen the latter.

The gray gelding was bound to find its way home. When it arrived with her boot hanging from the stirrup, someone would know she was in trouble. Charles would have riders out combing the prairie for her.

Surely they'd find her and everything would turn

out all right. But what if something went wrong? What if it was all up to her? She couldn't just wait to be saved. She had to keep moving.

The hot rays of the afternoon sun beat down on her. To protect her fragile skin, she'd slipped off her light jacket and draped it over her head and neck. It kept her from burning, but the underside was like an oven. Sweat had glued her thin cotton blouse to her skin. Her palms were scraped raw from the sharp grass and prickly weeds. The dry membranes of her throat felt as if they were cracking and curling like old paint.

She yelped as her hand came down on something sharp. Her stomach clenched in fear; but it was only a thorn. Dizzy with relief, she used her teeth to pull it out of her skin. She'd heard there were rattlesnakes on the prairie, as well as wolves and coyotes. And Stewart had mentioned something about Indians. Maybe he'd only said it to scare her. That would be like Stewart. But the dangers out here were real and deadly. Not least among them was the chance that she could die of thirst and exposure before anyone found her.

Arabella could feel her strength ebbing. Fighting the urge to rest, she inched forward, dragging her body along the ground. She'd lost track of time, but the angle of the sun told her it was getting late in the day. The thought of spending the night out here, alone in the dark, filled her with terror. And what if it stormed? She'd heard tales of terrible thunderstorms on the prairie. Nothing scared her more.

Now she could hear something coming toward her, approaching light and swift through the long grass. Was it a wolf? An Indian? Too weak to run or fight, she hunkered low and braced herself for the attack.

It came in the form of muddy feet and a slobbering tongue as the dog bowled her over. Struggling to right herself, Arabella heard the snort of a horse and a grating voice she knew all too well.

"What the devil are you doing out here?"

She would never have believed she could be so glad to see Stewart McIntyre.

He was off his horse now, crouching beside her. One strong hand lifted her, propping her back against his knee. The other hand tipped an open canteen to her mouth. Arabella drank greedily, gulping water like a winded horse.

"Easy…easy there…" He tilted the canteen away. "You'll make yourself sick. What happened?"

Her voice emerged as a croak. "Horse spooked and threw me. My boot caught in the stirrup—twisted my ankle when it tore loose. Hurts too much to walk."

"You were out riding alone?"

"Should I have taken Charles up on his offer to come with me?"

His look darkened as her barb hit home. "Never mind. Sit back and give me your foot. I'll have a look at that ankle."

Kneeling, he peeled off the dirty, threadbare remnant of her stocking which had dragged along the ground as she crawled. Cradling her foot in one hand, he pulled loose the stickers embedded in her tender flesh. For such a rough-spoken brute of a man, he had an amazingly gentle touch. Arabella closed her eyes as his big, callused fingers worked their way up her foot toward her ankle. Her breath hissed inward as he pressed the swollen spot.

"There?" He probed cautiously. Arabella clenched her teeth to keep from crying out. Stewart probably thought of her as a spoiled baby. She wanted to prove him wrong.

"It doesn't feel broken," he said, "but I'd guess you've got a nasty sprain." His free hand stripped the bandanna from around his neck. "We'll wrap it as best we can. When we get back to my house, we can cold pack it."

"*Your* house?"

"We need to get you out of the sun, and it's the closest place. I'll send a man to Charlie's to tell them you're safe." Stewart's hands wrapped the folded bandanna under the arch of her foot and twice around the ankle. The dog sat close by, watching.

"Is that your dog?" Arabella winced as he tightened the wrapping.

"I feed him. But Slocum's pretty much his own animal. You're lucky he decided to be yours today." Stewart tied the ends in a snug knot, then stood and pulled her to her feet. "It's too far to go for the wagon. You'll have to ride behind me."

As she balanced on her solid right foot, he lifted off his weathered felt hat and dropped it onto her head. "That should do a better job of shading you than that silly gewgaw the dog brought me."

She glowered from under the outsized rim. "I'll have you know that hat's the latest fashion in Boston. I paid a pretty penny for it."

"Now, why doesn't that surprise me?" With a mutter, he climbed into the saddle. One hand seized her arm and swung her up behind him, as if she weighed no more than a rag doll.

"Hold on tight." Tucking her jacket into a saddlebag, he kneed the buckskin to a brisk trot. For the first instant, the momentum threw Arabella backward. Recovering, she flung her arms around his ribs and hung on tight. Her straddled legs nested behind his.

A breeze had sprung out of the west, rippling across the long grass. How like the sea the prairie was, Arabella thought. Beautiful, dangerous, always changing yet always the same, not unlike the man who'd just rescued her.

Stewart's body was as solid as the trunk of an oak. He rode with ease, his big hands skilled and sure. His body smelled of prairie grass and clean, masculine sweat. Only the wide brim of the hat saved Arabella from the impulse to press her face against his back and inhale him into her senses. He was, in his own way, a compelling man, as powerfully male as the huge buffalo bulls she'd seen rumbling out of the hollow.

She'd always told herself she preferred gentle, refined men, like Charles, but Stewart's masculine closeness was having a strange effect on her. Where her pelvis rested against his taut rump, a delicious heat was spreading outward into her thighs. Enhanced by the motion of the horse, the tingling sensation spiraled upward into the core of her body. She stifled a moan. Common sense told her this was wicked, and that she should pull away. But without falling off the horse, she had no place to go. Besides, the sensation was… Heaven help her, she didn't want it to stop. Was this how girls like Sally got into trouble?

"How's your ankle?" Stewart slowed the horse to a walk, easing the sweet torment on her body. There was a roughness to his voice. Had he been aware of her response to him? Was that why he'd slowed down?

"It's no worse." Arabella had almost forgotten about her injury. As she remembered, her ankle began to throb once more. "How far do we have to go?"

"Not much farther. My ranch is over that next hill." He glanced at the sky, where clouds were scudding in from the west. "Good thing. Looks like it could rain in a bit. Have another drink." He passed her the canteen. Arabella took her time, savoring the sweet, clear water until it was gone.

"I never asked you. What were you doing out on the prairie before you found me?"

"Looking for strays."

"Did you find any?"

He chuckled, a surprising sound. "Just one."

"I saw buffalo. A big herd of them."

"Hope you didn't get too close. Those big bulls would kill you given the chance. And where you find buffalo, there are liable to be Indians tracking them."

Arabella shuddered. "Have you had much trouble with the Indians?"

He shook his head. "I stay out of their way, and they don't bother me. But it wouldn't take much to stir them up. A pretty red-haired woman, out there by herself..." He let the implication hang. "You were lucky this time, Arabella. You're not to go riding alone again, understand?"

She tried to ignore the burst of pleasure she felt at his protective tone. "For a man who has no claim on me, you're being downright bossy, Stewart McIntyre. Are you offering to go with me next time?"

"If that's what it takes—and if I don't ship you out on the stage before then."

"Ship me out? You sound as if that's *your* decision."

"Believe me, nobody wants you gone more than I do."

Though pleasantly spoken, the words stung. It shouldn't matter that this gruff giant of a man didn't want her around. But somehow it did.

They had come over the crest of the hill. Stewart's ranch lay on the plain below. Arabella wasn't sure what she'd expected, maybe a log cabin with a broken-down wagon in the yard and a deer hide hanging over the door. But the corral, barn and sheds looked immaculately built and tended. A small creek, bordered by willow and cottonwoods, ran through the property, shading a house that appeared to rise out of the land itself.

To please her, perhaps, Charles had remodeled his house to look like an Eastern home—the pillared porch, the white exterior with dark green shutters, the picket fence and paved walkway. Stewart's rambling home, built low to the land was all logs and natural stone, with an overhanging shingled roof shading the wide front porch. It looked as if it belonged here, like a natural part of the vast Montana prairie.

"Did you build the house?" she asked Stewart.

"Every stick and stone of it. I started when I came here, after the war. This was a wild place then, before the railroad. In some ways, it still is."

They started down the hill. The dog raced ahead of them, tail high through the grass. A hawk, circling overhead, flapped its wings and soared skyward. Beyond the outbuildings, cows and calves grazed in a fenced pasture. There was something welcoming about this spot, an air of peace that seemed to reach out to Arabella and embrace her. But how could that be, when its owner wanted nothing more than to see her gone?

She didn't understand it at all.

Stewart dismounted at the corral where Miguel, the shy teenage boy who helped out around the place, was waiting to take the reins. After instructing the lad to deliver the news of Arabella's rescue to Charlie's Ranch, he reached up to lift her down from the horse.

Even after her long crawl through the weedy grass, she looked beautiful. Her russet curls tumbled over her shoulders, awakening an urge to curl the silken strands around his fingers. The way her damp blouse clung to every curve of her perfect little body was enough to make his mouth go dry. From under the brim of his hat, her eyes blazed green fire.

He'd been acutely aware of her on the ride. The pressure of her bouncing crotch against his rump had triggered a heat surge so intense that he'd slowed the horse rather than lose his dignity altogether. And she'd felt something, too. He'd sensed it in the tightening of her arms around his ribs and the rapid jerk of her breath. She'd been all but panting. His imagination had gone crazy.

Lord help him, if he had a brain in his head, he'd hitch up the wagon and have Miguel drive the woman back to Charlie's place right now. But he could imagine the sympathy an injured Arabella might stir up there. Brotherly duty demanded that he keep the little bundle of temptation here with him.

Still sitting astride the horse, she lifted his hat off her curls and dropped it onto his head. Her hands braced against his shoulders as he swung her off the horse and caught her. She fit perfectly, her shoulders nested against his chest and her legs dangling over one arm. Since she couldn't walk, it seemed only sensible to carry her to the house.

When Stewart had built his house it had been with a future family in mind. He'd even imagined carrying a bride up this very path. But the years had passed, and it hadn't happened. Most of the women who came to this untamed country were either wives or whores, and the few eligible females were swiftly snatched up by more charming suitors. With time Stewart had come to accept his bachelorhood as a permanent state. After all, what could he offer a woman, with his scarred face and body and his solitary nature?

Sally's arrival had saved him from becoming a recluse. His vulnerable young sister had brought out his tender instincts and given him someone to nurture and protect. He'd always known she'd grow up and marry one day. But he hadn't anticipated the loneliness her absence would leave in his life.

Thunder, still faint, rumbled behind them as he carried Arabella toward the porch. Her head settled against his chest. His clasp tightened around her as he mounted the steps.

Arabella Spencer fit into his arms as if she belonged there. But she was an Eastern woman. She'd want an elegant Eastern husband—someone like Charlie who was soft, polished and courteous. She'd never choose a rough-spoken ex-soldier like him. Even if she weren't a threat to Sally's marriage, he'd be a fool to think of asking her to stay.

No matter how much he might want her to.

Chapter Four

Stewart's ranch house was even more striking inside than outside. Arabella had grown up with flowered wallpaper, draped windows, crocheted doilies and ceramic whatnots on every shelf and table. It was the way people lived, especially if they had a little wealth to show off. By comparison, the interior of Stewart's home was as stark as the prairie and, in its way, almost as beautiful.

Massive logs, oiled to a golden gleam, supported the walls and the open-beamed ceiling. The front, broken by wide glass windows, was formed of river stones, as was the cavernous fireplace at the room's far end. Gingham pillows, braided rugs and a bright, crocheted afghan—touches most likely added by Sally—lent color and warmth.

"I've never seen anything like this!" Arabella gazed around the room as Stewart lowered her to the buffalo robe that covered the couch in front of the fireplace.

He tossed his hat onto a nearby chair. "I was studying architecture when the war broke out. I never went back to school, but I always wanted to build something using my own ideas. This is it."

"But it's so different—people would love it! You could make a lot of money building homes like this!"

He shook his head. "The business would take away the pleasure. As for the money, ranching gives me enough for my needs. Now, let's have a look at your ankle."

Stewart pulled up a low footstool and sat down. He was so tall that his knees jutted like a grasshopper's. Arabella bit back a smile as he cradled her foot between his hands and began loosening the knotted bandanna. Such gentle hands. How would it feel, she wondered, to be loved by this big, gruff, surprisingly tender man?

But what was she thinking? Stewart viewed her as the enemy. The only thing he had in mind was to send her packing back to Boston.

She winced as he pulled the bandanna away. "The swelling's worse," he said. "Hold on, I'll get some wrappings and some cold water."

He left the room. Arabella heard him rummaging in what she presumed to be the kitchen. A moment later she heard the opening and closing of the back door. She waited, her ankle throbbing as her eyes explored the room.

Ceiling-high shelves crowded with books framed both sides of the fireplace. From where she sat, she could make out a few of the titles. There were books on history, architecture, travel and astronomy, novels by Charles Dickens and Jane Austen, Shakespeare's plays, Greek myths and volumes of poetry. Arabella had always loved to read. If Stewart was a reader, his sister probably was, too. Maybe she'd underestimated Charles's sweet, pigtailed bride.

Lightning flashed through the front window. Thunder crashed across the sky as the first raindrops spattered against the roof. Arabella shivered. She had yet to master her fear of thunderstorms. Her parents had been killed when lightning struck a tree, spooking the horse that pulled their buggy. The animal had plunged off a steep road, toppling the rig into the creek bed below. Only Arabella, a toddler then, had survived. She had no memory of the accident, but she'd been told about it. As long as someone was with her, she didn't mind a storm. But when she was alone, it was as if the terror had been etched into the marrow of her bones.

She was struggling with her nerves when Stewart returned with a bucket and a loose bundle of muslin wrappings. His wind-tousled hair was damp with rain. At the sight of him, her fear took wing.

"Blowing up a big one out there," he said.

Arabella remembered the youth he'd sent to Charles's place. "Will the boy be all right?"

"He should be. The ranch isn't far, and he can stay there till the storm's done. Sally will give him a good meal and a bed if need be." He glanced toward Arabella. "If the rain keeps up, there's a chance you could be stuck here overnight."

Her pulse slammed.

"There's a bed in Sally's old room," he added, as if reading her thoughts. "And if you don't mind cowboy grub, you'll find me a fair to middling cook. Now let's see about cleaning you up and packing that ankle."

With the sun gone, the room had grown chilly. Stewart took a moment to touch a match to the logs and tinder already laid in the fireplace. As the crackling warmth spread around her, Arabella settled back into the pillows. Beyond the front windows, rain streamed off the roof enfolding the porch in a shimmering gray curtain.

Along with the wrappings, Stewart had brought a washcloth. Dipping it in the bucket, he leaned toward her and began sponging her dust-caked face. His touch was light, the water deliciously cold. Arabella might have closed her eyes, but then she'd have missed the chance to study his arresting face. His eyes, set deep beneath the dark ridges of his brows, were the color of the rain, their pupils deep and penetrating. His features, sharp but rugged with high cheekbones, reminded her of a painting she'd seen in a museum—George Catlin's majestic portrait of a Mandan chief. Although he didn't really look like an Indian, Stewart had the same presence, the same quiet dignity.

Her eyes were drawn to the scar that slashed a lightning streak from his temple to the corner of his mouth. She knew he'd been in the war. Had it been a saber that marked him? A bayonet? She quelled the urge to reach up and trace the pale line with a fingertip. Maybe one day he would open up and tell her about it. But what was she thinking? After she left Montana she would never see Stewart McIntyre again.

"Hands." He dipped the washcloth again and wiped her scratched, bloodied palms. "I've got some pine tar salve in the kitchen," he said. "It works fine for horses—no reason it shouldn't work for you. But first, the ankle."

Settling back on the footstool he steadied her foot between his long legs. One hand dipped a length of wrapping in the bucket and laid it, still dripping, on her skin.

"Creek water. The cold will ease the swelling," he muttered without looking up. "You're damned lucky you didn't break a bone or snap a tendon. Maybe next time you'll be more careful."

"Are you saying there might be a next time?"

His glance was a warning. She chose to ignore it.

"I know what you think of me, Stewart. In your eyes I'm a Jezebel, out to wreck your sister's marriage. But you don't know me at all."

He continued wrapping her ankle. The cold was beginning to feel good now; and the brush of his fingers against her skin sent tingles of pleasure up her leg.

"Until I came here, I'd never known anything but love and kindness," she said. "If that makes me a spoiled brat, so be it. But it doesn't make me evil."

"Did I ever say you were evil?" He didn't look up but she could feel the tension in his hands.

"I grew up next door to Charles Middleton. He asked me to marry him when he was twelve and I was ten. There was never a thought that I might not be his wife one day. You can't imagine how I felt when I arrived here and learned how he'd betrayed me. I'll not easily forgive or forget what he's done."

Stewart tied the ends of the wrapping into a snug knot. "But he still loves you. I saw that last night. And for all I know, you still love him."

Arabella's temper surged. Wasn't the man listening to her? If words wouldn't get through to him, maybe she should try something else. Gripped by a sudden impulse, she seized the sides of his head, yanked him toward her and burned a hot, angry kiss onto his mouth.

For an instant he went rigid. Then his arms caught her close. His lips crushed hers, powerful and demanding. She'd been kissed by Charles, of course, and by a few silly boys at parties, but never like this. She'd always been so proper, so restrained— but something about Stewart made her lose control. She moaned as his mouth coaxed hers to open. The thrust of his tongue trailed flame along her sensitive nerves. Dizzy with a whirl of new sensations, she arched against him, offering her throat, her breasts, wanting to be kissed, to be stroked and touched by that compelling mouth and those big, gentle hands.

"Damn it, Arabella," he muttered. "I've wanted you from the first time I saw you!"

A response stirred in her throat. "I need…" The rest of her words dissolved in a moan as his hand cupped her breast through the damp linen blouse. Her nipple shrank to an aching nub under the pressure of his palm. Her free hand fumbled for the buttons. "Yes," she whispered as his thumb slid beneath her lace-edged camisole to brush and tease her bare nipple. "Oh, yes…"

Thunder rattled the windowpanes as the storm broke in full fury. Arabella's heart drummed in counterpoint with the pounding rain as he bent and kissed her mouth again. Her fevered body responded, hands pulling his head lower to her barely covered breasts. The heat shimmering through her veins was beyond anything she could have imagined. All she could think of was how badly she wanted more.

To aid the wrapping of her ankle, she'd bared her left leg to the knee. Now his palm found her naked calf, sliding upward to the lacy hem of her drawers. Arabella whimpered, feeling the yearning ache where she wanted him to touch her, and knowing that nothing less would be enough. When he seemed to hesitate, she found his hand and slid it beneath the loose fabric to rest on her thigh.

A groan escaped his throat. "Arabella, we mustn't…" he murmured.

Arabella's kiss stopped the words she was beyond hearing. Her hips arched against his hand. As her right leg moved aside, her foot struck something solid. With a clatter the bucket spilled onto the floor.

"Oh!" She felt the shock of the ice-cold splash. Pulling away, Stewart scrambled to right the bucket and sponge up the water with the leftover wrappings. When he stood, she saw that a wall had slid into place behind his eyes.

"Arabella, I…" She could see him trying to frame an apology, and knew she couldn't bear to hear it.

"Please don't," she interrupted. "We…we both got carried away, that's all," she added, desperate to save face.

He cleared his throat. "I need to see to the stock," he said. "It might take some time. Will you be all right to hobble around in here?"

"I suppose so." Shaken by his sudden shift, Arabella mouthed the words.

"The salve's on the kitchen counter, and there's stew warming on the stove. When you're ready to sleep, you'll find Sally's room down the hall. There's a necessity under the bed."

"Stewart, I—"

"Not now." Reaching out, he traced a fingertip along her cheek. "We can talk tomorrow, after we've both had time to come to our senses."

Without giving her a chance to respond, he turned and strode out through the kitchen. The back door slammed in the wind. Arabella reached for the afghan and pulled it around her shaking shoulders. Her cheek felt cold where his finger had brushed it. Thunder boomed across the sky like mocking laughter.

Merciful heaven, what had she done?

By the time Stewart reached the barn, where he kept a spare slicker, he was soaked to the skin. Not that it mattered. After what had happened in the house, he'd needed a good, cold dousing. Lord help him, he'd believed he was under control. Then

Arabella had kissed him and blown that notion all to hell.

What had she wanted? If she'd wanted to prove she could make him respond, she'd succeeded. For a few minutes there, his need for her had overwhelmed everything else. And oh, how she had responded… In that moment, her desire for him had been as real and as powerful as his craving for her. But it had been just a moment of passion, and nothing more. He couldn't let himself believe she might truly care for a man like him. He was too awkward, too homely, too old at thirty and, although well-off, most of his money was in the land. He was nowhere near as eligible and appealing as Charlie Middleton.

He needed to get himself under control. If he went back in the house right now, he'd be tempted to pick right back up where he left off—and he had a sinking suspicion that she'd let him. If he allowed their mutual passion to play out, if he fully explored the heat and desire between the two of them, then he didn't think he'd be able to let her go. Not back to Boston, not back to Charlie and Sally's house—not out of his arms or his heart ever again.

But that wasn't going to happen. With Miguel gone, he could find enough chores to occupy him for a couple of hours. He wouldn't go back into the house until she was in bed, safely tucked out of his sight.

Donning the slicker over his wet clothes, he saddled a horse and rode out to the pasture to check on the calves. Range cows were used to stormy weather, but the smaller, weaker calves could get chilled. Circling the pasture, he rounded up the cows with younger calves and herded them toward the open shed at the near end. Some hay tossed down from a storage rack would give the mothers an added incentive to stay put.

The horse he'd ridden would need a rubdown after the short gallop. The pigs and chickens would need attention as well, to make sure their pens weren't flooding in the storm. There was a weasel-size hole in the coop that couldn't wait till tomorrow. The milk cows were running low on hay; and that was only the beginning.

By the time Stewart finished the chores, night had fallen. Rain sheeted off the roof of the barn as he bolted the doors and turned back toward the house.

The windows were dark, but a lantern glowed on its hook next to the back door. Had Arabella lit the wick and hung it there? Since he hadn't done it himself, there could be no other explanation.

Shedding his slicker and muddy boots on the back porch, he stepped into the kitchen and closed the door behind him. He was chilled beneath his wet clothes. It was time he peeled them off and hauled his tired body into bed. But there was one thing he needed to do first.

Stealing down the hall, he paused before the room that had been his sister's. The door stood ajar. He eased it open.

Arabella lay asleep in the narrow bed, her curls spilling over the pillow. In the darkness, Stewart could just make out her pale face. With her eyes closed and her sweet mouth at rest, she looked as innocent as a child.

Gazing down at her, Stewart felt something tighten around his heart. From the start, he'd done his best to convince himself he didn't like her. But in the measure of things, Arabella was bright and spunky, with a ready wit and a courageous heart. He remembered her reckless plunge into the river to save her wedding gown. He pictured those small hands, scratched and bloodied from crawling across the prairie. And the way she'd turned to living flame in his arms…

Tearing his gaze away, he backed out of the room and left the door as he'd found it. He could drive himself crazy thinking about Arabella. But that didn't mean any good would come of it. She'd be leaving soon, and that would be best for them all.

Weary as sin, he dragged himself back to his own room, stripped off his wet clothes and crawled into bed.

Only after he'd left did Arabella dare to open her eyes. She'd lain perfectly still, heart pounding, while

Stewart stood in the doorway, gazing at her. What did it mean when he'd lingered a few moments in the darkness? Was he having second thoughts about what had happened between them and how he'd ended it?

She'd gone to bed hurt and angry. But as she felt his presence in the room, she'd found herself yearning to have him bend over and touch her. She'd imagined herself reaching up, pulling him into her arms. At least she might have spoken to him. Now it was too late.

She was in dire need of sleep. The day's misadventure had worn her out; but thoughts of Stewart had kept her on edge. Now that he was safe indoors maybe she could finally relax.

Fluffing the pillow, she turned over and closed her eyes. Lulled by the steady tattoo of the rain she began to drift…

A deafening thunderclap shook the house. Arabella opened her eyes with a gasp. What time was it? Was she still dreaming?

The dream had haunted her since childhood, returning again and again—no images or words, just the sensation of crashing through space, tumbling over and over to the boom of thunder and the echo of screams. Aunt Phoebe, who'd done some reading on the subject, said the dream could be the buried memory of the accident that had killed her parents.

Arabella would never know for sure. She only knew that, whenever it came, the dream left her terrified beyond words.

Lightning flashed hot blue through the bedroom window. Thunder roared across the sky, so loud it seemed to fill the universe. Suddenly Arabella was on her feet, bolting out of the room and stumbling down the hall in her shift—toward the one source of comfort and safety.

Stewart was a light sleeper by nature. He'd been snoring soundly, but the presence of someone in the room quickly roused him to full alertness. He raised his head and opened his eyes.

Arabella stood in the doorway, ghostly pale in her white shift. Her hair fell in tangles around her face. Her eyes were as wild as a spooked mare's.

"What is it?" he managed to ask.

Her lips parted, but no voice emerged. He could tell that she was shaking. Outside, the storm had redoubled its fury. Wind and rain lashed the house.

"What is it, Arabella?" he asked again.

Lightning flashed through the window. The thunderclap was louder than the cannon fire he remembered from the war. Arabella cowered in terror, wrapping herself in her arms. Her strength had always ignited a passionate response in Stewart, but somehow her vulnerability moved him even more deeply.

Stewart knew what he needed to do. He also reminded himself that he was naked between the sheets, a sure recipe for disaster. But then a solution dawned. Turning back the quilt, he exposed the top side of the sheet that covered him.

"Come here before you catch your death, girl," he murmured, brushing the surface he'd smoothed for her. She came with a little whimper, huddling into the bed as he covered her with the quilt. Stewart wrapped her in his arms. She was soft and warm and smelled faintly of lavender soap.

They lay spooned, chastely separated by a thin layer of cotton flannel. Stewart's body had responded at first touch, springing to full, quivering arousal. He did his best to keep his hips pulled back from her rump, so she wouldn't feel it and be alarmed.

The effort was pure torture. Arabella was the most desirable woman he'd ever known. But, so help him, the last thing Stewart wanted was to ruin her the way Charlie Middleton had ruined his sister.

Stewart's bed felt warm and safe but Arabella was still trembling.

"What's the matter?" he asked her again.

"Just a bad dream. The thunder makes it worse. I know it's silly but I can't seem to help it."

"Nothing's silly if it makes you afraid. Tell me about it."

Arabella's story began haltingly, then spilled out of her in a rush—how her parents had died in a storm, and how, despite no conscious memory of it, the tragedy still haunted her dreams.

"Sometimes I dream about the war." His lips skimmed her hair. "The thunder makes it worse—it reminds me of artillery fire. I tell myself that's silly, too. It was over a long time ago. But there's a part of my brain that doesn't quite believe that. Maybe it's the same with you."

She turned to face him in the bed. "Hold me tight, Stewart," she whispered. "Maybe the thunder will go away for both of us."

A groan quivered in his throat as his arms tightened around her. His skin was cool and smelled of rain. She realized for the first time that he was naked beneath the sheet. Somehow that seemed all right. More than all right. A freshet of excitement pulsed through her body.

He muttered something that sounded like "Maybe you should go back to bed." Arabella couldn't make out the words, but that didn't matter because in the next breath they were kissing, and she was lost in the taste of his lips, the roughness of his stubbled beard, the sheer masculine power of the man. Her arms slid around his neck, fingers raking his thick hair.

Now that they were face-to-face she could feel the rock-hard jut of his sex against her belly. The thought that *she* was causing that reaction sent a jolt of heat to the aching core of her body. Moisture slicked her thighs. The sensations that swirled through her were as old as nature, yet frighteningly new. A lady, she reminded herself, would leap out of bed or fight tooth and nail for her virtue. But she was lost in a storm of delicious yearnings. All she could think of was flinging aside every rule of propriety and common sense she'd ever known to give herself to this man.

"Stewart…" She tugged at the sheet. "Please, I need you…"

He exhaled raggedly. Shifting in the bed, he kissed her again, gently this time. "Lie still, Arabella," he whispered.

His hand found its way beneath her thin cotton shift to cradle her breast. She moaned as he caressed her, his skillful touch triggering ripples of pleasure. "More," she murmured as his hand paused to rest on the flat of her belly, then moved downward to cup the wet nest of curls that framed her secret place. Her hips strained upward. She whimpered with need.

His fingertips opened her gently, parting her labia like rose petals, taking time to stroke each one. She gasped as he found the sensitive bud in the center.

Brushing a kiss across her mouth, he moved his hand and began a delicate, featherlike caressing.

"Oh…" Arabella murmured. "Oh…!" The feeling was so exquisite she almost wept. Her legs parted. Her hips thrust upward, seeking more pleasure. He could have taken her easily, but that, she realized, wasn't his intent. He was holding himself back, doing this for her.

The pulsing deepened. She could feel the hot, liquid contractions in her womb, swelling like drumbeats. Almost sobbing now, she gasped his name. Something clenched like a fist inside her. With a little cry she tumbled over the edge.

Gently his hand withdrew. He leaned over her where she sprawled on the sheet, utterly drained. A ghost of a smile flickered at the corner of his mouth.

Her hand brushed the scar on his cheek. "I didn't know anything could be like this…" she whispered.

He skimmed a kiss across her mouth. "Go to sleep, Arabella. I don't think the thunder will wake you now."

She sighed and closed her eyes, already drifting. Outside, the storm's fury was moving east, leaving a soft rain in its wake.

Dawn came early on the Montana prairie. But even before the first dim rays silvered the clouds, Stewart was awake. He'd lain sleepless most of the night, feeling Arabella's warmth beside him and listening to the sweet murmur of her breath. He could be happy waking up like this every morning of his life. But he knew better than to think it was going to happen.

Rising on one elbow, he watched the soft light steal across her sleeping face. He loved Arabella. That was the plain, simple truth of it. He'd loved her since that wild night when he'd picked her up in the rain and delivered her soaked and shivering to Charlie Middleton's gate. He loved her beauty, her stubbornness, her courage. And he loved the vulnerability she'd shown in his arms last night. Her complete trust had touched him more than anything he'd ever known.

But even last night couldn't change the fact that she didn't belong here. Arabella Spencer was a city woman. She might think she could be happy on the prairie, but she'd soon come to miss Boston— the parties and dances, the fashionable shops, the company of friends, all the things Montana couldn't offer her.

Then there was the threat to his sister's marriage. For Sally, the presence of her husband's ex-fiancée would be an open invitation to heartbreak. He knew now that Arabella would never take Charlie back, but as long as Charlie continued to long for her, he could never make Sally truly happy. For that reason alone, Arabella couldn't be allowed to stay.

So he couldn't allow himself to want her—especially not as his wife.

Arabella stirred and stretched in the morning sunlight. Even with her eyes closed, she could tell it was going to be a beautiful day—especially if she could spend it with Stewart.

There was no reason she had to leave just yet. After she dressed and freshened up, she could offer to make him breakfast. Then, if he had time, she could ask him to show her around his ranch. But right now, all she wanted to do was move close and snuggle against his side.

Shifting in the bed she reached out to embrace him. Her hand groped in confusion, finding nothing where he'd been but the cool, empty sheet. Stewart was gone.

Startled wide-awake, she sat up. Only then did she see the folded sheet of paper tucked under his pillow. Her hands shook as she unfolded it and read the note, written in an architect's precise script.

Dear Arabella,
By the time you read this I'll be on my way to help the men with the spring roundup and branding. There's coffee on the stove and a tray of

fresh biscuits in the warmer. I've left instructions for Miguel to hitch up the buggy and drive you back to the Middleton Ranch. If I don't see you before you leave for Boston, have a safe and pleasant journey. I hope you'll think of me now and again, as I will surely think of you.
Stewart

Arabella's throat jerked. She reread the note, battling the urge to crumple it and stomp it into the floor. Temper tantrums were for spoiled babies, and she was a grown woman. It was time she started behaving like one.

Her hand wiped away a furious tear. After spending the night in his bed, this was the last thing she'd expected. She'd thought Stewart liked her, maybe even loved her. She'd drifted off to sleep with happy dreams dancing in her head—living here on the ranch with him, sharing his everyday life, waiting on the porch to welcome him at the end of each day…

What a silly, romantic little fool she was!

She'd given him a piece of her heart, and the wretched man had taken it and run off like a sneaking coyote.

Arabella wasn't accustomed to being cast aside by men. And now it had happened twice in the same week. Pride dictated that she toss her curls, pack her trunk and go back to Boston, where a bevy of rich, handsome, eligible men would be vying to court her. She could pick from the best.

But she would never find another man like Stewart McIntyre.

Chapter Five

"**Y**ou have such beautiful hair, Sally." Arabella plied the brush, letting the silky gold strands slide through the bristles. "Just wait till I'm finished with you. You're going to look like a princess."

Sally's laugh was musical. "I'm hardly a princess, Arabella. Pigtails will do me fine for the ranch."

"But you're the wife of a gentleman rancher now. There'll be times when you want to look like a lady."

Again, Sally laughed. "All right, have your fun. But remember our bargain. Today you get to do my hair. Tomorrow I get to take you fishing."

"I'll probably drown." Arabella curled a sun-kissed lock around her finger. In the three days since her return to the Middleton Ranch, she'd discovered how easy it was to like Stewart's sister. She was a softer, gentler version of her brother. Sally was bright, warm, practical and very much her own person. Despite the strained circumstances, she was exactly the wife Charles needed—a steadfast rock to balance his somewhat flighty nature.

The real challenge was getting Charles to see that. So far Arabella had managed to avoid being alone with her ex-fiancé. But his manner toward her hadn't changed. Sooner or later the confrontation would come. She would have to be ready.

"I'm still curious about what happened at Stewart's place," Sally said. "You've been mighty tight-lipped about it."

Arabella shrugged. "Well, there isn't that much to tell."

Except that I fell in love with him.

"Stewart's always been shy with the ladies," Sally continued, chatting on. "The more he likes a woman, the faster he runs away. I expect that's why he's never married. He'd make a wonderful husband and father. But that's not likely to happen—not unless some girl has the gumption to toss away her pride and go after him with all flags flying."

With all flags flying...

The hairbrush slipped out of Arabella's hands and clattered to the floor. The color rushed to her face as she bent to pick it up. It was clear that Sally had spoken for her benefit. But she'd never pursued a man in her life. In Boston society, that sort of thing just wasn't done.

Did she love Stewart enough to throw away her

pride? But why ask that question? His note had made it clear that he didn't plan to see her again. How could she pursue a man when he was someplace else? It wasn't as if she could ride out and track him down on the prairie.

Twisting Sally's hair into a shining coil, Arabella began pinning it into place. The motions were so familiar and automatic that they proved no obstacle to her wandering thoughts. Her time here was running out. Before long the roads would be patched, the bridges would be rebuilt and the stage would resume its scheduled run.

Would she be on it?

She blinked away a furtive tear. Once she'd been anxious to leave this wide-open country. But that was before she'd lost her heart. What she needed now, more than anything, was a reason to stay.

Stewart pushed back his hat and used his bandanna to wipe his sweating face. He'd spent the past four days roping and branding—and the past four nights dreaming about Arabella.

Those dreams—hellfire, they were enough to drive a man crazy. Arabella in his bed, her voluptuous little body meeting his thrusts as he filled her with his seed. Arabella at his side, holding his babies, railing at him and teasing him and filling his life with love and passion as their family grew.

He'd hoped that being on the range would help him forget her. But it hadn't worked. She'd been on his mind the whole time. More than he'd ever wanted anything in his life, he wanted that little green-eyed spitfire for his own.

So what was he doing out here with the cattle when the woman he loved could already be on her way back to Buffalo Bend? He'd never considered himself a stupid man. But he'd be an idiot if he let her get away without even trying to convince her to stay.

Win or lose, it was time he laid his cards on the table. Proposing to Arabella could be the biggest mistake he'd ever made. She could spit in his eye and tell him to go to hell. After the note he'd left her to find following her night in his bed, he wouldn't blame her. Worse, she could say yes and then later discover she couldn't really be happy with him after all. But unless he asked her, he'd never know what he might have missed.

It was a chance he had to take.

After leaving a few instructions with his men, he turned his horse toward the Middleton Ranch and nudged the animal to a trot. Roused from a doze under the chuck wagon, the dog shook its muddy coat and raced after him.

The fishing lesson had been a grand success. Sally had driven the buckboard to a small creek overhung by willows. There she'd shown Arabella how to string a line, attach the fly and cast it into a quiet hole. She had a collection of beautiful flies, hooked into the fleece of a sheepskin folder. Fashioned of tiny feathers, wound with silk thread on to a barbed hook, they were as exquisitely detailed as real insects. Some were nearly as small. Stewart had made them over the winter months, Sally explained. Each one was a painstaking work of art.

Casting the line had taken some practice. At first, Arabella's fly had snagged the willows more often than it landed in the water. But once she got the knack of it, she'd taken to the sport like a natural. Between the two of them, she and Sally had brought home a nice stringer of trout.

The morning's activities had worn Sally out. After lunch she'd gone upstairs to rest. Twenty minutes later, when Arabella had looked in on her, she'd found Charles's wife asleep on the bed with one arm curled protectively over her rounded belly. Arabella had covered her friend with a quilted throw, stolen back downstairs and walked outside, onto the front porch.

The builder of Charles's house had chosen the spot for its sweeping view of the countryside. From where she stood, Arabella could see all the way to the mountains, where black clouds were boiling over the horizon. Her ears caught the faraway whisper of thunder. Another storm, and it was moving fast. Soon it would be overhead.

Would Stewart be safe on the open range? She couldn't help worrying. But Stewart had spent years on the Montana prairie. To him, a spring thunderstorm would be nothing to fear. The only thing Stewart seemed to fear was *her*.

With all flags flying... Sally's words came back to her as she watched the clouds spread across the sky. Was that what it would take to win the man—an all-out, shameless pursuit? Was she up to the challenge?

A cool breeze struck her face, smelling of rain. As the distant thunder grew closer, Arabella turned and went back inside the house. Charles had stocked his study shelves with books. She could always pass the afternoon reading. Maybe that would take her mind off the storm.

The study was off the entry hall, across from the parlor. The door stood ajar. Arabella was about to cross the threshold when she glimpsed Charles at his desk, his head bent over his account books.

He hadn't seen her. It would be easy enough to sneak up to her room and avoid him, as she'd been doing all week. But sooner or later, the reckoning would have to come. With Sally asleep upstairs, now was as good a time as any for what she had to tell him.

Steeling her resolve, she opened the door. "May I come in, Charles?" she asked.

For an instant he looked startled. Then he rose. "Of course. Sit down, Arabella. Can I get you something to drink?"

"No, thank you. And I believe I'll stand. What I came to say won't take long."

"That's too bad. I was hoping you and I would get more time together." He walked around the desk and took her hand. "I have some news. Not welcome news for me, I'm afraid. One of my men rode a horse into town yesterday. He brought back word that the bridge is up again, and the road's been repaired. The next southbound stage will be coming through Buffalo Bend in three days."

Three days. Arabella felt her heart drop.

Charles's sky-blue eyes widened. "What's this? I thought you'd be happy. Does that downcast look mean you'll be sorry to leave me?"

She shook her head. "Charles, I—"

His hand tightened its grip on her fingers. "I knew it! You do still care for me, don't you?"

She tore her hand away. "Of course I still care for you! We've been best friends since we were children! That's why I can't let you go on making a fool of yourself!"

His expression froze. "A fool? Whatever do you mean?"

"Grow up, Charles!" She hurled the words at him. "You're married to a wonderful woman, and she's about to make you a father. Be a man, for heaven's sake! Give her the loyalty and consideration she deserves!"

He sighed, looking sheepish. "I do love Sally, you know. She's ten times better than I deserve. But, Arabella, I love you, too. I'll always love you."

"Well, I don't love you!" She watched his face go pale. "If you must know, I'm in love with somebody else."

He stared at her as if she'd told him night was day and the moon was made of butter—as if it had never occurred to him that her feelings could change.

"I'm in love with Stewart," she said.

"With *Stewart*? That big, overgrown—?" He shook his head in disbelief. "And does Stewart feel the same about you?"

"I don't know. I only know that if he asked me I'd marry him this minute."

As Arabella spoke the words she knew they were true. She loved Stewart to the depths of her soul, and she couldn't leave without giving herself another chance with him.

"That's why I'm telling you now, Charles. I don't know what's going to happen with Stewart, but if I stay, things will have to be different between us. We could end up being neighbors. Your wife could end up being my sister-in-law. But no matter what happens with Stewart, you have to understand that there will *never* be anything but friendship between you and me ever again. Do you understand?"

His eyes had taken on that lost puppy look. Once it would have melted her heart. Now it made her want to grind her teeth. "But we still *can* be friends, can't we?" he asked.

"Of course we can. But nothing more. You'll be giving all your love to your beautiful wife and your child." She thrust a finger at his chest. "For heaven's sake, Charles, don't you know what a lucky man you are to have a woman like Sally? Breaking her heart would be the worst thing you could ever do."

He sighed again. "You were always the wise one, Arabella. You're right. I am lucky. And I'd be crazy to risk losing my wife and child through my own foolishness. All I can do is wish you well. You deserve the best life has to offer."

"Thank you. So do you."

"Friends?" He held out his arms for a hug.

"Friends." She stepped into his embrace. They'd been companions most of their lives; but looking back over the years, it seemed they'd been more like brother and sister than sweethearts. It was time for both of them to move on.

"Be happy, Charles." Arabella was stretching upward to plant a sisterly kiss on his cheek when she heard a footstep and the subtle squeak of a door hinge.

Startled, she turned to see Stewart standing in the open doorway, unshaven and dusty from the range. His face was rigid with shock.

He couldn't get out of there fast enough. Without a word, Stewart stepped back into the entry and strode outside, letting the front door slam behind him.

He'd always been a man of action, a man who'd charge fearlessly—even recklessly—into any situation, no matter the odds. But now, all he could do was run.

Lord, how could he act sensibly when he couldn't even think straight? He had to get away from here before he did something crazy. Vaulting into the saddle, he kicked the horse to a gallop and headed for the gate.

"Stewart!" Arabella had rushed out onto the porch. "Stewart! Stop! This isn't what you think!"

As he thundered down the drive, he willed himself not to look back at her.

Arabella collapsed on the top step of the porch and buried her face in her hands. Her intentions had been entirely good. How could she have made such a mess of things?

Stewart had long suspected her of scheming to break up his sister's marriage. Now she was certain that he believed he'd seen proof of it, and he wasn't the sort of man to change his mind. She had lost him for sure; and after she heard his story, Sally would never want to be her friend again. The best she could do for all concerned was leave.

Hot tears scalded her cheeks. She smeared them away with her hand. At least Charles hadn't followed her outside. He was probably scared of what Stewart might do to him.

The storm clouds that roiled overhead matched her mood. Sheet lightning flickered against the blackness. Out of habit, she counted between the flash and the thunder. Four seconds. Four miles. Not so close yet but the wind had freshened. The storm was moving in fast.

She could no longer see Stewart. Horse and rider had vanished behind a low hill. From there they could be headed in any direction. Even if she tried, she'd have no hope of catching up with him.

Something cool and wet touched her arm. The dog, its fur coated with dust and mud, pressed against her side. It must have come here with Stewart and decided to stay.

She stroked its head, heedless of the smudges on her yellow dress. Whining, it pushed its nose into her hand. "What is it, boy?" she asked. "Are you trying to tell me something?"

The dog's tail thumped against the porch. Pawing at her skirt, it gazed at her with eager, golden eyes.

Such an intelligent animal. Arabella remembered how it had run off with her hat and led Stewart to her rescue when she'd fallen off her horse.

Could the dog lead her to Stewart now?

Lightning cracked across the sky, chased almost immediately by an earsplitting boom of thunder. Terror gripped Arabella's throat. The storm was closing in. If she left now, she would be in the open—but so would Stewart.

Stewart knew the prairie well, but that didn't make him immune to danger—especially if he was feeling betrayed and prone to recklessness. What if something were to happen to him? What if he were to die—like her parents had died—without ever knowing that she loved him?

Arabella was on her feet now, running across the yard with the dog at her heels. Raindrops spattered the ground as she dashed into the barn. The gray gelding that had thrown her was in its stall. Despite her bad experience, she knew the animal was swift and sturdy. She would choose it any day over the carriage horses and the showy bay Charles favored. But no more sidesaddle for her. She found a well-used Western saddle, lifted it onto the gelding's back and buckled the cinch.

Outside the barn, she hiked up her skirts and mounted the nervous horse. The dog was dancing with anticipation. "Find your master, boy," she said. "Go!"

The dog was off like a shot, with Arabella flying along behind. The rain was coming down hard now. Within seconds it had plastered her clothes to her skin. The memory of her nightmares stirred and rose—the thunder, the screams… She willed them away. All that mattered now was finding Stewart and forcing him to hear the truth.

She could only hope he would listen.

Stewart had ridden straight out onto the prairie. He hadn't wanted to go home, where Arabella's sweet fragrance still lingered in his bed. And he was in no condition to go back and face his men. All he wanted to do was crawl into a hole and lick his wounds like a wild animal.

What was he going to tell Sally? Nothing, for now, he resolved. There was too much danger that her distress could harm the baby. But the next time he caught Charlie Middleton alone, he would threaten to shoot off the bastard's balls if he didn't behave himself. As for Miss Arabella Spencer…he didn't know what to think, or what to believe. It was as if the world had turned upside down. His eyes and his mind told him one thing, but with all his heart and soul, he didn't want to believe it.

Lightning cracked the roiling sky. The boom of

thunder seemed to shake the earth. The strike had been close—too close. In a storm like this one, the open prairie was a dangerous place to be. It was time he headed for shelter.

Rain streamed down as the clouds opened. Stewart scanned the country around him. He'd been riding aimlessly, but he recognized the hollow between two low hills. In a shallow canyon was an abandoned homestead with an old sod shanty. Last time Stewart had seen it the shanty had barely been standing, but as least it might offer some protection.

Pushing the horse to a gallop, he made for it.

Numb with cold and terror, Arabella urged her horse through the streaming rain. The dog was a brown blur in the long grass. It was all she could do to keep the creature in sight. What if it wasn't leading her to Stewart at all? What if it was just out for a run?

A hundred yards to her right, lightning struck a burned-out tree stump. The crack of thunder was like a cannon going off inside her head. The gelding screamed and reared. Arabella clung to its neck, sawing at the reins. Seconds crawled past as she struggled to quiet the frightened animal. Little by little, she managed to bring the horse under control.

Exhausted, she sagged in the saddle and glanced around for the dog. The shaggy mutt was nowhere to be seen. Fear crawled up her throat as she whistled and called. There was no bark, no rustle in the grass; no response at all. Arabella was lost in the storm.

She had little choice except to keep moving. But with the deadly lightning so close, she realized it would be safer to dismount and lead the horse. Now that she no longer knew where she was going, there was no reason to hurry.

Speaking calmly to the skittish gelding, she slid to the ground and took the reins. Her boots were spongy with water, the sharp-edged grass knee-high. She was soaked to the skin, shivering with cold and nauseous with terror. Her sprained ankle, which was still healing, had begun to throb. But she didn't dare allow herself to rest. If she sat down she might not have the strength to get up again.

Was Stewart somewhere out here, cold, miserable and alone just as she was? Arabella battled a growing hopelessness. Even with the dog, finding him would have been a matter of luck. Now not even luck would be enough.

She needed a miracle.

Stewart huddled in the driest corner of the old soddie. Most of the roof had caved in, but at least the walls lent some protection from the wind and the lightning. Too bad he had no walls against the bittersweet memory of Arabella in his arms.

Could he have been wrong about what he'd seen? Now that he'd had time to think, the question tormented him. She'd come running after him to explain, but he'd stormed off without giving her a chance. What if he'd stayed long enough to listen? If he'd misjudged her, he could pay the price to the end of his days.

The horse snorted and stirred in the shadows. Stewart had led the animal inside the walls to protect it from the lightning, which had been known to kill men and animals on the open plain. He remembered Arabella's story of how her parents had died, and the fear that was buried inside her, deeper than memory. At least he'd left her in a safe place. No matter what she might have done, he could never wish her harm.

He loved her too much for that.

The horse nickered, pricking its ears. Stewart was instantly alert, moving toward the Winchester he kept slung from the saddle. Before he could reach it, a wet, muddy canine hurtled through the crumbling doorway, flinging itself on him in a paroxysm of joy.

Stewart managed to shove the squirming, licking animal to arm's length. "Fool dog," he muttered, "don't you even have the sense to stay out of the rain?"

The dog wheeled toward the doorway, whining and yipping. It was a behavior Stewart had come to recognize. "What is it, boy? Do you want me to follow you?"

The dog yipped and trotted outside. Knowing it would be safer to go on foot, Stewart slung the rifle over his shoulder and hurried into the storm. Whatever the mutt wanted him to see, he could only hope it wasn't far off.

Minutes later he spotted the bulky outline of a horse through the rain. His heart plummeted as he recognized the gray gelding from the Middleton Ranch. It was the horse Arabella would have taken if she'd come after him.

With a prayer on his lips, Stewart plunged ahead. Arabella was terrified of thunder and lightning. She would never have ventured out in a storm like this one—not unless she was crazy enough to love him.

He could have stayed and listened to her. Instead he'd mounted up and galloped away. If the worst had happened, he'd have no one to blame but himself and his damned foolish pride.

He had nearly reached the horse when he saw her. She'd fallen to her knees in the grass, her head drooping forward. Was she praying or merely exhausted? It didn't matter. Nothing mattered except that she was alive, and he'd found her.

At the sound of her name she looked up. Stewart strode forward, caught her in his arms and lifted her like a child. Shivering, she curled against his chest.

She was so precious, and he loved her so much. He would do everything in his power to make her happy.

"Stewart—" She looked up at him. Her lips were blue with cold.

"Hush, it's all right. Don't try to talk, Arabella." He strode toward the old sod house, the horse and dog trailing behind.

"No, I have to tell you." Her hands gripped the front of his rain-soaked shirt. "When you saw me with Charles, he was wishing me well, as an old friend. That was all. I'd just told him that I…" She hesitated. "That I was in love with you."

"Hush, I know, my love." All doubt vanished as he spoke. "I should have known all along. If you'll forgive me, I want to spend the rest of our lives making it up to you."

She pressed her head against his chest as he carried her into the crude shelter and settled against the wall. "Let me warm you," he whispered as he held her close.

The rain would soon be letting up. Already, through the clouds, Stewart could see a glimmer of sunlight. Before long the storm would pass. Then they would mount up and ride home side by side, under a blue Montana sky.

Maybe there would even be rainbows.

Epilogue

One week later

The setting sun had turned the clouds to flame. Ribbons of gold, pink and vermilion streamed above the western peaks, casting the prairie in a rosy glow. A flock of wild geese, flying north, winged across the sky.

Arabella rested her head on her husband's shoulder as the buggy pulled over the last hilltop. "Look," she whispered. "Even the sky is celebrating with us."

"I think the sky is telling us it's almost bedtime." Stewart chuckled as he lifted the reins to drive forward.

"No, wait." Arabella laid a hand on his arm. "Give me a moment to look down at the place from here. It's so beautiful. And I'm seeing it for the first time as my new home."

"Whatever pleases you, love." He slipped an arm around her shoulders, pulling her close. The ranch house nestled below the hill, a perfect symphony of logs, stone and glass that harmonized with the land where it lay. The windows glowed in the golden light.

"I think I realized I was in love with you when I first saw your house," Arabella teased.

"Well, now you have both—the house and me. I hope you're pleased with yourself, Mrs. McIntyre."

"More than pleased. Now let's go home."

Arabella's wedding had been far different than she'd imagined. There'd been only a few days to plan it before the circuit preacher came through. Grandma Peabody's silk wedding gown was splotched with water stains that not even Sally had been able to remove. Arabella had chosen to wear it anyway, for luck. The wreath of wildflowers in her hair had matched the bouquet she carried down the aisle of the little white church. She had never felt more beautiful. And when she looked up into Stewart's eyes to recite her vows, his love had flowed through her like warm sunlight.

In attendance at the simple ceremony were a few friends from town, as well as Charles and Sally who'd smiled and held hands the whole time. A special guest of honor, Stewart's dog, had been bathed, brushed and adorned with a garland of ribbons and daisies around its shaggy neck. During the ceremony, the wayward mutt had wandered off to romp in a puddle with a canine friend, then returned to the church, leaving muddy footprints down the aisle. A wedding picnic at Charles and Sally's had capped the festivities.

In other words, the day couldn't have been more perfect.

Stewart pulled the buggy up to the front walk and turned the horse over to Miguel, who waited with a shy grin on his face. Arabella was about to climb to the ground when Stewart swept her up in his arms.

"Remember the first time I carried you into this house? I was wondering then how it would be to carry you home as a bride," he said.

Arabella laughed. "As I recall, I was thinking along the same lines. Let's find out."

She nestled against Stewart's chest as he carried her across the porch. Some things, she'd learned, didn't work out according to plan. And life's unexpected gifts could be the dearest blessings of all.

* * * * *

Dear Reader

You can't imagine how excited I was when asked to participate in this anthology. I've written a few very short stories for magazines, but I've never written in novella length. My excitement grew when I learned I would be able to link this story to the series I've been working on for Mills & Boon® Historical Romance.

The question about my writing I'm asked most often is, 'Where do you get your ideas?' My answer is always, 'Everywhere.' The inspiration for this novella came from my husband's sister. She married his best friend—his childhood friend. That happened after what we all laughingly call 'the miracle'. She was an unashamed tomboy, who had a date one Saturday night when my husband and his friend happened to be heading somewhere as well—being a man, my husband doesn't remember where. As they were readying themselves to leave, my sister-in-law came downstairs, all prettied up for her date. His friend looked up and lightning seemed to strike him. He asked a now infamous question. Watch for it, because Dylan asks it too. My sister-in-law, who is now my best friend, answered in much the same way as Rhiannon Oliver.

I hope you enjoy this tale inspired by our family history. There's always something exciting happening in Tierra del Verde, so watch for other instalments of the characters who settled the Wild West in Texas's beautiful Hill country. You can find out what sent them West in the first books of the series. They're at www.millsandboon.co.uk

Dedication

To Deb and John. Thanks for the inspiration.
I love telling your story! Hope you have
many more happy years together. All my love, Kate.

Chapter One

Tierra del Verde, Texas—March 1879

Rhiannon Oliver pulled the buckboard to a stop in front of Wheaton General Store. She glanced up and down the main street and smiled a little sadly. The town had grown because of the stagecoach line having put them on their route. Sadly a few families had moved on because of the growth.

Unfortunately with progress came problems. Strangers drifted in and out of town more often now. Which forced her to continue wearing a disguise of britches and loose shirts that had come about accidentally when her figure had begun to blossom six years ago. With her mother long dead, neither Rhia nor her father had known what to do other than pretend she was a son. But she wasn't.

Since her father's death two years earlier, she'd had no one to rely on but herself. Her friend's mother had filled in, so in some personal matters she hadn't been completely bereft of a woman's counsel. A woman alone was in danger, however, so what had been a convenience for her father now had to be continued for her safety.

Recent Comanche raids worried everyone, too, especially since no one had been able to track the raiders or find evidence they even existed. Some called them Ghost Warriors. Some looked at the bigger operations with suspicion but the source of the murderous raids remained a mystery.

Rhia just kept putting one foot in front of the other trying not to let resentment take root in her soul because no one saw past the disguise. Two cowboys walked along then, passing her without notice. Rhia sighed. Yep. *Still invisible.*

She set the brake and jumped down. Her gaze fell immediately upon a poster tacked to the upright of the covered boardwalk. Spring Social. April 4. Rocking R. Five To Midnight. Apparently Alex Reynolds and his wife were hosting again.

She would stay home. Again.

Tying her old horse, Jessie, to the hitching rail, she watched with a smile as Scout, her border collie and constant companion for as long as she could remember, took a flying leap from the wagon's seat to the boardwalk. Rhia grabbed her basket of eggs and ran lightly up the steps. She and Scout entered the general store together—the way they did everything else.

"Good afternoon, Abby," she called out to the proprietor as the screen door smacked shut behind her. "I hope you need eggs."

Abby Wheaton peeked around the back room doorway, her green eyes sparkling. "I just sold the last to Reiman House. Your timing's perfect." She pushed the curtain aside, carrying several dresses. "Let me hang these before they wrinkle then I'll be right with you."

Rhia set her basket on the counter and went to the empty display table where Abby started to lay the dresses. The scent of freshly ironed cloth rose from the neat stack. "Here," Rhia said, "let me hold them while you hang them. It would be a shame to see them wrinkled."

Scout padded over to the stove and lay down as Rhia took the dresses by their hangers. She handed them to Abby one by one, admiring each while Abby hung them. Rhia found herself wishing for at least one of the pretty garments Abby had made. Ready-made dresses was an idea Abby had brought with her from the East. "These are really lovely, Abby."

Abby looked over at her, eyes narrowing shrewdly. "You know, I let those britches fool me for a while. You'd love to be able to wear dresses."

Rhia laughed, her nerves showing in the shakiness

of her voice. Abby had stated a fact not a question and now Rhia felt a bit like an unmasked bank robber. She shrugged, pretending indifference. "Daddy taught me never to buy on credit. If this year's wool prices stay where they are, maybe I'll be back for one of these," she said, but it probably wasn't wise to step out from behind the mask.

"Oh, I remember the penny-pinching days."

That was what was nice about Abby. Though married to the town's banker, a man of means, she came from working stock, the daughter of a Pennsylvania coal miner. She knew what living without meant.

Rhia came to a dress that looked like it might fit her. She hesitated and took a moment to gaze at it. "Raul and I plan to start shearing tomorrow," she said, hearing the wistful tone in her voice and praying Abby hadn't.

Abby took the dress and looked over the pretty blue frock, giving Rhia an extra moment to covet it. If she bought anything, it should be new shears, not an impractical dress she shouldn't wear in public.

"Are you coming to the spring social?"

The tinkling of the bell over the door made Rhia glance over her shoulder. She nearly sighed aloud. Dylan Varga. She couldn't remember a day since meeting him when she hadn't loved him. He was her best friend's older brother and, with womanhood, her puppy love had deepened and begun to fill her entire being. Unfortunately, she might as well be part of the shelving for all the notice he gave her.

Maybe if I dropped the disguise that'd change. But that presented complications. She'd promised her father to make Adara a success, which meant living alone. She couldn't fail him. That was far more weighty a worry than risking a final rejection from Dylan.

She glanced Dylan's way again, holding the remaining dresses in front of her like armor, hoping to avoid that stomach-flipping effect his nearness always caused.

Dylan took his hat off, his black hair shining in the sunlight, and closed the door. Then he smiled. Oh, no. Now she even felt it when all he did was smile in her direction.

"Good day, Mrs. Wheaton," he said, then to Rhia he added with a grin, "You thinking of buying a dress, Rowdy? You don't want the sun to fall out of the sky, do you?"

She notched her chin. Rowdy. He'd named her that the first time he had to rescue her when she'd climbed too high in a tree. She'd liked it, that pet name he called no one else—but it had grown tiresome. His sister wore pants while working at Belleza, their family sheep ranch. Her pants were the more costly Levi Strauss jeans. At $1.25 a pair,

Strauss's jeans cost what an acre of good Texas land did. Farrah's father could afford what Rhia couldn't.

That her clothes didn't reflect the real her rankled. She wasn't a tomboy like Farrah. She wanted to dress like a woman but her position as a woman alone wouldn't allow it.

"Actually," Rhia heard Abby say, "we're looking for the right one for Rhiannon to wear to the spring social. I hope you'll be escorting your sister since your mother and father won't be attending."

His golden eyes widened at Abby's whopper but he refrained from any smart-mouthed comments about Rhia wearing a dress and attending a dance. "The don won't step foot on the Rocking R because I work there," Dylan replied. "He demanded Alex Reynolds fire me. Alex being Alex refused. Still, I don't think the don would forbid Farrah from going. I doubt she'd want to go, but I'll ask."

"Oh, she'll come," Abby assured Dylan. "Now if you'll excuse us, I need to get Rhiannon settled in the back. Come along, lovie." She ordered compliance with a look. "I'm sure Mr. Varga won't mind waiting a moment."

Stunned, Rhia stared at the back of Abby Wheaton's head then followed meekly. What would it hurt to try on one or two of Abby's pretty frocks? She didn't *have* to buy one. Thankful Dylan wasn't too close, she walked past him. Having him too near was another thing that caused her stomach to do that strange dance. Surely she could outlast Dylan's business there. It would give her a chance to wallow in all that pretty finery.

"Abby, I told you I can't buy a dress," she whispered. "You know how Daddy felt about credit. And are you sure Farrah is going? She hates socials."

"Oh, she'll be going or my name isn't Abaigeal Kane Wheaton," Abby said, stepping close and working at the buttons of Rhia's oversize shirt. "You're leavin' here with a dress. We'll take a little bit each time out of your egg money till it's all paid off. You won't even notice it missing. I know what it's like to be ashamed of my clothes. You deserve this. Don't be denyin' you want to go. Or that you want to be impressin' that big lug out there. Callin' you 'Rowdy.' I never heard such a thing. Now strip and try on one these dresses. I'll be right back with a crinoline after I've waited on him and sent him on his way. We're going to knock him senseless come the fourth," Abby whispered.

Rhia stared after Abby. The woman was a force to be reckoned with. Especially since Rhia had never wanted anything as much as she wanted to knock Dylan senseless with that blue dress and what she looked like in it. Rhia hurried to get it on praying it fit—forgetting all the reasons it was a bad idea.

Chapter Two

At almost dusk on April 4, Dylan waited impatiently in the gig outside his parents' hacienda. His mother had stuck her head out the door for just a moment to ask him to wait there. Which really meant the don still wouldn't receive his own son.

She'd also told him Farrah had asked her friend Rhiannon Oliver to ride along. It was going to be a bit of a tight fit in the two-person gig.

God, at least Rhia always managed to scrub off the stink of working with sheep. He knew that smell having been forced to care for them while growing up. Instead he always caught the faint scent of wildflowers whenever he was in the same room with her.

Strange.

He looked up and saw his mother staring out at him from Farrah's upstairs bedroom window. He smiled and blew her a kiss. His thoughts swung back to her and her difficult position between the warring men in her life. And guilt followed. He couldn't imagine being separated from his own child and he was sorry for his part in her heartache. But he had to live life his way and that didn't include sheep ranching.

His mind slid to his sister. What had sparked her attendance tonight? Farrah's pretty face and tall stature managed to make her in a pair of Levi Strauss's blue jeans a sight most of the men around Belleza and Tierra del Verde enjoyed seeing. Of course, knowing they'd be looking elsewhere for work kept the men on Belleza from acting on any attraction they felt toward her. Farrah's prickly demeanor took care of the rest.

Farrah's surprise companion tonight put them off with her appearance alone. Unlike Farrah, Rhia had always been too plump and too unkempt. From a couple years after her mother's death, every time he'd seen her, she'd had a beat-up old Stetson rammed down on her head. She made herself real inhospitable to a man, no matter that she was a good, hardworking person. To his knowledge no man had ever given Rhiannon Oliver a second look. Of course, he doubted Rhia minded. All she seemed to care about was following in her daddy's footsteps running Adara.

The door opened and his mother came out again. He jumped down and went to her. God, he'd missed her.

"The girls will be along," she said. "Your father said I could come get a hug."

Dylan wrapped his arms around his mother and held her for a long moment. *"Cabra vieja,"* he growled.

His mother whacked him on the shoulder as she stepped back. "Who are you calling an old goat?"

"The don." He kissed his mother's smooth cheek. "Certainly not the prettiest woman in the state of Texas."

She clearly fought a smile. "Flattery won't get you out of hot water. You should be ashamed. He's your *father.*"

"You're right, but I loved my grandmother too much to call him a son of a bitch."

"Language," she scolded. "One of you has to bend first. He's not going to live forever, then it'll be too late."

"Talk to *him.* He's the one who refuses to compromise. He won't even let me into the house so I *can* talk to him. I'd have been happy to stay. He's the one who needed to bend. Instead he escalated this. He disowned me. All I asked for was a piece of land to raise horses."

His mother sighed and stroked his cheek. "I know. You have your life and dreams just as he did when he left Spain." She forced a smile. "He had to give up his dreams for you the way his father did when we came here. But enough talk of problems. Smile. You're the luckiest man in Tierra del Verde tonight." She stepped to the side. "You'll be escorting the two prettiest young ladies in Texas to the social."

Dylan looked first to Farrah walking toward him. She did indeed look like a lady for once with her chestnut hair waving around her shoulders and wearing a pretty dress instead of jeans.

Then his eyes slid to Rhiannon as she drew closer.

His heart turned over in his chest.

She was dazzling. Not a bit plump. And the dark-as-night hair she usually kept hidden under that beat-up hat was so silky it even managed to capture the last dying rays of the sun. It hung down her back in adorable waves and framed her face while flirting with the breeze. Her creamy complexion made his fingertips yearn to touch its softness. He was suddenly grateful to that hated old hat for the shade it had provided. Her ebony lashes, thick and full, framed her cornflower-blue eyes.

She wore a pretty blue dress with a full skirt he'd swear was the same color as her incredible eyes. The sash around her middle accentuated her slender waist and hips. He retraced the path of his perusal back up to her eyes where he found himself ensnared.

Why had he never noticed how pretty she was?

Why had he never noticed her at all except as some-one to tease? "Rhia? Where the hell have you been?"

Her chin notched up. "I've been ready to leave for an hour. Farrah and your mother were arguing over her dress. Why blame me?"

"No. No. I'm not. I meant…uh…where did you come from?"

She looked at him as if he'd lost his mind. "From Farrah's room?" she said real slowly the way folks talked to someone not quite right in the head.

Maybe he *had* lost his senses. He'd certainly lost his touch. He was usually a lot more polished with a woman who'd caught his eye. But then again, the soiled doves at the Golden Garter weren't exactly a good test of his prowess.

"I meant you look…nice," he finished, knowing that wasn't a strong enough word but settling. As tongue-tied as he felt God alone knew what might have popped out.

Silently he took Rhia's hand to help her into the gig he'd borrowed from Alex. And nearly gasped. What the hell was that? If his eyes hadn't told him different, he'd have sworn her touch had set his hand afire. By handing her up first he'd insured that she'd be pressed close to him in the two-seat gig. He ought to be able to untie his tongue on the way so he could charm her into walking in on his arm.

A few hours later Dylan watched from the side of

the room as yet another admirer claimed Rhiannon for a dance. They were like bees drawn to the last flower of summer. He'd only gotten to partner her in one dance and that had been a square dance.

Checking his watch, he realized the night was nearly over. He tried to take comfort from the knowledge that she'd walked in on his arm and would be leaving the same way. But it didn't help that George Bentley had her hand in his as the caller signaled them to allemande left then promenade.

Finally Bentley had to let go as they each moved on to other partners. Dylan felt better about it as it was Joshua Wheaton, the town's banker and husband to the miracle worker who'd made Rhia's pretty blue dress.

Funny, Dylan wouldn't have thought Rhia could dance—if he'd thought about her at all. Or that she'd be so delicate and pretty under what she usually wore. He ached to hold her in his arms and wished he could claim her for a waltz.

He looked across the handsome gold room with its gas chandeliers and wall sconces. They made the place almost as bright as day. Alex Reynolds stood near one of the open windows.

Dylan walked over and breathed in the scent of the early blooming wildflowers. Alex was his boss but he'd become more friend than employer since Dylan had played a part in rescuing Alex's wife from a kidnapper. "Do you think those yahoos know how to play a waltz?" Dylan asked, nodding toward the piano player from the Golden Garter and the three others sawing on their fiddles.

Alex grinned. "They'd better. They promised to practice it all this week. I have the last dance reserved with Patience. It's supposed to be the waltz. You going to try for a chance to lead out the belle of the ball?"

Dylan followed Alex's gaze to Rhia. She *was* the belle and he wanted her in his arms. He found himself moving back toward the dance floor, making sure he stood right where Rhia and her partner stopped. Quickly stepping forward, Dylan cut off George Bentley's approach. "This is the dance you promised to me," Dylan lied.

Miraculously Rhia didn't call him on it. She did look confused, though, when she said, "Oh, yes. I suppose I must have forgotten." Her breathing was a bit labored, too. He should lead her to the lemonade table to cool off but he was feeling selfish. He wanted her all to himself.

The little quartet struck up an odd version of a waltz. Though he'd heard it played more expertly, it was sweet music anyway. Because Rhia was in his arms, looking into his eyes.

"I can't believe I finally have the belle of the ball all to myself."

"Hardly a belle and I doubt this is as grand as a ball. You've visited both sets of your grandparents. Farrah told me how grand everything is in England and Spain."

He grinned. "Tonight, my belle, here with you like this, it all seems pretty grand to me." He couldn't seem to curb the things he said to her any more than he could take his eyes off her. "You look so beautiful tonight. I'd like the opportunity to get to know you better, Rhia."

Chapter Three

Rhia stared up at Dylan aware of everything in the room and nothing except the feeling of being held by him. The musk-and-lime scent of his nearness. The sparkle in his golden-honey-brown eyes. The security of his strength surrounding her.

She didn't know what to say in answer to the words she'd dreamed of hearing almost her whole life. "You've known me since I was six years old," she finally managed to say. "I hardly remember a time when we didn't know each other."

He shook his head. "I've known the girl running tame after Farrah. I've let her ride along when I took my sister into town. I've waved to her across the street. I've teased her and called her Rowdy. But I don't think that's who you are. There's more to a person than recognizing them or even knowing they like the ices at Reiman House or the licorice at the General Store. I don't know your hopes. Your dreams."

And I don't know yours, either, she thought as she stared into his rich, honeyed gaze. Really all she knew about him these days was that he and his father were on the outs, but not why. And she knew that being near him flustered her, made her nervous. But not in a way that made her feel…afraid. It was an exciting kind of nervousness. Like riding full out while a thunderstorm was bearing down on you.

But she never courted danger.

She was careful. Farrah said too careful. She planned each move she made. Until she'd looked at a blue dress and thrown caution away with her disguise.

Rhia forced herself to examine why she'd done what she had but she came to no conclusions. Dylan's proximity seemed to scramble her thoughts and tie her tongue in knots. Yet his words hadn't thrilled her as she'd thought they should. Why?

The music came to a halt and she was saved from needing to make further comments when the voice of their host thanked the men on the instruments and all the guests for coming to celebrate spring.

The evening was over.

Farrah rushed up then. "The band played longer than planned. We should be going. Papa will be waiting up and you know how grouchy he is when he's kept up so late."

Rhia wanted to protest but Dylan, who'd continued to hold her in his arms, abruptly let her go and jerked back. The loss of his heat made her shiver in the warm room. She felt instantly bereft and resentful of her friend's intrusion.

"I'll bring the gig around," Dylan said. "The stable boys are probably harnessing up the mare right now." He nodded to them and walked away.

"You certainly made use of all those dance lessons Mama forced on us over the years," Farrah said, looking a bit cross.

Rhia considered her friend. "She forced them on *you*. I liked them."

Farrah frowned but joined arms with Rhia and they moved toward the doorway and down the stairs that led to the big rear yard where the many wagons and coaches were parked. There was already a bustle of activity as guests began to head home.

"Why should I let some man lead me around a dance floor as if I'm too stupid to know where to put my feet?" Farrah complained, taking up the argument again. "It's a metaphor for the way they treat us. What's wrong with wanting to be the master of my own fate?"

"Nothing." Rhia patted Farrah's hand. Don Alejandro ruled his home with an iron fist. Nothing was beyond his control. She was as independent as Farrah wanted to be but Rhia knew it wasn't all her friend thought it was. "Life on your own isn't as easy as you seem to think it is. If I make a mistake, I could lose everything. Raul follows my orders but never does more than what I specifically tell him to do. Angus is just plain cantankerous. He refuses to take orders at all." She shook her head. "He's always liked sheep more than people."

"You seem to handle it so easily I forget Adara could fail. Are you worried about coming out from behind the disguise? The men flocked around you tonight like a swarm of bees to a newly opened bloom."

"I feel...exposed," Rhia admitted. "And confused. I kind of wish I'd resisted dressing up and coming tonight. The other half of me wouldn't have missed it for anything." They reached the busy yard. A breeze blew softly from the west carrying a sweet scent on the air. "When Abby made me try the dresses on, it was to needle Dylan. But I'd already been thinking how sick I was of hiding behind baggy men's clothes. I'd gotten to where I was more afraid of ending up some strange smelly hermit than of the consequences of being seen for who I am. I'm still not sure what I feared more but now there's only one possible consequence left to face."

Farrah squeezed her hand. "Are you afraid no one will come calling or that whoever does won't treat you as an equal once you marry him?"

"I didn't think ahead. I just reacted, you know?

Abby all but shoehorned me into the first dress. But when I looked in the mirror, I wanted to be the person staring back at me. I didn't think further than that." She gazed at Dylan where he waited. "There's only one man I'd want to come calling anyway," she muttered under her breath.

"Maybe I should give that man a little push in your direction," Farrah said.

She'd heard! Rhia stopped dead in her tracks, pulling Farrah to a stop, too. Farrah was unpredictable and likely to do anything once she got an idea in her head. "Don't you dare say one word to him. I'd be mortified. Promise me."

Farrah sighed. "Fine. Now let's go. Papa's going to be fit to be tied that I'm out this late. Which means he and Dylan will have another fight."

She followed Farrah hurrying toward the gig where Dylan awaited. But George Bentley came rushing up the path from the side garden. "Miss Oliver, I wondered if you would—"

"Sorry, Bentley," Dylan said as he stepped between them. "I have to get my sister and Rhi— Uh… Miss Oliver home then be back here to catch some shut-eye. Days around here start with the dawn. We don't keep bankers' hours."

Rhia nearly groaned in relief at Dylan's interruption. George seemed nice but he was a bank teller as Dylan had just pointed out. They had nothing at all in common.

She scrambled into the gig with Dylan's help and Farrah followed. He walked around the gig and looked up with a smile. "Now to take the two prettiest ladies in Texas home."

Farrah emitted an unladylike snort but all Rhia could think about was what he'd said. And this time she wouldn't let sour thoughts intrude.

That was pretty hard to do, though, because it was the last thing Dylan said on the whole ride. He just drove and seemed to brood. Silent. Stiff. Farrah peppered the air with meaningless small talk.

But she'd been a bit uncommunicative herself, caught up in her confused thoughts. When they arrived at Belleza, Rhia was shocked, having ignored the passing scenery. Farrah's smug grin told the story of what she'd missed. Her former friend had apparently talked Dylan into dropping her home first. Now Rhia would be alone with Dylan.

I'll throttle her.

Rhia was as close to heartbroken as she'd been since her father took his final breath. Dylan would never be interested in her even all gussied up and looking her best. Couldn't Farrah see that? Rhia stiffened her back. Well, so what! She didn't need him. She didn't need anyone.

Still, she didn't know how she'd live in Tierra del

Verde knowing that at any time she might see him courting some woman who'd moved there, then hearing of their marriage or later about the birth of their children.

She tightened her hands where she had them tangled in her lap. Becoming a smelly hermit didn't sound half bad right then. She should have stayed hidden. She'd come out into the open. Exposed herself. Probably weakened her standing as a landowner. She'd certainly made herself look vulnerable. And all for nothing. Now she'd have to face the consequences. Alone.

Then she got to wondering what she'd done earlier to put Dylan off. He'd insisted she dance with him and she hadn't stepped on his feet or lost her place even once while they'd danced. Had her anger over trivialities shown in her manner while they'd been dancing? It must have. He'd changed somehow after the band ceased playing. The moment Farrah had given him an excuse, he'd all but fled the ballroom. Which meant, unplanned and ill-timed as this night had been, she'd exposed everything for nothing.

The ride to Adara wasn't as silent as the ride to Belleza but it was full of the same kind of meaningless small talk. Just as they topped the rise overlooking Adara's homestead, Rhia took one last deep breath, sure it would be the last time she got to enjoy

Dylan's earthy lime and leather scent along with his warmth pressed against her shoulder.

Then she noticed the silence and all thought of her failure that night fled. The ominous feel of impending disaster crawled over her. She put a staying hand on Dylan's forearm. "Stop," she whispered. "Something's wrong. The sheep are too quiet. Especially for a night with a full moon."

Dylan canted his head listening, too. He hadn't acted on her hunch alone but at least he'd listened for the worrisome silence. Would he have questioned another man or taken him at his word?

Then, without another whispered word between them, he pulled the gig to the side of the road into the shadow of a big oak. "Wait here." His reply barely audible, he pulled his revolver from the holster on his hip, flipped it over and offered her the pistol grip. "Tie up the rig and hide. Use it if you have to but, Rhia, save a bullet." Then he yanked his Winchester from under the seat, jumped down and headed into the shadows.

The sharp sound of Dylan cocking the Winchester brought his last words to her thoughts. *Save a bullet.* What he'd left unsaid was—*for yourself.* A woman alone was in danger.

Chapter Four

Dylan ducked under a low-hanging branch of a big old oak. Moving through the dense woods, he kept his steps as silent as possible. When he emerged from the cover of the brush, it was with a sinking heart.

In all directions the full moon revealed Rhia's northern-slope flock—still, silent, slaughtered. He made his way to a shadowy form on the ground. Angus, her grizzled old shepherd. He'd been murdered and it looked like the work of the Comanche.

Most of the tribe had signed a treaty but apparently this band of renegades had something other than peace in mind. He'd just bent down to close Angus's sightless eyes when a thought occurred to him. Comanche raided for food, horses, useful goods and, yes, murder and mayhem. But it was unlike them to kill innocent animals in this wasteful way. They'd have stolen as many as they could for hides and food but they'd never kill this many animals so indiscriminately.

Puzzled, he looked below toward *the* homestead and sniffed. The breeze carried no smell of smoldering lumber. Adara's house, barn and cabin looked to be intact. Yet in every other raid so far, the band had torched the buildings.

He rose turning slowly, deep in thought. With almost all the residents of town and the surrounding area attending the dance on the Rocking R, Rhia's nearest neighbor, flames lighting up the sky and the smell of smoke on the breeze would have brought men running. But why would a renegade band of Indians know about the Spring Social?

Wanting to get back to Rhia, Dylan moved through the dead flock to the access road. He walked back up the hill. When he saw the faint silhouette of the gig, he called out, "Coming in," not wanting to get shot full of holes.

Rhia crept out and went to the mare's head, taking hold of the bridle, the revolver in her grip. "What happened?" she demanded, a small quaver in her voice.

"I'm sorry, Rowdy. There's been a raid. Angus is dead." He saw her flinch and her shoulders sagged when he added, "And your northern-slope flock is wiped out. I don't know about the others. The buildings look intact from up here but I didn't want to take the time to check and leave you alone and vulnerable."

That Rhia didn't argue a bit about her being vulnerable told him she was badly rattled. He took the revolver from her lax grip and put it back in his holster. "I'm nearly sure the attackers are gone," he went on but didn't add, *because Angus is already cold.* "Let's go see how bad it is."

Rhia nodded and silently walked to the seat of the gig. Shaking, she needed his help to climb up. Her expression looked as if she held on to her composure by a tenuous thread. He was tempted to leave straightaway but decided there was no use having her imagine it as worse than it was.

He climbed up next to Rhia and snapped the reins. They'd gotten as far as the yard when two figures stepped out from behind the big elm tree that dominated the site. Dylan nearly had his revolver out of its holster before he recognized Raul Hernandez and his wife, Consuela.

The two approached. Raul had his sombrero in his hand, looking apologetic. His woman had a belligerent tilt to her head. "We are sorry, Miss Rhia," Raul said. "We can stay no longer. Angus is dead, no?"

Dylan nodded when Rhia stayed silent, staring toward the destruction filling the clearing ahead.

"We leave now," Consuela Hernandez said. "They will get us *all* if we stay."

"How did they miss you two?" Dylan asked.

"We hide in the cave near the stream," Raul replied.

"Didn't you even try to help Angus?" Dylan demanded of Raul. The man's face crumpled and he looked away. Dylan liked to think he'd have tried but did any man know how he'd act until death came knocking?

"He would not have come to help Raul," Consuela snapped.

More composed now, Raul explained, "I have Consuela and the *bebé* she expects. I stand no chance against so many. Howling and shooting comes from the north and warns us. Before we get to the cave, Angus…he no longer screams. They come look for us as if they know we are here but the cave the *señorita* shows us is well hidden."

Consuela nodded, looking around at the mess Dylan's eyes had finally adjusted enough to see. "They go through *sus casas*, Señorita. They make much mess but take only money jar and *armas y balas*."

Dylan frowned, thinking. "Guns and bullets make sense, but money?" Then he glanced next to him to see if Rhia had picked up on the inconsistencies. But she just sat there. Silent as her dead shepherd and sheep. Completely unlike the Rhia he knew. He wanted to wrap her in his arms and keep her safe.

The thought shocked him. Was it the dress or had he seen a part of her she usually hid from the world? He'd never thought of her as needing protection. She'd always been so strong and capable. This feeling was as out of place as the peculiarities of the raid were.

He stifled a sigh at the destruction littering the clearing ahead. Torn curtains hung out of broken windows. Pieces of crockery and cloth items had been trampled into the ground.

"I have to go for the sheriff then take Rhia to Belleza. You two can pack up and use her wagon to get to town." He wasn't happy about the couple's desertion of Rhia but he couldn't say he didn't understand. They'd had quite a scare. Lesser men had cleared out after the first raid last year.

"You can talk to Sheriff Quinn or Ranger Kane about what you heard and saw when you get there."

Dylan turned to Rhia. "*Querida,* can I get you anything from the house before we leave?"

She glanced toward the house again, then just shook her head. He'd expected an argument or maybe even tears. They'd have scared the bejezus out of him but her soundless answer, like the lost look in her eyes, was as haunting as the ranch's silent little yard.

Minutes later he'd turned the gig around and headed toward town. After reporting the raid to the law, he'd take her on to Belleza. She was nearly as close to his mother as she was to Farrah. He wasn't looking forward to dealing with his father but tonight it was Rhia who mattered.

He also had to talk to the old man about taking precautions. They could just as easily have attacked Belleza. At least Rhia had been thinking ahead. He was sure Raul and Consuela were only alive because Rhia had shown them the cave where they'd all played as children.

His thoughts went back to Farrah and his mother. The most ferocious guards on Belleza were the dogs whose job it was to protect the sheep from predators.

Dogs.

Dammit! He hadn't seen evidence of Rhia's dog, Scout, on that hill or Angus's dogs, either. He hoped they'd successfully run from the sound of the guns. Maybe it was just as well he hadn't thought to look. He didn't think Rhia could take another loss tonight.

With Rhia sitting next to him frozen in shock, Dylan was at a loss as to what to say to her. So, as he had on the way to Belleza after the social, he drove in stony silence fighting the instinct to hold her and promise to always keep her safe.

He'd been so consumed with desire for her earlier he hadn't thought about the poor timing of her sudden emergence as a desirable woman. Now because of the waltz and, influenced by her nearness, what he'd said during it, he had to be very careful how he offered comfort. He didn't want to hurt her but he wasn't ready to take on a wife. Especially not one who stubbornly clung to the idea of making her father's dream come true by making a success of Adara. She couldn't be the woman for him no matter how much he wished it were otherwise.

The stop in town to alert Ryan Quinn about the raid took only moments, then they headed for Belleza.

As he drew the gig even with the front door of his parents' hacienda, it flew open and the don stormed out in full high dudgeon. "I care not if the rest of the females of the area are allowed to dance at that Englishman's to all hours. What were you thinking to bring your sister home so late? And what have you been doing with Rhiannon Oliver all this time? What if someone discovers you've been—"

"Shut. Up." Dylan's voice cracked into the air and shocked the old man into silence. "Get Mama," he told Farrah who'd followed her father out of the house. Dylan jumped to the ground and scooped Rhia unresisting into his arms. When he turned, his father blocked his path to the house. Dylan wanted to simply walk away as he usually did but tonight was different. Dylan ordered, "Stand aside. This is no time for you to get on your high horse about bloodlines. Rhia's had a nasty shock. Adara was raided while she was gone."

Miraculously his father gave way but he followed them inside, demanding, "Why bring her here?"

Dylan refused to react to the don's coldheartedness. He set Rhia on the small divan and stepped back as his mother and sister rushed to her. He turned to face his father and through gritted teeth said, "I brought her here because she needs Mother."

By moving to the beehive fireplace in the far corner of the room, Dylan forced his father to follow. The sound of Rhia answering Farrah's question calmed him a bit. All he could think was, suppose she'd been there when they'd struck. There was no question in his mind that she'd have tried to help Angus. She'd be dead now, or worse. A captive.

"Are they all dead?" the don snapped.

"The couple who lives there are lucky they escaped with their lives but they've moved on. Old Angus is dead. The whole place has been ransacked. I couldn't leave her there," he whispered fiercely. "Surely you can see that." Dylan ran an angry hand through his hair and leaned even closer to the stubborn old coot. He felt like shouting but had to whisper so Rhia wouldn't hear. "At least half of her flock is dead. If you're turning her away, I'm sure Alex and Mrs. Reynolds would be happy to take her in."

That got the old man's back up. "I wouldn't consider turning away a neighbor in need."

"Funny. That's how you sounded." Knowing his father, what the don meant was he wouldn't consider allowing Alex Reynolds to outshine him.

"I've asked her to sell Adara to me several times

since Henry Oliver died. I knew she'd never make it out there."

He'd probably offered half what the place was worth. Dylan glanced at Rhia. She already seemed better, looking angry and determined. The knot in his stomach eased. Rhia would recover from this. If the don tried to push her toward selling out now, she'd probably hand him his head. But that thought brought the knot right back. The next thing she'd do was head on home. Alone. She had a stubborn streak that ran deeper than anyone he'd ever met.

Except maybe himself.

He had to take the don's mind off making another offer for Adara. And he knew exactly how to do it. "You have to take steps to increase Belleza's security. Your men aren't trained with guns. It's dangerous."

The don's face darkened in anger. "I refuse to arm men of a lower class. How I run Belleza is no longer your concern."

Farrah stood and the other two followed suit, beating a hasty retreat, exactly as he'd hoped they would if he stirred up trouble. His sister and mother had witnessed enough battles. Dylan usually walked away when the don started shouting. This time, he'd stick till his father heard him out.

"I may have given up my inheritance to Belleza, but the safety of my mother and sister is at stake.

The way I see it that gives me the right to comment on how well you protect them. These raids aren't stopping. They're getting even uglier. What makes you think you're not going to face what others have? Arm the shepherds. Failing that, hire guards you feel you can trust! If you don't, *you* might not live to regret it. But *Mama and Farrah* may. Do you really want your last thoughts to be of them as Comanche captives?" He couldn't help but be pleased to see the old man pale.

"I'm borrowing a horse," Dylan said and stalked toward the door. Maybe he'd finally won one of their arguments.

An important one.

Chapter Five

Rhia settled with Farrah in Elizabeth Varga's sitting room as they'd been doing since she and Farrah were in their teens. She glanced around. The architecture of the room, like the rest of the home, was Spanish, but the decor was unashamedly British. Farrah's mother clung to her roots as did her husband. The mix might work for them but not for their children who were unashamedly Americans. Texans.

"I'm so sick of the arguments between Papa and Dylan," Farrah lamented. Rhia focused on her friend. She sounded disconsolate and looked near to tears.

Elizabeth Varga shook her head and reached over to squeeze her daughter's hand. "They love with great passion and disagree the same way. It is their nature. Dylan will never follow your father's path and your father sees Dylan's stand as a criticism of him. I only hope Alejandro comes to understand his son before it's too late. If a rift grows too wide, a bridge can never be built to traverse it."

Though Rhia agreed with Elizabeth's wisdom, she grew distinctly uncomfortable with all the personal talk. She didn't belong at Belleza. Don Alejandro didn't even want her there and never had. She'd heard him protest her arrival somewhere in the distance. She'd always known he objected to her but she ignored his insults because Farrah needed their friendship as much as Rhia did.

She wasn't letting him chase her away now any more than she ever had, she assured herself. But she couldn't stay there. She had problems to solve. A lot of problems. It had nothing to do with bruised feelings.

It didn't.

Angus needed burying. Poor Angus. He'd died as he'd lived. Alone among his sheep. Her father hadn't been the first to have a man on his payroll who preferred to remain anonymous but it was so very sad that she didn't have more than his Christian name to put on his marker.

Hearing of his death had been a shock. She'd always hoped to reach him. To hear his reasons for being so secretive. Now that would never happen. She would mourn the emptiness that had existed between them. Lost opportunities to love were always the saddest.

"I have to get back to Adara. Raul and Consuela left, which means the place is deserted," she said when she realized the two women had fallen silent and were staring at her.

"You can't go back there alone," Farrah insisted.

"Of course I can. I can't let the place and the remainder of the flock go unwatched. And I have to find out about Scout. I can't believe I forgot to look for him. Dylan would have told me if he'd found him dead, wouldn't he?"

"Of course he would," Elizabeth said and squeezed her hand. "And you'll go *nowhere* tonight, young lady. Especially not to look for a dog."

Scout might only be a dog to most folks but he was her only family. If she'd been at Adara instead of that darn dance, he'd have been safe at her side in the cave. She should have looked for him earlier but the wanton destruction of her parents' dream had stunned her. She'd gone numb all the way to her core, unable to break through what felt like a wall. It had been as if someone had locked her inside her head. It was still nearly as frightening as the all-encompassing effect the raid would have on her life.

Now all her anger, fear of the future and desperation about Scout—emotions she should have felt earlier—came rushing to the fore. This time Rhia sat straighter, determined to fight back. She rose. "The don doesn't want me here. I have to leave."

"Do you think I let that man rule me?" Farrah's mother said, conviction in her tone. "This is my home as well as his. I want you here. He'll welcome you to our breakfast table in the morning or he'll sleep in his study for a week. On his very short settee!"

Hardly noticing Farrah's chuckle, Rhia protested, "But Adara—"

Elizabeth Varga took her hand. "Let Dylan handle Adara tonight. I'll make sure he plans to go back and that at least one of our men goes along to see to your flock." She gave Rhia's hand a little squeeze. "Think. You cannot go there alone with my son for propriety's sake. It's bad enough he took you to town with him to inform the sheriff. And Farrah may not travel along as a chaperone. It's too dangerous and I won't have you all at risk. These Ghost Warriors could be watching."

They could be. All right, she would stay. Rhia sat down with a sigh and got a pat on the shoulder as a reward. It actually felt good to be pampered. It was the first time in years she had been. Rhia took an instant to savor the moment. Foggily she recalled Dylan caring for her earlier. Had he really called her *querida*? Or had it been hopeful, desperate thinking on her part?

"Farrah, find your brother," she heard Elizabeth say, "and remind him Scout is missing."

But at that moment a triumphant bark echoed through the house. Popping to her feet, Rhia smiled. "Scout." Toenails rapidly clicked up the stairs and along the hall toward her. In seconds she was on her knees, wrapping her arms around the exuberant dog. "You're all right! They didn't hurt you or take you." She took his head in her hands and looked into his golden eyes. "I was so worried."

She heard a masculine chuckle as Scout licked her face and neck. Dylan stood in the doorway, a slight smile curving his beautifully sculpted lips. "I see he found you. I'm sorry I didn't think to look for him earlier. He must have followed us all the way to town and then here. I'm heading back to Adara. The don is lending me two men to help out. But he won't have a dog in his hacienda. Suppose I take Scout along with me?"

"You can take us both."

"No, he won't," Elizabeth said. "I've told you why. Go on with you, Dylan. And, son, good for you for storming in when you arrived. Did you manage to fix anything between you and your father?"

Dylan's lips thinned as he shook his head. "Let's go, Scout."

Rhia signaled Scout to go with Dylan. Scout protested with a high-pitched whine and a sloppy tongue lick on her cheek. She shook her head. "Go on, buddy. Go with Dylan." With his head down and a last wistful look over his furry shoulder, Scout followed Dylan close on his heels.

The next morning finally dawned with light creeping across the ceiling. Rhia had been staring at it for hours. If she'd slept at all, it had been in tiny snatches. Dylan's mother had meant well but Rhia's thoughts had bounced from problems to losses to Dylan and back to problems, losses and Dylan throughout the night.

Exhausted, she admitted to herself she would probably sell Adara if not for the deathbed promise she'd made to her father. Having sworn to make his dream of success come to fruition, she had no choice but to plod ahead. Which meant she would now have a lot of unexpected expenses to deal with just to make the house habitable again.

Joshua Wheaton was a fair banker and would no doubt let her take out a mortgage on the free and clear property but that didn't sit well. One more setback like this one and she could lose it all if a bank held title and she found herself unable to make the payments.

To avoid that, she'd have to use credit at businesses around town to replace some of what had been destroyed. If she owed a little here and there and couldn't pay it back right away, she wouldn't lose Adara.

Rhia pushed herself out of bed. Her body felt leaden as she put on the dress she'd worn to the social, having no idea where her usual clothes were at that moment. She went down to eat at the table in the courtyard where the family took many of their meals. The don made his usual bid to buy Adara for much less than it was worth. Even though exhausted with the day barely begun, Rhia needed to stand on her own feet. Having lost her appetite, she asked to borrow a wagon so she could go into town to try to hire a shepherd. The don lent her an old wagon and she left for town.

During the ride, she tried to steel herself for the inevitable. Unless she found and hired a man of Angus's advanced age, there was bound to be talk. With the help of the Ghost Warriors, she may have traded invisibility for notoriety in one short night. Never in her life had she so regretted a decision as she did buying the blue dress and going to the social.

Her emotions felt like a fish just pulled from a stream, flopping back and forth, leaving her unable to decide how or what she felt. She tied up the wagon at the town square, blinking away useless tears. Used to invisibility, she couldn't help notice the attention she drew as she walked along the pathway.

Straightening her shoulders, Rhia moved across the square to the posting board. She tacked up her notice for a shepherd, distressed that no one had posted as a job seeker.

She decided to walk over to Abby's General Store and leave the ancient, badly sprung wagon at the square. Once again she noticed folks watching her. But then she heard two women talking and could have sworn they'd used her name before realizing she was behind them. One of them glanced back and, looking a little shamefaced, grabbed her friend and pulled her to the side. But then, as if some silent communication went between the two, they put their noses in the air and stepped back even farther, holding their dresses aside lest their hems brush Rhia's as she passed. Perplexed, she walked on.

Between the square and the bank, three different men who'd partnered her the night before stopped her, voicing varying degrees of concern for her welfare and reputation. Others stopped her, too. The topics ranged from invitations for meals at the hotel to outright insulting proposals of marriage without even the meal. All the men had two things in common—they all had plans for Adara that were contrary to hers and they mentioned they were all willing to overlook her having been seen alone with Dylan in town the night before. To a man, they assured they didn't think anything untoward had happened but it felt to Rhia as if they were trying to push her down the aisle by offering to rescue her from shame. She turned them all down, of course. And explained to each one in the most reasonable tone she could muster that Adara had been raided and that she'd needed Dylan's help to summon the sheriff and his gun in case the raiders were still around.

Not only was it all infuriating, but the haunting fact was that the only man she was interested in walking down an aisle toward was Dylan. And he persisted in seeing her as a sister, no matter that he'd professed to want to get to know her better and had later called her *querida*.

"Miss Oliver," George Bentley called as he rushed toward her from the side door of the bank. In seconds he'd blocked her way on the boardwalk. "You simply must have tea with Mother and me. She has a reputation for strict adherence to propriety. It would make my day and go a long way to taming these preposterous rumors."

She frowned. They must all know about the raid and about Angus's murder. None of them knew she and Angus hadn't been close. That she wouldn't be deeply grief-stricken by his death. How could they be so thoughtless? She stepped to the side.

"I'm sorry, Mr. Bentley," she said. "This isn't a good time." As she tried to pass him, he took hold of her arm.

"Because of your losses? I understand. Any rancher

would be upset at your business setbacks but your reputation is more important."

"Business setbacks? More important?" She gave him a long hard look. "A man *died*, Mr. Bentley. Raul and Consuela could easily have been killed, as well. I lost nearly half my stock, not to mention that most if not all of the mementoes I had from my parents are damaged if not utterly destroyed. I'd advise you to let go of my arm before I'm tempted to push you into that horse trough behind you."

He let go with an affronted huff and Rhia walked on. She was about to pass the bank's front doors when Lucien Avery stepped onto the boardwalk. Avery was a wealthy rancher with a large spread out near her place. If she wasn't mistaken he'd danced with her the night before, too. "Good day, Miss Oliver. I just heard about your terrible misfortune. I wanted to extend my deepest sympathy for your losses."

Finally a man who isn't shockingly callous. "Thank you, sir."

"Have you given much thought to your future in town with all this talk? I imagine you'll want to move on. After all, Don Alejandro will never allow his son to marry so far beneath his station even if the two of them aren't on the best of terms. I'll be happy to purchase your property to facilitate your departure."

Rhia fisted her hands. "I'm not interested in—"

"Now, now. Don't be too hasty," he cajoled. "You haven't heard my offer. I'll give you ten percent over the highest offer you get from anyone else."

"You'll have to look elsewhere for more water for your cattle, Mr. Avery. My parents are buried on that land. Adara isn't for sale. And I don't give a hoot in hell what the don thinks of me. Never have. Never will. Excuse me."

He stepped in front of her as Mr. Bentley had. "If your reputation doesn't concern you, you should at least think about how lucky you were not to be a casualty last night. You could be as dead as your shepherd is right now. This is a dangerous time for a young woman alone."

She stared at him. Concern? Or threat? She couldn't tell so she forced a smile. "I'm tougher than I look," she told him and this time he stepped aside.

By the time she'd reached the sanctuary of Abby's store, Rhia had sworn off men entirely and off the women of the town as potential friends, too. Tierra del Verde had changed more than she'd thought.

Chapter Six

Hell-bent-for-leather, Dylan rode into town with his sister. An hour earlier, Farrah had torn onto Adara shouting as if the hounds of hell were on her heels. Rhia had left for town unescorted. What she thought she'd accomplish there was anyone's guess.

Since he wasn't happy that Farrah was out riding around alone, either, he'd let her ride along rather than take the time to take her home as he had the night before.

They reined in their mounts and jumped to the ground next to Belleza's old supply wagon where it stood tied to the hitching post near the town square. But Rhia was nowhere to be seen.

Mr. Johnson hailed them. He was the town's undertaker and barber and the worst gossip around. He said he'd seen Rhia tack something up in the square. Dylan went to look and found her advertisement for a shepherd. When Dylan got back to Farrah, Johnson was telling her that quite a few men had stopped Rhia to talk and she'd seemed upset by whatever they'd said.

After that Dylan walked his gelding, Rory, along the street on one side, checking in shops, looking down alleys. Farrah did the same thing on the other side.

Joshua Wheaton stepped out of the bank and said something to Farrah, then walked across the street toward Dylan. His sister followed in Josh's wake.

"Can I assume you thundered into town looking for Miss Oliver?" he asked.

"She rode in from Belleza alone," Dylan explained. "Did you see her?"

Josh nodded. "I saw Lucien Avery stop her just outside the bank. She seemed upset by something he said then she hurried over to my wife's store."

"When Papa offered to buy her out at breakfast she got really upset. Maybe Mr. Avery offered, too," Farrah ventured.

Dylan frowned. Dammit. What was wrong with their father? Had he no compassion at all?

Josh frowned, too. He also looked thoughtful. "I was going over to Abby's store, to make sure everything is all right," he said, "but Miss Oliver may need a friend."

"I'd better go check on her," his sister said. "Don't take too long to calm down, brother mine. She isn't likely to stay put for long and you wanted to keep her away from Adara." Farrah mounted and wheeled her mare off toward the general store.

Dylan narrowed his eyes in thought. "I'd love to know what Avery said to upset her," he muttered.

Wheaton raised an eyebrow. "I'd guess your sister is right. He probably offered to buy her out. Or he could have mentioned the gossip that's circulating. Maybe both."

Dylan tethered his mount to the hitching rail and looked at Josh. "What gossip?" he asked.

"Someone saw her in town last night with you. And the news spread like a wildfire. I had to go over to the saloon to talk to Walther about his mortgage on the Garter. Even the men in there were talking about her. And not in a good way."

"Dammit. For crying out loud. Was I supposed to leave her alone out there to contend with the dead?" Dylan gritted his teeth. Why hadn't he taken the time to leave her with his family before he headed into town? He had to fix this. He turned toward Abby's General Store and Josh fell into step beside him.

"I'd never dishonor Rhia in any way. People should learn not to say anything if they can't say something good."

Josh gave a sharp nodded. "I know. But she left the social with you and hours later, she came riding into town still in your company."

"Came riding in after we discovered her place torn up and her shepherd dead. Pardon me all to hell if I wasn't thinking about anything but getting Quinn and Kane out there and not leaving her there alone."

"I know. You wanted to protect her but you did the opposite. Folks are adding two and two and coming up with five or six. Eastern mores are moving west. Wagging tongues aren't going to be stilled easily. Maybe you should think about marrying her. Just last month you were grousing that the women coming in on the stage were either bound for the Garter or looking for a big ranch owner."

"I meant I'd be looking in a year or two and I didn't like how things were going," Dylan protested. "I'm not ready for marriage. I haven't saved enough to buy a place."

"She wouldn't be opposed to working by your side, building Adara into a fine horse ranch."

"Yes, she would. Rhia's dead set on seeing her father's dreams of a successful sheep ranch realized. And you know how I feel about sheep. I don't want my kids teased and tortured the way I was."

"Well, my friend, I have to tell you, she won't live this down alone."

His mother was going to skin him alive for putting Rhia in this position. He was ready to skin himself. Where had his penchant for careful planning gone last night? "Am I supposed to give up my dreams because of a few thoughtless decisions?"

"Maybe it would just be a dream postponed. There's some more land out by her place available. You could do there what you wanted to do at Belleza. And at least you care about her. From what I heard over at the Garter, there will be other offers coming but not good ones. If you don't help get her out of this, she's going to wind up ostracized or with someone who not only doesn't care about her but who doesn't respect her or her dreams."

Josh was right. This wasn't about him, was it? He'd always wanted only good things for Rhia, even when he'd thought she was peculiar, because she was one of the kindest people he'd ever met. And now, through his carelessness, her chance to be courted properly by one of the respectable men who'd partnered her last night was ruined. She deserved better than people treating her poorly.

Rhia's fixation on raising sheep aside, last night he'd been sorry her emergence as an attractive woman hadn't fit into his timing and plans. He'd even been annoyed with all the men partnering her. Because, dammit, even though he wasn't ready to take on a wife, he'd wanted her. That waltz he'd insisted on had proven that to him.

So timing aside, there was only one course of action. He'd have to offer to marry her. There didn't seem to be any way around it. Feeling a bit like a condemned man and conversely like the luckiest yahoo in town, Dylan looked at Josh.

And Josh grimaced. "Take a little advice. Give Miss Oliver a choice even though neither of you has one. But make no mistake, you've got to talk her around to seeing this as the only way it can be."

Dylan sighed. He knew Rhia. She was going to dig in her heels and dare anyone to criticize her. But he knew how cruel people could be. They would indeed condemn her. His thoughts somersaulted more than his stomach as he strode toward Abby's store.

How in hell was he was supposed to talk Rhia into marrying him when he was so ambivalent about marrying her? He wanted her. Sure. But he wouldn't lie. It was attraction. Lust. He certainly didn't love her nor did he want to. He'd seen the heartache his mother's love for his father had caused her. All he could claim was that he cared about Rhia's welfare and that he wanted her physically. If she rejected him, he didn't know how he'd keep her safe from the circling vultures.

He winced. If she said yes to his proposal, he would become a sheepherder after all. *Madre de dios!* He glanced up and wondered if the One the priests called *Lamb* of God was up there laughing at him.

Probably.

Chapter Seven

"Farrah, try to understand. I have to go home." Rhia put down the now empty teacup. Abby had promised tea would make her feel better. It hadn't. Because there she sat in Abby's back room, wondering how many times she'd have to repeat the same thing. This time she added what they both knew to be true but had never acknowledged. "Your father doesn't want me at Belleza. You know he doesn't. And he never has. He thinks I'm beneath him and therefore beneath you. Now he'll hear all this talk and be sure of it. He'll say my being there will sully your reputation by association."

"Since when do you care what my father thinks?"

"Normally I might go back to Belleza just to watch him stiffen up when I get too close. But I'm not that strong right now."

"Why don't you stay with us?" Abby offered as she walked in from the front of the store where she'd been taking care of a customer.

Embarrassed that she appeared to be so needy, Rhia shook her head. "Thanks, Abby, but I promised my father I'd take care of the ranch. Town is too far from Adara. Besides, I've had all I can take of town people for a while."

"Then you have to stay with us at Belleza, at least until you can hire replacements. You can't be out there alone," Farrah said again.

"That could take weeks," Rhia argued. "After word of Angus's death gets around, I doubt anyone from these parts will hire on with me. That means sending a letter or a wire to San Antonio to advertise in the *Express*. In the meantime, I can't leave my mother's home all torn up and open to varmints— the four-*or* two-legged kind."

The bell over the front door jingled another arrival. Abby sighed. "Why did everyone in town have to pick today to need something?"

"They're probably coming in the hope of getting a glimpse of the fallen woman," Rhia sneered.

"Where is everyone?" Dylan called out.

Abby stood and pointed at Rhia. "You stay put," she ordered and rushed out to the shop. "We're back here having a bit of tea."

"We? Please tell me that includes Farrah and Rhia," he said, worry rife in his tone.

Farrah frowned and said, "He sounds upset, doesn't he? I'd better go see what's wrong."

"Maybe he heard his name linked with mine," Rhia grumbled. Before they'd found Adara raided, he'd seemed to regret everything he'd said to her all evening. After, he'd started talking to her like a big brother.

Farrah rolled her eyes and went into the store.

Which left Rhia to ponder her options. Was her name really so ruined that life would become more difficult for her or was it just a few—well, all right, several—small-minded citizens without enough to occupy themselves? And as far as going home, at least there she wouldn't have to deal with unearned scorn. Besides, would she really be in that much danger at Adara? Was there any reason to think they'd be back?

She should just go ask Dylan what he thought. She needn't mention the talk in town today. She doubted anyone would really repeat any of those things to him. They'd all be too cowardly. So he'd never know.

Unfortunately she didn't have the energy to even stand much less walk out to the other room. Instead she propped her chin on the heel of her hand and closed her eyes. What was wrong with her? She couldn't let any of this defeat her. Her problem was that both of these trials had come upon her within hours of each other.

No, she wouldn't let it get to her this way. Rhia started to push herself to her feet to go ask Dylan's opinion but he stepped into the room. Rhia settled back into the chair.

He seemed to fill the room with his essence. Shrink it. "Rough morning?" he asked, tilting his head just a little. His every gesture was so familiar. So dear.

"There weren't any postings up in the square for shepherd work or really anyone looking for a job. Farrah tells me you buried Angus. Thank you. I'll visit his grave as soon as I get home."

His eyes locked with hers. "Thanks aren't necessary. I'll show you the grave. You'll miss him even though he was…"

She managed to chuckle. "Grumpy. Cantankerous. Difficult."

"Well, yeah. But he was a constant in your life and the last one left who started the place with your father."

She swallowed. "I know, which is why I—"

"I need you to listen to me," he interrupted, settling in the chair across from her at the small table. Then oddly he fell silent which seemed strange, as he'd wanted her to listen. Had he heard what they were all saying? God, she prayed not. Dylan leaned his elbows on the table and clasped his hands lightly. "You're in a bad position right now. I wanted to help. I never meant to make it worse but apparently I have."

"Then you've heard."

"What? You thought I wouldn't? It's about me, too, you know."

"But it isn't really your problem."

"You think I can let my thoughtlessness ruin your life and do nothing?"

"Dylan, I come into town once a month. Stop at Abby's for supplies and leave. I'll just come to the back door for a while—"

"No back doors. You did nothing to be ashamed of. I'm the one who has to fix this and there's only one way I can." He took a deep breath, reached a hand toward her, only to let it fall back to the table. "I want you to marry me."

She could hardly catch her breath for the pain. How could the six words she'd longed to hear falling from his lips hurt so badly? All because he didn't love her. He couldn't even look at her.

He was being forced by circumstance.

By gossip.

By his own chivalrous nature.

Rhia started to shake her head but he stopped her by raising a staying hand. "Wait," he ordered, "hear me out. Adara would remain yours to run as you see fit. I'd never take that from you. I just want to protect you and your reputation. You can't hide what everyone saw last night. That horse has left the barn."

Her response, full of resentment, burst from her

lips unbidden. "You never even *saw* me before last night." And, as it was too late to take back the accusation, she went further. What the heck! *In for a penny, in for a pound, Daddy always said.* "Don't pretend you'd be sitting there if I hadn't looked so different last night."

He blinked. "You're mad that I didn't see through your disguise? Not my fault you did such a good job all these years. But you showed up looking like you do with your hair done up all pretty. It changed everything. They all see you as a woman. A lady."

"A lady who spent the last two years running her own place. Alone."

"Dressed as a no-account squatter. Then everyone saw you all prettied up and we all realized how many years had gone by. And then came the raid and you were so fragile all of a sudden. It scared me witless. I was so worried about you I didn't think to take you to Belleza before going to town."

She was so busy trying to work out exactly what he'd said and if there was a compliment buried in there somewhere, she nearly missed what he meant. "So you want to marry me to do penance for not thinking like a few mean-spirited people around these parts?"

"You are the stubbornest! There's *plenty* of talk. Not just a few gum-flapping idiots. Josh was in the Garter and heard your name bandied about. *In a saloon, Rhia.* You won't stay a lady in anyone else's eyes with you living out there alone with no husband. Especially not after all that happened last night."

She clenched her hands into fists. "This isn't fair."

"No. It's not. But like Josh says, the town's changing. Growing up. Getting civilized. With that comes rules. *And* gossip. A woman can't break rules, Rhia."

"And because of some Eastern idea of propriety with nothing to do with living in Texas, you think you should marry me?" Stunned, bleeding inside, she managed to add, "You're from nobility. In your father's eyes, I'm the child of a guttersnipe from London's Seven Dials section and an Irish housemaid from Five Points in New York City. The don would pitch a fit."

Dylan grinned, his golden eyes sparkling. "Now you're just trying to seduce me with a chance to get the don's goat even more than I already do. See, you're the perfect wife for me." Then he grew serious again. "Women coming west by train don't understand this place. You know what hard work it takes to make a dream rise out of a scrap of land. You're what I want in a wife and in the mother of my children."

"I know I'm not the perfect wife for anyone. You just feel obligated."

That turned him serious again. "Look, I'm not

going to pretend what I don't feel. I respect you too much for that. But I'd like to think I measure up in the husband department a little better than the early-morning bunch over at the Garter. And a hell of a lot better than that drifter in there who hasn't taken a bath in a month of Sundays."

He did. And he knew he did. "This isn't fair to *you*." It was she who didn't measure up to what he really wanted. Was there ever anything worse than being only an obligation to the man you love? Of course it wasn't unfair to her. He'd always been her dream lover. She'd lain in bed and hugged her pillow, pretending it was him for so many years, she no longer found it odd to wake still holding on for dear life to a sack of goose feathers.

"*Querida*, life doesn't have to be fair," he whispered, his brown eyes clearly assessing her. "Just *good*. We can be good together. We respect each other. I'd like to think we like each other. Lots of folks don't have that starting out."

"By not fair I meant what if you meet someone you love someday but you're already stuck with me?"

"Not going to happen. I don't want love. It just makes for hurt feelings and broken dreams. I won't pretend I don't want a real marriage but that can wait till you're more used to me as more… As more than a brother."

Brother. There, he'd said it and her heart sank a bit

more. She'd never seen him as a brother. That was his feeling he was talking about. A blush heated her face and she looked away but nodded so he wouldn't try to explain further. God, could this get worse? She *was* ready. She'd been *ready* for years. And he thought she was a *lady*? He clearly wanted one because this was all happening because he thought he needed to save her reputation. If he'd thought she wasn't a lady, he'd never have offered marriage. He'd have laughed at the gossip.

"I'll send one of the don's men for that piece of garbage he lent you. I'll see the livery readies your buckboard. Farrah can ride with you and I'll follow," he said. "Maybe on the way, you could talk to her. Or maybe wait and talk to Mama."

Would this never stop getting worse?

She found herself asking the very same thing of Farrah on the ride back to Belleza.

"But it's wonderful. We'd be sisters!" Farrah exclaimed.

"How can you not understand? He. Doesn't. Love. Me," Rhia said between her teeth. Then she slapped the reins so hard against the horse's hide they took off in a jerking dash. She had to saw back on the reins and use the brake to slow them down again.

Farrah laughed. "He will soon then. How could he not?"

"Before last night I hid who I was. Now he sees me

as more than I am—as a lady—and he still doesn't love me."

"More than you are? You are a lady. Being a lady is about more than pretty manners, lovely dresses and fancy hairdos. Or the right ancestors before you add that. It's about purity and goodness and kindness—all qualities you have in abundance."

Rhia huffed out a breath. "But he doesn't even *want* to love me. He said he doesn't want love. Oh, and he can wait for a *real* marriage till I get used to him as more than a brother so forget him being attracted to me."

Farrah sighed. Took a breath then said, "That was nice of him, wasn't it?"

"I never thought of him as a brother. That's his feelings for me so forget any passion on his part. I'd settle for a little passion, hoping love would follow no matter what he says he wants or doesn't. But I may as well *be* his sister for all the desire he feels."

Farrah squeezed Rhia's hand over the ribbon of leather threaded through her fingers. "He'd probably shoot me for saying this but he didn't take his eyes off you all last night."

"Probably the same protective way he watched you."

"He didn't even glance my way. He didn't forget I was there, he practically forgot anyone else was.

I may not want to attract a man but I know what it looks like."

"Oh…" Now that changed things a little. Maybe he truly had been talking about her feelings.

"But what about your father? I can't let Dylan make things worse on my account. He'll never get back in your father's good graces if we marry. I said as much to him but Dylan made a joke of it. Like he's happy not in the don's good graces."

"Don't confuse my father with yours. They're as far apart as the East is from the West. Dylan's only concern at Belleza is Mama and me. You can't live your life to suit anyone but you, Rhia. That isn't what this is really about. I know you love my brother and have for years. Ask yourself this—how will you feel when he marries someone else and you're all alone on Adara?"

Rhia closed her eyes. "I already have thought of that. Angus would seem cheerful compared with the shrew I'd become. But it still hurts not to have love returned. And to hear it said so plainly as he did."

"I've seen every day of my life how much that hurts. Dylan feels as he does because of Mama. Our father swept Mama off her feet but what he loved was her dowry. What Dylan doesn't understand is that he's half in love with you already. He just doesn't recognize it because he has no idea what love looks like. You know more about love than anyone I know. Opposites are supposed to be perfect for each other. You two are. You can teach him about love. So are you going to accept or not?"

Rhia mentally asked herself again. Could she watch Dylan marry someone else, knowing he could have been hers? The answer was still the same. Defeated, she sighed. "I guess I only have one other question. Considering that your father already doesn't talk to Dylan unless he's forced, what do we do about arranging a wedding?"

Farrah grinned. "We leave that up to my mother and Dylan. Our job will be to make sure you outdo the dress you're wearing. I'm going to enjoy seeing my brother finally happy."

From your lips to God's ears, Rhia thought.

Chapter Eight

Rhia brought the wagon to a stop in front of Belleza's hacienda and Dylan rode around them to the hitching post. Quickly tying Rory off, he hurried over to help the women down. And nearly stopped dead in his tracks.

Women. They really are *women.*

In the last day his world had shifted. The *girls* he'd waited for last night had suddenly grown up in his mind. How had he failed to notice the years passing in their lives yet remain aware of his own age?

Reaching up, he grasped Rhia around her slim waist and lifted her to the ground. It was a near thing but he resisted the urge to pull her against him and let her slide along his body. If he'd lost that battle, she'd know what a struggle it would be to give her the time he'd promised.

If indeed she consented to marriage at all. What woman wanted a shotgun wedding when they'd done nothing to deserve it?

Farrah cleared her throat, having jumped down on her own while he'd stared down at Rhia. "I'll go get Mama," she said. When he glanced at her, she wore a knowing grin and winked before spinning away.

They must have talked about his proposal. He covered his latent desire with a teasing grin. "Got an answer for me, Rowdy?"

She nodded. Opened her mouth to speak but not much by way of sound came out. She cleared her throat. "On one condition." She seemed to force the words out. "Promise you won't let Belleza swallow up Adara. I promised my father I'd make it a success for him. I promised, Dylan."

"I'd sooner cut off my right arm than be in league with my father." He didn't add that he'd rather try to herd chickens than go back to tending sheep but he couldn't provide for her safety at Adara if he spent his days working miles away at the Rocking R. She needed his gun as well as his name. "Adara is yours," he said and added, "you have my solemn promise." Somehow he'd save enough money to add land and horses and see that his part of the operation grew so their children wouldn't suffer the way he had.

"I'm willing to accept your proposal but with one more condition. I run Adara. I might want to bounce ideas off you but the decisions will be mine."

"I already told you the operation is yours. I'm man

enough to take orders from a woman." He hoped he hadn't sounded as gloomy as he felt. He'd be working sheep again. *Damn.*

His tone must have sounded okay to her because she looked up at him with such gratitude and caring in her eyes it took his breath away. He leaned forward, drawn to her by that expression, intent on the sweet experience of their first kiss. Her pretty cornflower eyes drifted closed, her thick sooty lashes the perfect foil to her porcelain-doll complexion. He'd brought his lips within an inch of hers when his father's strident voice jerked them out of the moment.

"Dylan! I demand to know what you told that upstart sheriff!"

Dylan stepped back and turned toward the hacienda as the don stalked around the corner with Farrah tripping behind him.

"Why?" he asked. Sheriff Quinn and Kane, the Texas Ranger now assigned the area, had both spent a couple of hours at Adara looking at tracks, the wounds on the dead animals and helping him bury Angus. Just as Dylan had thought, there were things about each of the recent raids that didn't add up to Comanche being involved. The Hernandezes' survival made no sense. Day or night, no one hid from the Comanche.

Instead of pushing Dylan further and probably

knowing it was a waste of breath, the don glared at Rhia. "What about you?" he demanded.

Before Dylan could object to the don's disrespectful tone, Rhia said, "I barely spoke to him."

She seemed unsurprised by his father's treatment—used to it in fact. Which could only mean the don always treated her this way.

Dylan's anger grew. "Don't take that tone with Rhia. It isn't a way to talk to any woman, especially not your future daughter-in-law," he added, waiting for the explosion Rhia had predicted. Now he understood why she knew he'd object.

The don's face darkened even more. "You cannot—"

"Watch it!" Dylan snapped. "I *can* and *will* be more than proud to take her as my wife and it'll be as soon as I can arrange it. As I said last night, this is America. We're all equal no matter where our parents came from." He flicked a look from his father's eyes to his feet and back up again. "And thank God we aren't judged by *who* they are, either. That isn't a position I'd ever want to be in considering how rude you are."

Farrah jumped in then clearly trying to once again be the peacemaker. "Papa, Sheriff Quinn probably heard you'd offered to buy Rhia out from Joshua Wheaton. I mentioned you'd made Rhia another offer this morning. I saw the sheriff ride into town but he stopped to talk to Mr. Wheaton. Then the sheriff turned around and rode out again. I guess to come here. Dylan, I'll go tell Mama your happy news."

"So this is why the Anglo sheriff questions *me*? *Me*, Don Alejandro Alvaro Varga. Do I look like a Comanche? A thief? A murderer?"

Dylan coolly pretended to study his father then shrugged nonchalantly. "Better be more careful what land you try to buy, *Don Alejandro*, especially from raid victims. It could be misconstrued." Since he'd promised not to tip Quinn and Kane's hand, Dylan turned away to watch his mother rush from the hacienda. For her sake, Farrah's and his own he prayed his father wasn't involved in the deepening mystery about who was behind these raids. They would all be so ashamed if the don was responsible.

His mother wore a wide smile, obviously thrilled with their marriage plans, clearly unaware of the don's mood. Remembering the shadows of destruction at Rhia's place, he extracted a promise from Rhia that she would remain with his family and not attempt to return to Adara. In turn, he promised to keep watch over the place, couching his request in a need to maintain the greatest measure of propriety before the wedding.

Ignoring the don, his mother scolded Dylan again for his carelessness last night and instructed him to make arrangements for a wedding in a week or two. Then she bundled Rhia and Farrah inside as the don was getting all set for another tirade. Dylan ignored him and mounted up but he glanced back as Rhia entered the hacienda. A worried feeling stole over his soul. He felt as if he'd left a prize foal with one hoof poised over a snake den.

That feeling, while unsettling, gave him hope for the future. As he'd told her, many happy marriages had begun with less than they had between them. He had always cared about her so protecting her with his name already began to feel less like a life sentence. He went whole minutes without a spirit of doom settling over him. It was a doom that always stemmed from business concerns. He truly was attracted to this new Rhia who'd emerged at the social. He'd only tried to step back because of bad timing financially and Rhia's plan to keep Adara a sheep ranch.

Worries and recriminations were a waste of time and energy. He had no real choice. He'd made a huge blunder by taking her into town with him and now he had to fix it. Still, life might turn out pretty good eventually. Just not like he'd planned. He sighed and prepared to get on with arranging a wedding for as soon as possible not in a week or two as his mother suggested. He wanted Rhia away from his father.

Dylan encountered Father Santiago on the road

as the priest was leaving town. He'd been called to another of the missions he served to perform the last rites and probably a funeral mass for the same person. From there he'd go on to make his regular rounds. Though he sympathized with Dylan's reason for speed, commended him for facing his responsibility and even agreed to skip reading the banns, he could do no more to speed things along. He'd be back in time to marry them the following week on Friday or Saturday.

Dylan rode to the Rocking R to draw his last pay from Alex then rode back to Adara, to assess the damage and make a list of supplies. Once there he stood in the midst of the wanton destruction, grateful he had a week to make repairs before Rhia saw the destruction in the light of day. As the list grew, Dylan's hope of buying the land to the east dimmed. Every pane of glass was broken, the furniture, the doors, the dishes. The list went on. And on.

As he picked up the broken pieces of Rhia's world, he remembered something. Rhia always referred to the sweet little house as her mother's. She always referred to the surrounding land that made up the enterprise portion of Adara as her father's. But they'd both been gone for some time.

So why was no piece of this place Rhia's?

Not the broken dishes, the dented pots, or even the faded curtains that had been torn asunder had changed from the days his mother used to take him and Farrah for visits. There was no trace of Rhia anywhere.

He picked up the broken pieces of a teapot to toss them into the waste bin but he stopped, remembering the first time he'd met Rhiannon Oliver. It had been his eleventh birthday and her sixth.

His mother had urged them into the carriage for a ride to welcome Henry Oliver's wife and daughter to the area. Henry Oliver had come ahead to build a house for his family then he'd sent for them.

His mother had brought a pie along that day. Dylan had felt so grown up having been given the job of keeping the treat safely balanced in his lap all the way there. That sunny day Mrs. Oliver had greeted them with a broad welcoming smile, inviting them into the little house to share the pie and a cup of tea.

From that very pot—the pieces of which lay in his hands.

He, Farrah and Rhia had become fast friends after that day as had Theresa Oliver and his mother. For six years they'd repeated the ritual, especially on that day of the year, until Mrs. Oliver died in childbirth along with her baby when Rhia was twelve.

Dylan sighed and wrote "glue" on his list for town so he could mix up a batch and fix the teapot. He only hoped he could put the shards of Rhia's life back together as easily. And that his own life didn't wind up as full of unwanted feelings as he felt at that moment.

* * *

Dylan paced to the window of San Rafael's tiny sacristy then turned back toward where his grooms-men sat slouched nonchalantly in their chairs. He, Josh Wheaton and Alex Reynolds all wore nearly identical black suits but his friends wore nearly identical grins. Amused by his nervousness.

In truth, he hadn't had time to even think about the wedding his mother had insisted upon because he'd been working so hard trying to put Adara's homestead back together. Or as back together as his savings had allowed.

They only had a plate apiece and a few dented tin cups and bowls. But the walls were painted on the inside as were the clapboards outside, along with the doors and window trim. Abby had made curtains and cushion covers for the chairs as a wedding gift.

Dylan raked a hand through his hair then tried to loosen his collar a bit. He'd thought he'd settled himself about the marriage so his nervousness was a surprise. He'd barely had time to sleep. He probably wouldn't sleep tonight, either.

Tonight, Dylan repeated to himself. That's what had him nearly jumping out of his skin. If she even smiled at him, he wasn't sure he'd be able to keep his hands off her. And a broken promise was no way to begin their marriage.

Chapter Nine

Rhia stood in Abby's bedroom looking into the mirror at the stranger staring back at her. The white silk gown was so beautiful it made her eyes flood with tears. She fingered the delicate lace that formed the high neck of the gown.

And it truly sank in. She covered her mouth, blinking away tears. Rhiannon Oliver, the girl who eight days earlier had arrived at the Varga hacienda in britches to dress for the spring social, was about to marry the man of her dreams.

Farrah's mother had insisted on buying the dress—a betrothal gift, in memory of Rhia's mother, who couldn't be there.

So how could I refuse?

She turned to the side, admiring the way the straight princess front belled out a tad in back then fell into a train trimmed in flounces of Brussels lace. Cuffs of matching lace fell to her wrists from the middle of her forearm. Her veil was made of light net and lace and was attached to silk flowers.

"Beautiful," Farrah whispered behind her, her tone almost reverent. "Dylan isn't going to see another person in that church once he catches sight of you."

Rhia whirled, her heart leaping with joy. "Oh, you came. I was so afraid your father wouldn't let you."

"I told you we'd be here. Mama went to see Dylan at the mission."

Rhia could see Farrah looked worried behind her smile. "Your father didn't come."

"Don't let that bother you," Farrah said. "It won't upset Dylan."

Rhia sighed. "I didn't want to be responsible for widening the rift between them."

"Mama's wrong, *hermana*. That rift is a canyon. And you aren't responsible. Papa is."

Through gathering tears, Rhia smiled at being called *sister* by her best friend. "I'm so sad for Dylan. I always knew Daddy loved me."

"Dylan will have *your* love, now. It'll be enough."

"He told me outright he doesn't want love in this marriage. I don't think he believes in it."

"He believes it exists. But you're going to have to love Dylan until he knows he can trust in it. He already trusts in you."

She'd loved Dylan for years already. That wasn't about to change. She would give him all the love and time he needed. She'd need patience. "I can do that," she promised, praying she wouldn't have to wait too long.

"Don't you look just like the picture?" Abby said from the doorway, her green eyes sparkling, her smile wide and pleased.

"The dress is gorgeous," Farrah said. "My brother will be awestruck."

Abby laughed. "And isn't that what a special gown for a woman's wedding is supposed to be all about? I've been waiting for a special bride to wear this one from the day I saw it in the catalog."

Rhia turned and rushed to give Abby a hug. "I don't know how to thank you. Or how to repay you for all your kindness."

Abby blinked away the mist of tears. "I'm grateful for this week at your side as I doubt I'll ever have a daughter to fuss over." She swirled into the room, letting out a watery laugh. She and Farrah both wore the kind of full-skirted dress Western women favored. Abby's was emerald and Farrah's was sapphire.

"And don't we look wonderful in *our* new dresses, Miss Farrah?"

Farrah gazed at herself in the mirror and crossed her arms. "Just so we're clear. I wore this for your sake, Rhiannon Oliver."

Abby rolled her eyes at Rhia and laughed. "So,

we're all set?" she asked. "My brother has the carriage all hitched and ready to take us to the church."

Rhia took a deep breath. "I'm as ready as I'm gonna get."

"Stop," Farrah shouted. "I nearly forgot. Mama says you have to have…ahem…something old, something new, something borrowed, something blue and sixpence in your shoe," she recited in one breath. "It's for luck." She dug into her reticule and pulled out a tarnished coin. "Mama kept this sixpence from her wedding. And since it's old and borrowed and your dress is new all you need now is something blue."

Abby chuckled. "And I have that for you in the hall. From Dylan. It came with a note." She rushed out then back in with a bouquet of flowers tied with a blue satin bow. "I added the blue and a bit of arrangin'. He is a man and therefore ham-handed," she teased.

The flowers were wonderful and bright. Wildflowers every one. Rhia's hands shook as she opened the note.

Rowdy,
I felt pretty terrible this morning because all I have to give is a ring to show my esteem. Then, as I headed for town, I noticed Adara is in full bloom.

The daisies made me think of how small and delicate you look but how strong I know you are. The bluebonnets remind me of your eyes when they darken up because you're riled. Then I noticed a few Indian blankets scattered around. I didn't think they matched the others but I remembered an old-timer called them fire wheels. Fiery. That's you past riled all the way to furious. I'll try to avoid that. I promise. Last time you tried to bean me with my own baseball. Remember?

I hope having these will be a little like having a small part of your parents with you. I also hope this wedding with all the trimmings makes up for how mean some people were to you.
Deepest regards,
DV

Rhia blinked away tears that had gathered as she'd read. Esteem. Regards. She prayed that would be enough if his love never came her way. She clutched her beautiful bouquet and prayed for patience all the way to San Rafael's.

When she got there and peeked into the sanctuary there were more of the same flowers on the altar and she found she could smile again. How many flowers had Dylan picked? He must have denuded every meadow on Adara! And he *must* care. He must care *a lot*.

How far behind could love be?

A few minutes later Rhia stood alone in the nave still clutching her precious bouquet, watching Abby and Farrah walk down the aisle of the sanctuary ahead of her. The pews were full of people who'd watched her grow and had lent their support through the last week. And there were the newcomers from the East who hadn't known her. They'd turned a tragedy into a scandal and because of them Dylan was about to sign away his life and she her heart.

Just as despair nearly swamped her again, the strains of the same music she and Dylan had waltzed to floated from the balcony overhead. It was the same group of men from last week's Spring Social. Dylan's doing, she was sure.

She saw him then, stepping in front of Father Santiago up by the altar. He held his hand out. But, standing there with no support, she couldn't seem to take that first step. Clutching her flowers, her connection to her parents, she took one step toward Dylan and their uncertain future.

Maybe he realized how hard it was for her to be alone right then because he walked up the aisle toward her.

They met halfway.

It was late afternoon when she and Dylan rolled to a stop at the top of the hill overlooking the heart of Adara. The Wheatons had hosted a late-morning breakfast at their house for everyone who'd attended the ceremony. Mr. Reiman over at the hotel had even sent over a fancy cake as a gift. They'd put what was left of it and their other gifts in the back of the fancy rig Josh and Abby insisted they use. Because Scout and cake were a bad combination, she'd left him behind for a day or two with the Wheatons. Dylan would get Scout when he returned the rig.

"Close your eyes, Mrs. Varga," Dylan purred into her ear, making her shiver. Making her want.

Then apprehension spread through her. It was time to return to reality. Rhia closed her eyes with a silent sigh. This was near where she'd waited while Dylan investigated the silence that had shrouded Adara. She didn't really want to look at the house anyway. She knew destruction lay below.

As he started the rig downhill, Rhia found herself dreading the first sight of her mother's house. Though her memory of that night was foggy, she'd seen the debris in the shadows. Her father had been so proud of the sweet little house he'd built for his beloved wife.

Trying to brace for destruction, she imagined the windows boarded-up, maybe the door fixed but scarred. Dylan was only one man after all. That he'd tried was all that mattered.

"Hoah!" Dylan called and the horse stopped. The seat shifted, telling her he'd scrambled down. Then he took her hand from below. "Keep 'em closed and stand up so I can get you down."

She stood, wobbling a bit. "Dylan Varga, I feel like I'm six years old again and you're torturing me with blindman's bluff."

He took her by her waist and, laughing, lifted her down as if she were still that tiny girl. "Oh, *querida*, you are no longer a mere girl." His voice, so close and deep, made her open her eyelids in the next instant. Then as his lips moved toward hers, she let her suddenly heavy eyelids drift closed. This kiss, unlike that first chaste one he'd given her in church, had her stomach flipping and her toes curling. Like the other kiss, this one ended too quickly. Dylan jumped back so suddenly it left her teetering. "Open your eyes!" he said abruptly.

Startled, reeling with confusion, bereft of him, she opened them and stared at him. She didn't understand him at all. Especially not his strained grin when he gestured toward the house.

She looked then, and blinked in shock. It didn't look like her mother's house. Not anymore. But it gleamed.

"I hope you like it. All the paint is Patience and Alex's wedding gift."

The previously dull, whitewashed clapboards were painted the color of buttermilk. All the trim, the shutters, and front door—the *new* front door—were bright white.

"I know it looks different," he said, "but—"

"It's beautiful," she interrupted sure by his tone he was worried. "How on earth did you do all this?"

"I had some help. Josh and Alex pitched in a couple of days. Then Abby's brother Brendan Kane came out and it turns out a Texas Ranger can be an able carpenter. A few cowboys from the Rocking R spent some hours here, too. Everyone felt awful about the raid and the gossips in town."

He paused then, as if nervous. It was the first time she'd considered him unsure of anything. Then he said, "Oh, and I hired Juan away from my father. Juan was sick of being screamed at and belittled, so we have a shepherd who's also good with horses. He cleaned up the Hernandezes' cabin and moved in. He took care of the livestock and the dogs leaving me free to work on your house. Our house now."

"Still, this was a lot of work. I could have helped. It wasn't necessary for you to work so hard on your own."

He grimaced. "Yeah. It was. There was a lot of damage, Rhia, and I didn't want those memories to linger. We have to look forward. It doesn't matter what put us here. We need to do our best with the lot we've been dealt."

She hated that she was the lot he'd been dealt while

she'd gotten her fondest wish. Some men would have been in a vindictive frame of mind, put her to work on the mess and brooded. But, though Dylan hadn't wanted this marriage, he wanted to make the best of it. She still felt guilty that Dylan had given up his job, his freedom and further infuriated his father. All for a life he'd never have chosen freely.

Dylan led her to the front porch where he'd even added some of the pretty fretwork Abby had on her house. "Ready?" he asked, turning back to her after opening the door.

She nodded bracing herself for all the damage he hadn't had time to fix inside. She took a deep fortifying breath then it came out in a long squeal when he swept her off her feet. "What are you doing?"

He laughed and she felt the sound rumble through his chest. His golden-honey eyes danced with mischievous delight when he smiled down at her. "Have to do this. Mama made me promise not to let evil spirits pester you."

"I never knew your mother was so superstitious. First that 'old, new, borrowed and blue' rhyme. Now this. That coin they made me put in my shoe has given me a blister. You'd better not drop me, Dylan Varga."

He laughed as they cleared the doorway, then he bent to set her on her feet in the front room. She looked around. The board and batten interior walls were freshly painted in the same buttery color as the outside. The seat cushions of the sofa had new cotton duck covers. The curtains had been replaced with the same color gingham and there were matching seat cushions on two new rockers positioned across from the sofa.

"Where did the chairs come from?"

"Brendan Kane made them. They're a wedding gift."

She blinked against tears stinging the back of her eyes. "I hardly know him. Everyone's been so kind. Well, not everyone, but this goes a long way toward making up for what those townsfolk said, doesn't it?"

"To my way of thinking, it does," Dylan said. "Brendan promised to help me build new tables for the parlor when this raiding calms down."

The little front room looked wonderful but over the smell of fresh paint she noticed the faint odor of kerosene. "I guess the lamps broke," she said and looked down. The rag rug her mother had made just before she'd died was missing.

"I soaped up and rinsed the rug but it's still airing out on the corral fence."

She bit her lip, nodded and looked toward the kitchen. It, too, was clean as a whistle but there used to be six chairs and now there were only two. She walked to the kitchen and braced her hands on the backrest of one of the ladder-back chairs. The shelves were mostly empty of dishes and bowls. But in the center of the table sat her mother's sunny-yellow teapot with a little bouquet of daisies and bluebonnets in it. The teapot had been lovingly glued back together. She sighed and ran her finger-tip across a flower petal.

Dylan had tried so hard. She forced a smile. "Thank you," she whispered but her voice broke.

He was there in a heartbeat, his arm around her shoulder. "I glued it and put a tin can inside so at least it could be a vase. The flowers…it was the strangest thing. Yesterday there wasn't a bloom to be picked and this morning the whole meadow was wild with color."

"I guess Adara wanted me to have a pretty wedding bouquet and flowers at the church. Thank you for listening to her."

"Her?"

"Mum teased Daddy that Adara was her rival for his affection. But it was just a tease. After she was gone, I used to hear him cry in his room at night. At least now they're together."

"I put a bunch of their things that were torn up and broken in the barn. I thought you should get to decide what to keep and what to say goodbye to. There are enough unbroken pieces for me to put two more chairs together."

Rhia nodded, looked up at him and smiled. "I'll look over all of it soon but it's okay. You're right, it's time to build new memories—a new life."

He blinked and let go of her, stepping back in the same moment. "Uh…right." His eyes widened. "Oh, the bedrooms. I forgot them." He raked a hand though his thick black hair. "I took the smaller one. I'll put your things in the bigger room. That reminds me, I should unhitch the wagon and check with Juan. And bring everything in, too." Then in a blink he was gone.

He'd all but *run* from her at the mere mention of the bedrooms. She'd told herself she could handle his subtle rejection. They were still only friends. Not even partners. Maybe she shouldn't have told him she would make all the business decisions. Maybe she should have shared some of the burden of the place.

Maybe when she trusted his methods with the sheep more and when he trusted her heart more, they'd be more to each other. Then they'd share burdens and their love. She had to be patient.

But with his indifference standing right there where he had a moment before, the loneliness she'd been battling for such a long time seemed to swallow her whole.

She'd been stuck miles away from town, working day and night, hardly seeing anyone except the silent

Hernandezes and occasionally Farrah. Now, when she finally had someone to share her life with, he'd jumped away like she was a rattler about to strike.

Drained after so many ups and then one last, huge, downhill slide into despair, she stumbled into the place that had always brought her solace. Her parents' room. She'd hoped that through some miracle it had gone untouched. But the bed was all that remained. Not even her mother's quilt had survived. She'd watched her mother piece it together back in Philadelphia while they'd waited to travel to Texas.

Tears came in a torrent then and she threw herself across the bed. She wept for all that was gone. For the years alone. For all the lonely, loveless years that seemed to lie ahead.

Oh, God, what have I done?

A hand pressed on her back and rubbed. "Shh," she heard over the sound of her own anguish. "Rowdy, stop. They were just things. We'll get new ones as soon as we can afford to."

She rolled over, going from anguish to anger in half a heartbeat. "Things? You think I'd cry over *things?*" She screamed out her pain. "It's not their things but what they represented. My parents. People who loved me. Now even those are gone."

"I'm sorry."

She couldn't stop. She had to tell someone, tell *him* what was buried in her heart. What she'd never let herself admit even to herself. "Do you have any idea how alone I've been? Angus growled at me or ignored me. Raul just took orders. Consuela said it would be too hard to move on if we became friends. I'd come in from the field and she would tell me what she'd made for dinner and had done in the house, then she'd rush off to their cottage. This last week was the first meal I ate with anyone except Scout in two years. We're going to have to teach him to eat off the floor again because I took to putting his bowl on the table. At least that way there was a pair of eyes looking at me."

Rhia sat up. Dylan's eyes, his lips were mere inches away. "It's like the center of me is empty. I feel so…so hollow."

"Oh, Rowdy," he whispered and cupped her cheek, then spanned those terribly lonely inches in a blink and covered her lips with his. His firm, roving mouth on hers started to fill some of those empty places inside her.

But not all. "Fill me," she whispered against his lips when she felt him start to pull away. "Fill me up so I know I'm not alone anymore."

Chapter Ten

Dylan did the only thing he could think of in response to her pain. He kissed her. Gently. As innocently as his raging need for her would allow.

But those tortured words in her hoarse, anguished voice echoed in his head, threatening his tentative control. He lifted his head and stared into her tear-filled eyes. Those tears shimmered, reflecting luminescent blue in the sunlight that flooded the room.

Then she said, "Fill me. Fill me up so I know I'm not alone anymore."

And all his good intentions about taking it slow and waiting for the physical part of their marriage flew right out that brand-new window next to the bed. He reached for her. Tunneling his fingers into her fancy wedding hairdo, he dropped his head again, unable to resist taking her sweet lips now that those words had fallen from them. He should say something but didn't trust himself to utter even a word. He hoped she understood what it was she'd asked for. A man couldn't resist starting the rest of his life in the face of this much temptation.

And so he took her mouth with his, more forcefully this time, parting her lips, swirling his tongue past them, reveling in her sweet taste. He dragged one hand out of her hair, fingers of the other still tangled in her curls. He caressed her cheek and neck with his knuckles using a featherlight touch. His hand shook as he fought for control. Or was that her quaking?

Dylan hadn't any idea. Lost in the feel and taste of her, he no longer knew where she ended and he began. He slid his fingers gently, lightly, over her neck and lower, over the soft slippery silk of her dress. It was wondrous yet torturous because he knew her skin would feel so much better. Then he cupped her breast and knew it was his hand shaking.

Her gasp when he fondled the lush globe nearly drove him mad with desire. He rolled her nipple between his index finger and his thumb, earning a sensual moan and himself a gnawing ache he had to wait to assuage.

She moaned again, fisting her hands in his hair, and threw her head back. "Fill me," she begged again, breaking his heart with her need for a connection to another person. He'd never realized before today how alone she'd been. He was grateful she'd turned to him for the warmth and affection she needed.

Grateful he would be the one to teach her about passion.

His control on the thinnest of tethers now, he pulled back and looked into her eyes. The blue had darkened to the color of the paintbrush that bloomed all over Adara's meadows.

"No," she sobbed, "you can't stop. I need more. I need *you*. I need to belong to you. I need you to belong to me."

He groaned against her neck. And just like that, everything he'd sworn to keep in check bubbled up, spilled out.

Set him on fire.

For his little wildflower.

"I need you, too, Rowdy girl," he gasped. "But we have to get you out of that pretty contraption you're wearing." Before he turned savage and tore her beautiful gown, he urged her off the bed to stand between his thighs. He started working at the satin buttons running down her back but his hands shook enough to make him fumble. He cursed roundly, earning him a muffled giggle.

He took a deep breath, trying to settle down before he sent tiny buttons flying everywhere. What kind of cruel person had designed this means of torturing bridegrooms? Ought to be staked to an anthill, that was for sure.

Finally, after a few tries, the first button gave up the battle and fell open. Then another. He got the knack after that. But he was on fire, his erection was so hard it was practically screaming for freedom. By the time he'd bared her to her waist, undid the hook of her crinoline and untied the damn tiny drawstring of her pantaloons, his whole body thrummed. His need was so strong it scared him. Thank God his tiny new wife didn't have one of those corset contraptions on.

Maybe he should run for the hills but now that he'd gone this far there'd be no stopping. Running for the hills sure didn't make any sense to the rest of him. He couldn't remember why he'd said they should wait. Stupid idea. He needed her more than he needed to listen to reasons that no longer mattered.

Not with her shivering. Quaking. Calling his name.

And not with her whole beautiful back from neck to her cute round bottom bared. Not with her right there for his taking. Unable to resist the call of all that creamy skin, he nibbled his way from her nape all the way across the sharp planes of her shoulders and listened with pure satisfaction to the sweet music of her gasps and moans.

Nope. He wasn't going anywhere but right there with her.

Needing to see her, all of her, he stood and ran his hands down her arm taking all that silk and lace along for the ride. In seconds the dress, crinolines and drawers were in a pool at her feet and all she wore was her shoes and stockings. She turned in the circle of his arms, and he looked his fill of her curvaceous, compact body. The best things—the very best things—really did come in small packages.

A blush stole everywhere his eyes roved. She tried to look him in the eyes but looked down then sucked a shocked little breath. He guessed she'd caught sight of his erection, straining for freedom. Then the little torturer of his youth—not about to play a passive part—reached out and ran her knuckles over him.

He cursed.

She giggled.

Then biting her lip, her expression a little uncertain, her breath coming out in little pants, she went to work on the buttons of his trousers. He stood there rooted to the floor, panting like a stallion scenting a mare. But when he sprang free into her hand, he spit out another curse, scooped her up and lowered her to the mattress in the space it took for his next breath.

He'd planned to take off her shoes and undress himself but then he caught sight of her hot gaze on him and followed her down instead. Kissing those swollen lips couldn't wait. Neither could trailing his mouth down to her pert nipples.

He braced himself on one forearm and cradled her breast in his palm then drew her taut nipple into his mouth. Soon he moved on to the other as she raked her fingers through his hair, then kneaded the taut muscles of his arms. He'd never felt anything like having her hands on him as she panted with growing excitement.

Nearly at the end of his tether, he ran his hand downward, exploring the firm skin of her hips and belly until he came to her nest of black curls and found her center—wet and ready.

She shouted his name, trembling under his fingers and pulling at his shirt, running her small hands up his ribs and over his back. She seemed to be urging him on. He stood that. He did. He even helped her get his shirt off. But the sensuous feel of her silky skin against his and her cry of "Closer. Please, closer" in a low raspy voice completely undid him.

After that every thought but the most primitive fled. He shoved his pants farther down on his hips and pushed her knees apart with his. He entered her as carefully as he could but her gasp this time was of shock and pain, not glory.

As if doused by cold water, he froze, managing to ignore his own need in favor of hers. He kissed the tears that flooded her eyes, letting their personal history take over. "That full up enough for you?" he teased.

She gifted him with a watery chuckle. "A...a little too, I think."

"No," he soothed. "It'll get better, wildflower," he whispered against her lips, "give it some time. You tell me when you're ready for more." He closed his eyes reaching for a memory to help him keep that promise.

Just like that, he was back there on the spring day he'd taught her to swim in Adara's clear cool lake. Looked like he was teaching her something new this spring, too. "You'll see, wildflower. I'll see it gets real good real, real soon. That's no brag, I promise."

"And you never break a promise. Right?" She moved under him a bit as if testing the waters.

It was a point of honor for him. He never did.

He kept this promise, too. It got a lot better for her and him. Right after he kissed her again and carefully moved in her. She let out a beautiful little gasp. It was full of delicious joy followed by a tiny shriek, hot with need. His own need flooded back with a vengeance. He wanted to race for the end but forced himself into a slow rhythm. He felt the surprising strength in her when she wrapped her arms around him and in the undulating motion of her body as she caught his rhythm. It took him by surprise when she started to shudder and quake under him, around him. He'd never felt such unbridled happiness knowing he'd brought her such pleasure. Needing to watch her face as she came apart for him, he braced himself and arched his back to look down into her beautiful face. And then he had to follow her or die.

And if he had, it would have been with his boots on.

Chapter Eleven

Rhia threw her arm over her eyes, trying to block out the sunlight and cling to her dream—she and Dylan making sweet love. Though she was desperate not to lose the dream, it started to fade as her sleepy senses pushed past the fog that dulled her mind.

There was sunlight on her face. She usually woke to the subdued light of dawn. She frowned. The sun rose on the other side of the house. Curiosity drove her ahead, willing her to face the day.

She opened her eyes and stared up at the ceiling. This was her parents' room. An ache registered in her muscles. Muscles she'd swear she'd never used before. It hadn't been a dream. She slid a hand across to where Dylan had slept. He wasn't there but still, it all flooded back.

Dylan. The wedding. His kindness. Everything that had led to him trying to comfort her.

Her love for him and her own need to belong to someone had welled up from some deep place inside her, overwhelming her pride. He'd made love to her but didn't love her. She blinked back welling tears. Her pain was no excuse. She'd agreed to the terms of his proposal. As he had to hers.

So, instead of finding a way to thank him for his rescue from her uncertain circumstances and scorn, for relinquishing his chance to ever find a woman he could love the way she loved him, she'd thrown herself at him—begged him. Which made her no better than a soiled dove at the Garter, trying to earn a dollar.

Remembering the way he'd made love to her and the number of times he'd turned to her in the night, she thought sadly that Dylan was a passionate man. Which only meant she'd tempted him beyond endurance. She wasn't foolish enough to think his passion had anything to do with feelings for her.

Her face heated. How was she going to face him? Abby had tried to fill in her spotty knowledge of the human mating ritual but she hadn't told her a thing about the awkwardness she'd feel the next day.

She imagined Dylan had let her sleep as yet another kindness. Rhia shook her head. Though the idea of hiding in there with the door bolted held real appeal, it was time to do what she'd always done— put one foot in front of the other. She rose to face the day.

There were eggs to collect, sheep to be sheared

and probably fences to check. She washed, dressed in her same old baggy work clothes, and felt the sharp pang of hunger before she remembered she no longer had a cook.

That stopped her in her tracks. Had Dylan thought she'd be the kind of wife who could cook? Sew? Knit? If so, he was in for a rude awakening. After her mother died, Rhia had lost count of the meals she'd burned. She'd get it all going just fine, then her mind would skip to the ranch work that needed doing. She'd follow that thread of a thought on into deeds and forget about the kitchen until smoke leaked from the house. Which was why her father had always hired a shepherd with a wife to cook for them.

Spying the leftover cake from their wedding, Rhia cut a big hunk, and ate it on the way to the shearing shed. She noticed Dylan's mare, Annie, in the corral and stopped to give her a quick pet. Then she chatted with Juan about where they stood in the shearing and some of the load lifted from her shoulders. Dylan had thought to shear, and skin the sheep she'd lost to the raiders, which would recoup some of her losses.

Grabbing her shears, she got right to work on a ewe she pulled from the holding pen. Shearing time was measured by the number of sheep handled, not by the clock. She and Juan worked in silence but for the din of the bleating sheep.

Fifty ewes later, Rhia's arms and back ached as she caught a particularly stubborn sheep and finally rolled it over to rest against her knee. "Why are you fighting me?" she crooned as she started clipping its belly. "Don't you know how hot you'd be in a few weeks if we don't get this done?"

"She's probably just hoping to make your life even more miserable than it already is with this job to do," Dylan said from behind her.

Startled, feeling at a distinct disadvantage bent over a recalcitrant sheep the way she was and still dreading facing him, she lashed out, "I wasn't aware my life was all that miserable. I'm sorry if you feel I've dragged you into a pit of misery."

"I didn't say that exactly but I had hoped after yesterday I'd seen the last of the no-account drifter." He nodded toward her clothes. It sounded as if he was teasing but she couldn't help thinking there was more than a grain of truth to what he said.

Which meant she was doomed. How was she supposed to keep her promise to her father and look like the person she'd been last week? She couldn't.

Rhia stared at Dylan over the struggling sheep. She'd been raised to respect hard work as the path to success and security. She hadn't been raised to care how she looked or to sit around being waited on. In other words, she wasn't a lady like Dylan's mother.

Too bad! He'd said he didn't want that. Apparently he'd been wrong. She guessed she wasn't the only one having emotional revelations suddenly crop up the way her loneliness had.

He'd been determined to rescue her. He'd said the perfect wife for him had to know what it meant to put in a hard day's work. That's what he'd gotten.

All he'd gotten.

Distracted, the shears slipped in her palm. She dropped the sheep before she hurt it and rounded on Dylan in a pure fury. "Now that tears it!" she shouted and heard a door at the other end open then shut. Juan had fled. Smart man.

"I look like a no-account drifter? Suppose you go over to the Rocking R and herd cattle wearing a dress. Or pick up a pair of sheers here with your skirts tangling in a ewe's hooves, then tell me how your day went."

Dylan took a breath. "Look. I'm sorry for the re-mark about your clothes. It just drives me crazy to know you wore that getup to hide and that you're still hiding. I want more for you than that. But the truth is, we need you to help with the shearing to get to market before my father drives prices down be-cause of the volume he'll have for sale. I rode over there. He hasn't started shearing. I'm sorry I hurt your feelings."

She nodded. "What exactly did you mean by calling my life miserable? Do you see this marriage as having dragged you into misery?"

Dylan's eyes widened and he raked his fingers through his hair. "You don't know what the don and I fought about, do you?"

"You call him *the don*," she said, her tone sarcastic as she planted her hands on her hips. "That pretty well says it. I figured you two had another battle and he ordered you off Belleza. So you went to work for the Rocking R."

She could see anger build in his eyes as he shook his head. "You have it backward. He disowned me because I went to work on the Rocking R. And I did that because I hate sheep and anything to do with them. They're smelly and stupid and cause trouble wherever they're raised."

Rhia could feel the blood draining from her face. Who was this man she'd married? Did she know him at all?

Apparently not.

She put a hand in the middle of his chest and pushed him back out the shed door. "Get off my place, now. You set me up when you took me to town the night of the raid. It got you ahead of all those others in town who lined up to court me all of a sudden. Which means you didn't marry me to save me from disgrace. You planned to take over here so you could bring cattle here. You want to destroy my parents' dream."

Eyes narrowed, lips thin, Dylan took a vibrating breath. Then another. "You're wrong, Rhia. You don't know what it's like to grow up being tormented for being the son of a sheepherder. They just left you alone 'cause you were a girl and you were rarely in town.

"You talk about your parents' dream. Well, I had one, too. I gave it up to try to help you make their dream and yours come true. But I wanted more for me and eventually my wife and children than the stigma cattle ranchers tack on to those who run woolies. The town's growing. Changing. Look at the gossip over you and me going in to report the raid. There's a school now. I wanted my kids to be able to go there and not get tripped in the street or not get pushed in the mud because of how their father earns a living. I'd think any woman would want the same for her children.

"As for me leaving Adara, we consummated this marriage, Mrs. Varga. And you asked for it. So I guess you're stuck with me." He turned and stormed away.

Oh, God. What have I done?

"Dylan," she called but it came out as barely a

squeak. Her breath, her anger, and all the starch drained right out of her along with her ability to stand. Numb, she slid downward, the outside wall of the shed at her back. She hugged her knees. "Dylan," she whispered.

Too drained to even cry, she just sat. And tried to think. Was she sorry for Dylan or herself? Had she betrayed her parents by loving Dylan? Or had Dylan betrayed her?

She didn't know.

She didn't know anything anymore. So she sat there and watched the breeze stir the leaves on the big elm overhead. And thought of nothing—nothing at all.

Not much time could have passed when she felt Dylan crouched down in front of her. "Rowdy, honey, I'm sorry." He touched her arm.

She lifted her head and stared into his earnest golden eyes.

"Despite my feelings about raising sheep, you're the boss of this outfit and it's your dream we'll work toward. And what I said about last night was plain unforgivable. But I hope you'll forgive me anyway. Last night was special." He smiled. "I hope for both of us."

She nodded and tried to smile back. How could she hold back forgiveness when everything she'd done since she'd seen that darn blue dress had trapped him in a life he clearly hated?

"Thanks," he said quietly.

"Your dream, Dylan. What was your dream?" Her voice sounded so thin and reedy it shocked her.

"I wanted to breed horses. That's what Annie was all about. She'd throw gorgeous foals. Alex has a stallion he was going to let me breed to her. I'm good with horses. I could train them and if I cut some of the ones with good lines out of wild herds, I might be able to breed in mustang endurance. With horse racing getting more and more popular, I think I could do really well."

"Maybe someday we could buy more land. I've been trying to save for some. I'm sorry, Adara isn't big enough for both right now, but maybe some-day," she said.

He nodded but there was a deep sadness in his eyes he tried and failed to hide. "Enough of that. Let me see that hand."

She blinked. "Hand?"

"There's blood on my shirt from when you pushed me out of the shed. You must have cut your hand or you have some mean blisters. Now let me see your hand."

Her hand did sting some.

She put her palm up and he spit out a curse. "It's

both. Let's get you up to the house and get this looked after."

He was so sweet and gentle. He took care of her hand but then he got all polite and stiff, his eyes still sad. He excused himself. He had things to think about, he said. Then he made her promise not to go back to shearing. Next thing she knew he was out the door. And she was alone.

Not knowing what to do, she figured she'd try to cook dinner. Since she was supposed to stay in the house, maybe she could keep from burning it to a cinder.

It wasn't easy with her hand all bandaged but she had the stove going and a stew on to simmer within an hour. At loose ends in the sparkling-clean house, she went to make up the bed and blushed at the evidence of last night's activity. She stripped the sheets, grateful for the new ones the Presbyterian minister and his wife gave them as a wedding gift.

As she tucked in the blankets, she wondered about the damage to her mama's pretty quilt. Yesterday Dylan said he'd put the damaged things in the tack room of the barn. That was something she could do with herself.

In the barn she stopped to pet Jessie's velvety old nose. Dylan's mare, Annie, trumpeted for attention and Rhia went to the stall and stroked her neck and cheek. "You really are a beauty."

With a deep, defeated sigh, Rhia left the stalls and headed for the tack room. She found the quilt right off and was relieved she had enough skill with a needle to fix it. Mum had kept swatches of their old clothes Rhia could use to make repairs. They were in a yellow wooden box Daddy built. Mum had been going to make a quilt for the baby. Then they'd both been gone. Now Daddy was gone, too.

It wasn't hard to find the bright yellow box. The lid was crushed and broken. She lifted the pieces with care and laid them aside in the hope that Dylan could glue it the way he had the teapot.

She smiled at the memory of the wildflowers he'd had waiting for her on the table. In her bouquet. On the altar at the church. Dylan had made their wedding day special even when she was the last woman he'd have chosen to marry.

Feeling sad already, she got even more so as she looked through the swatches, remembering the clothes they'd come from. Her dresses. Her mother's. Her father's shirts. At the bottom of the pile lay a letter addressed to her grandparents in New York. They were both gone, too.

She frowned down at the envelope and ran her fingertips over her mother's handwriting. Curious, Rhia opened it. The date explained why it had never been posted. Mum had written it the day before her death.

In it she talked about Adara and the reasons they'd

decided on raising sheep. It wasn't for any great love of them. Her mother confessed to not liking them a bit. She called them smelly and stupid.

Rhia fought a smile. Dylan's exact words.

Her parents had picked sheep because it was easier to build a herd. Required fewer men. And there were the drives north with cattle on long dangerous trails they'd considered and rejected. It hadn't mattered to them what made Adara a success, as long as they gave their children a good future.

Rhia closed her eyes, she'd been so wrong.

Then a thought occurred to her and she knew exactly what she intended to do about it. Their birthdays were tomorrow.

The only question left was could she do it on time?

Chapter Twelve

Dylan sat staring at the lake. It spread out before him, so still it perfectly reflected the trees surrounding it. They remained the bright green only seen in spring.

Spring.

Supposedly the season of promise. Of renewal. Of life. Not destruction, heartache and pain.

If only he'd kept his mouth shut. Rhia hadn't needed to learn about his hatred of raising sheep or his reasons for it. She had so many worries with the uncertainty of starting a life together. Clearly a lot of men had made their true interest in her clear in town last week. They'd all wanted her land. It made sense that she'd read the motives of those men into his actions toward her.

So she'd lashed out in anger.

He frowned and looked down at the stone in his hand, then hurled it into the lake. No, she'd been feeling more than just anger. Hurt had added teeth to it. He'd never seen her strike out in anger at anyone, even as a child. He rubbed his hand over his chest where she'd shoved him backward out of the shed.

It surprised him that he could read her so well sometimes and not at all the rest. Like he'd understood she was hurt as well as angry but not why. He got to his feet, unable to sit while his thoughts had him so churned up. He stared at the lake and shoved his hands in his pockets. Could you wound someone who was indifferent to you? He didn't think so.

He paced to the water's edge. It made no sense. She hadn't responded to his proposal as if she had any feelings for him. It had taken his sister to talk her into the marriage. Even the censure the people in town hadn't been incentive enough. Had his unemotional approach put her off? Could it be she cared about him as more than a friend?

A thrill shot through him at the idea that she might love him. Why that would be, he didn't understand. It wasn't as if he wanted to love her in return. What kind of person did that make him?

Not one he was proud to be. He wasn't a taker. That *wasn't* who he was. Agitated, Dylan started walking along the shoreline needing the motion. The action.

He kicked a stone. He *hated* that he'd hurt her.

Even the act of taking her virginity had made him cringe for her pain. He thought back to the second time he'd made love to her. He'd looked in her eyes and his heart had turned over with wanting for what he'd seen there.

He stopped and blinked. Love was something he'd sworn he'd never want. Yet he did. He wanted hers. He hadn't wanted to love anyone, either. But he must love her. What else could cause this aching need to be with her? To protect her? To make sure she was happy?

He loved her. With all his heart.

What a prize idiot! He'd left his family over sheep but had married her in spite of them. He'd do anything to keep her safe and make her happy. Anything!

He stopped walking, suddenly sick to his stomach. She must feel awful. There were only two things she could give him as his wife. One—her love—was something he'd said he'd never want. The other— her body—he'd said he could wait for as if he'd been indifferent.

She must think she'd gotten everything with this marriage and he'd gotten nothing. He spun around and started back the way he'd come. He had to tell her. But how? How to let her know and ease the guilt he now understood?

He swallowed. There was only one way to fix this. And that was to show her he loved her above everything. He had to do it. She had to know nothing was more important to him than she was.

That only left one question. Could he do it by tomorrow and give her the best birthday gift possible? The gift of knowing how much he loved the woman she was.

He arrived back at the house and found only the scent of burning food. A pot sat on the hot stove untended. Burning. He grabbed a hot pad and ran it outside then went back in to open all the windows.

Where the hell was she? "Rowdy?" he called.

No answer.

He checked the bedroom thinking maybe she was tuckered out from the hard morning she'd put in. Nothing made your back hurt more than a day shearing woolies. But Rhia was nowhere to be found. Which meant she was working. With those hands!

He stomped out to the shed but she wasn't there. While he was there he took a look at her shears. They were in bad shape. It was a wonder she had any unblistered skin left on her poor hand.

He checked the barn next. And heard a scuffing sound in the tack room. Was she never still? He grinned. She had been last night after each time they'd made love. She'd been played-out and satiated, her body pliant. He liked that he could affect her the way nothing else did.

Dylan looked into the tack room and drank in

the sight of her sitting on the floor, surrounded by a large pile of ruined goods. She was busy sorting. "Hey there, wildflower. You forget something?"

"I'm not shearing. I came out to see how bad the quilt Mum made was damaged. I think I can fix it. That got me started on going through all this."

"I meant did you forget something at the house?"

She frowned, her forehead wrinkling adorably. "The house? No, I—" Her eyes widened and she dropped whatever it was she'd been looking at. "Oh, my God, dinner." She scurried up and moved toward him and the doorway. "Get out of the way."

He grabbed her around her waist. "It's too late. I'm not sure even the buzzards want whatever was in the pot."

She let her head drop on his shoulder. "Stew. It was stew. I'm the worst wife ever. I didn't make us dinner last night or breakfast this morning and now I burned tonight's dinner."

He kissed her exposed neck. "I liked what I had for dinner last night," he murmured, thinking he could as least hint at how much she'd pleased him in bed. "Let me be the judge of your success as a wife. I think there's some ham in the springhouse. Let's slice it up and make sandwiches then top it off with wedding cake."

"I had cake for breakfast," she confessed.

He chuckled. "So did I. I didn't want to wake you.

And cake has milk, eggs, flour. It's really puffy griddle cakes. Right?"

She groaned against his chest. "Stop, Dylan. I still ruined good meat and vegetables. I never told you why we always had a cook after Mum died. I can't cook. If I could remember I was in the middle of cooking, I could probably make a passable meal, but something always steals my attention."

He gave her a little squeeze to reassure her. "How many women can shear sheep, repair a fence *and* keep a kitchen? It's okay. We'll cook together. I'll make sure you don't get distracted and help with the chopping. I'm good at that. I used to hide from the don in the kitchen. Cook put me to work. We'll be partners inside and you're boss out here. How's that for a deal?"

She nodded. "I'm sorry."

He let go, stepped back and tilted her chin up with a crooked finger. "Stop apologizing. If I'd been the one cooking you'd wish it had burned."

They supped by the lake on thick slabs of bread, ham and more of their wedding cake. When she got cold, he warmed her up until she burned. He muffled her cries with his mouth and gloried in her response. But he didn't tell her how he felt. Not then. Not on the walk back to the house. Or before, during or after they made love again.

He wasn't sure she'd believe words. He wanted to

show her. Prove how much she mattered. And by tomorrow afternoon, she'd believe him.

Dylan rose early the next morning and crept from bed as he had the day before. He'd told Rhia he was going to take Annie to the blacksmith in town to cover his real plans. He saddled Rory, put a leader on Annie then headed for the Rocking R. His heart was a mite heavy but he knew he was doing what was right.

He concluded his business with Alex quickly and left for town with a wad of cash on a mission that needed Abby Wheaton's touch. After he'd finished there, he'd hurry back to give his bride her birthday gifts.

Chapter Thirteen

Rhia lay in bed fighting a smile and pretending to sleep as Dylan snuck out of the room on cat feet. As soon as she heard the front door shut, she jumped up, washed and dressed in her pretty blue dress. She grabbed the last of the cake and ran to the barn, to hitch up old Jessie.

She felt lighter than air as she all but danced through the chore. The decision she'd made, the dinner by the lake, the closeness they'd shared afterward, had changed something between them. Or maybe it had just changed something in her.

What did it matter if Dylan never *said* "I love you"? He showed her with more than just passion, though there was plenty of that. He treated her as if she were precious to him. He cared. Deeply. It was in his every action. Words came cheap. It was actions that mattered.

Actions had always been enough between her and her father. He'd shown his love but rarely talked about it, yet she'd been secure in that love. She was going to choose to believe Dylan loved her.

Shortly she'd be dealing with the reason why Dylan didn't understand love. His father.

The cut on her hand burned, protesting her grip on the seat as she climbed onto the wheel of wagon, then swung into the seat. Once seated, she took up the reins, thankful Jessie was such an easy animal to control. Dylan had been so worried about her hand, he'd made her promise to stay away from the shearing in the shed, another example of the way he cared for her. She smiled. She'd had other plans for her day anyway.

She was off to change Adara's direction. Change the dream to suit a future with Dylan.

A weight lifted from her shoulders even as she stopped in front of Belleza's hacienda, ready to face the don.

Farrah rushed outside. "Happy birthday," her new sister called. "I planned to ride over with gifts later. What on earth are you doing riding around by yourself? Dylan's going to be fit to be tied."

Rhia laughed. "If your father agrees to my proposal, I don't think Dylan'll even think about how it came about." She climbed down with Farrah's help, not yet used to wearing skirts. Rhia eyed her friend's Levi Strauss jeans with envy. Remembering Dylan cupping her bottom last night, Rhia had a feeling he wouldn't cringe if she wore those.

They walked into the inner courtyard. "Papa," Farrah said, "Rhia's here to see you."

The don looked up from his meal, his eyes narrowed. "Have you learned you married a man with no means? If you come to plead his case, you waste your time, *señora*."

"Dylan doesn't need anyone to plead for him." She stood straighter. Prouder. She was through deferring to this old toad. "I've come with a business proposition." She saw Farrah melt into the interior. "I have two hundred and fifty ewes. Twenty yearling rams. And fifteen mature rams. They're good stock. And for sale." She named her price and saw his interest before he schooled his features and tried to bargain her down. When she threatened to sell elsewhere, he capitulated.

She left with thirteen hundred dollars and an escort to the Rocking R. There, Alex Reynolds listened to her offer to buy the half-Arabian stallion Dylan was so interested in. Clearly confused at first, Alex finally shot her one of his irreverent grins and agreed to her price. She paid him three hundred dollars and he promised to get the balance of her money safely to the bank for her. Then he sent her home with an escort to control the big high-spirited stallion.

Dylan had never even dreamed of owning the stallion and soon he'd be culling the wild mustang herds for mares to breed with him. Dylan would be in business. They might have a few lean years but they'd be together and their children wouldn't be taunted as he had been.

She was thrilled to get home before him. Determined, she stoked the fire in the stove and got out the ingredients for a cake. It came out of the oven without a single singed spot. While it cooled, she made boiled ham, carrots and potatoes. Then she iced the cake and had just set it on the table when she saw Dylan, trotting down the lane. He must've needed to leave the mare with the blacksmith but Scout was with him.

She clasped her hands together and started out the door but stopped and ran back to take the dinner off the stove and set it on the warming shelf. When she stepped outside Scout raced up onto the porch barking his enthusiastic greeting. She ruffled his fur and hugged him while watching Dylan enter the barn. She rushed to the barn and she found Dylan scratching his head and staring into the stall holding Midnight.

"Happy birthday," she said, sneaking up behind him and grabbing his muscular arm.

He whirled around, more than a little confused. "What's he doing…?"

"I changed the dream. To *your* dream. I sold my sheep. To your father. We get to finish this last shearing. We can use the money from that and what's left from the sale of the flock to build your corrals and fence your paddocks. And I guess build a stable and anything else you need."

He stared at her for a long moment, then he erupted in laughter. She'd expected him to be happy but not to laugh like a crazy man. Next thing she knew, he grabbed her and took them flying into a hefty pile of fresh hay. She screamed as she landed on top of him, then he rolled onto his side, laying her in the fragrant hay. They stared at each other.

"You've been busy, Rowdy. But so have I." He jumped up and rushed to his horse, pulled a roll off the saddle they dug into his saddlebag. He rushed back and sat next to her, handing her a box. "Happy birthday to you."

She opened the box and found a set of new shears. She sputtered a laugh. "Abby'll take them back. I'm sorry if I spoiled your surprise."

He handed her another, much bigger bundle. She untied the cord and delved inside. There were two pairs of the Levi Strauss jeans she'd coveted just that morning and two blouses. There was also a pretty yellow dress. All of which said he understood her.

Except... "I thought you'd spent all your savings fixing the house. This isn't on credit, is it?"

He snorted out a laugh. "Nope. I sold Annie to Alex."

Her eyes widened. "That's why he looked so confused. And amused. He could have warned me!"

Dylan chuckled. "Too much fun for him to spoil, I'd guess."

"He'll sell her back, right?"

Dylan nodded then he took her gifts and set them aside, pulled her into his arms and over him as he fell back into the hay. His expression turned serious as he cupped her face with both hands. "I love you, Rhiannon Varga."

She stared. "Did you—? You love me?"

He grinned. "More than life. Hell, more than I hate sheep and that's powerful. I married you in spite of them, didn't I?" His eyebrows pulled into a V. "You forget something, wildflower? You love me, don't you?"

It was her turn to grin. "Dylan Varga, I've loved you for what seems like my whole life."

"And I'm going to love you for the rest of mine," he promised and sealed the deal with a long, lingering kiss.

* * * * *

SOMETHING BORROWED, SOMETHING TRUE

Lisa Plumley

Dear Reader

Thank you for reading SOMETHING BORROWED, SOMETHING TRUE! I'm thrilled to be a part of the *Weddings Under a Western Sky* anthology, and I'm happy to introduce you (or welcome you back) to my favourite Old West town, Morrow Creek! I've written several books set in this cosy Arizona Territory town now, and it's always a pleasure to return for a visit.

If you like Nellie and Everett's story, and would like to know more about my books, please visit my website at www.lisaplumley.com, where you can read free first chapter excerpts from all my historical, contemporary and paranormal romances, sign up for my reader newsletter or new book reminder service, catch sneak previews of my upcoming books, request special reader freebies and more.

I'm also on Harlequin.com, Facebook and Twitter, so please 'friend' me on the service of your choice. The links are available on www.lisaplumley.com. I hope you'll drop by today!

Chapter One

"The first thing necessary to win the heart of a woman is opportunity."

—Honoré de Balzac

April 1884
Morrow Creek, northern Arizona Territory

When a man couldn't pick out his own blasted fiancée from the crowd of people on a train platform, it was probably time to rethink a few things. Like the way he was living his life. The honorable intentions he clung to. And the damnable, meddlesome *vaqueros* he employed, depended on, and trusted... far too much.

Standing hip deep in confusion at the Morrow Creek train depot, Everett Bannon reckoned this was what he deserved for letting down his guard. He deserved cinders and sparks. He deserved hordes of travelers, cheery train whistles, and puffs of sooty coal smoke. He deserved a mail-order bride—arriving on today's 10:17 train from San Francisco—that he *hadn't* ordered.

The *vaqueros* at his ranch had ordered her. *For him.* Secretly. Giddily. Most of all, inconveniently. Now it was up to Everett to deal with the imminent arrival of one Miss Nellie Trent—and to squash her expectations that they were to be wed.

He hoped she didn't bawl. He couldn't cope with bawling.

Feeling altogether provoked by this unexpected turn of events, Everett paced the length of the depot platform. The springtime sun shone down on him. The morning breeze threatened to steal his hat. Travelers streamed past—but none of them wore the red hat "with a jaunty blue ribbon" that his hypothetical bride-to-be was supposed to be sporting. None of them gazed at him with knitted brows, trying to match his rugged face to his farcical written description. None of them brightened at his approach. None of them seemed hopeful...and therefore vulnerable.

Everett knew all about romantic hopefulness. He wanted no damn part of it. Not anymore. His calamitous experiences with his former ladylove, Miss Abbey O'Neill, had taught him that. He was better off without sentimental mush like loving. And needing. And hoping. So, he reckoned grumpily, was Miss Nellie Trent—wherever she was.

"Patrón!" Casper—one of his interfering ranch hands—clomped his boots in Everett's wake. "Wait! You forgot your armband!"

Turning, Everett was nearly blinded by the hank of blue fabric that Casper foolhardily waved at his face. It was frayed. It was spotted. It stank of saddle leather and stale tobacco.

It could have been worse. It could have been a sock.

Squinting at it, Everett wasn't entirely certain it *wasn't* a sock. It did have a particularly hard-used aspect to it—the same quality that every ranch hand's worldly goods acquired after some time in the bunkhouse. What's worse, Casper seemed—even more foolhardily—hell-bent on tying it on Everett's arm.

He jerked away. "I'm not wearing that."

Casper blinked in surprise—something Everett should have expected. After all, the lanky boy was the newest, greenest, and—therefore—most reckless of all his ranch hands.

"You *have* to wear a blue armband, *patrón!*" Casper said in a tone of earnest concern. "How else will Miss Trent find you?"

"I'll find her myself." *Then I'll send her away.*

Stubbornly Everett set his jaw in silent confirmation of that plan. That was the reason he'd come to the depot at all. He intended to meet Miss Nellie

Trent, explain the mistake his *vaqueros* had made, buy his "fiancée" a return train ticket…and hope she was a reasonable woman who wouldn't kick up too much of a fuss about canceling their impending "wedding."

"Heck, this will help with finding her!" Not the least bit daunted by Everett's refusal to be earmarked for love, Casper fixed the length of blue fabric around his arm. He wrenched a firm knot with a yank of his cowpuncher's fist, all but brimming over with misguided optimism and youthful naïveté. "There. Now you look the way you're s'pposed to look to meet your bride!"

With a saint's forbearance—because Casper was too gullible to know any better, and because the older men had doubtless been the ringleaders in this whole imbroglio, even if they were letting Casper stick out his neck—Everett shook his head. He sighed. "For the twelfth time…I'm *not* getting married."

"I know you're fixin' to send her away, *patrón.* You told us so already this morning." Casper broke off to rub his nose with the heel of his hand, the gesture unaffectedly boyish. He grinned. "If I recall correctly, you told us Miss Trent would be 'back on the train before her feet touched the ground.'"

Everett *had* said that. He'd also said a lot more during this morning's kerfuffle, when the men had revealed their unasked-for matchmaking. In rejecting their scheme, Everett hadn't bothered with mollycoddling. The words *damn fools, pack your duffels* and several colorful profanities had been spoken.

"I meant what I said." It was his way. Always had been. "I don't want a wife. I don't need a wife. I won't have a wife."

"You'll change your mind when you see her," Casper alleged with an imprudent grin. "I bet five dollars you would!"

Everett frowned. "You have a bet running? On me *getting married*?"

Casper and his compatriots nodded. Casper did so gleefully. The others... *Hellfire.* They nodded gleefully, too. Everett didn't know what the world was coming to when a man couldn't even trust his own *vaqueros* not to stab him in the back with Cupid's arrow.

Audaciously a few of them had even followed him on horseback along the mountainous road between his sprawling ranch and the town of Morrow Creek. Presently more than half his troublemaking ranch hands loitered between the train tracks and the bustling ticket office—hoping, he knew, to see the spectacle of their hard-nosed *hacendado* being overcome by love.

The odds of that happening were very long indeed. Once, Everett had thought he was a typical

Western male: gruff but affable. Now he knew he was not. Despite the longtime admiration of his men, he was…lacking. At least to the *feminine* mind, he was. The day he'd learned that had been one of his worst.

No right-thinking woman wants to live on a hard-scrabble ranch with a burly, unrefined oaf for a husband, Everett.

Honestly. Did you think I would settle for this? For you?

Those had been Miss Abbey O'Neill's parting words to him. The memory of them still stung. Not long after that, she'd absconded from town to elope with Astair Prestell, the famously cultured author, during his whistle-stop speaking tour of the territory.

Although Everett did not miss Miss O'Neill in the way he'd thought he would—unaccountably, he did not miss her at all—he didn't like knowing that he'd turned up wanting. In any arena.

Far better, he'd decided, to give up on "love" for now.

But his men had no compunction about meddling in their *hacendado's* affairs. They'd banded together, contacted a mail-order marriage bureau and written several letters to his "fiancée" on Everett's behalf. He still didn't know exactly what those letters had said—what they'd promised. The possibilities of that concerned him. Who knew what a miscreant bunch of whiskey-swilling, knuckle-dragging *vaqueros* from a half dozen different countries and cultures considered to be "romantic"?

The possibilities made Everett shudder. When Miss Nellie Trent arrived—*if* she arrived—she might be expecting a very peculiar courtship. What sort of woman agreed to that? To *him*?

"Don't look so worried, *patrón*. This is one bet *I* aim to win. *Fácil.*" Smiling at Everett, Pedro patted the pocket where he kept his bankroll, apparently ready to risk everything on the outside chance his boss would find love. Before coming to Morrow Creek, Pedro had been a faro dealer in the southern presidio of Tucson. Swarthy and debonair at almost fifty years old, the man still sported the heavy silver rings that proved his expertise at the gaming table. "Not even you can resist a pretty woman. You won't be able to help yourself. Just like me."

To prove it, Pedro winked at a passing woman wearing a full-skirted pink dress and carrying a parasol. She blushed. She giggled. Finally she relented and coyly waved at him.

"*Da.* Sooner or later, wedding fever strikes everyone," Ivan opined in his lingering Russian accent, oblivious to the flirtation that Pedro had embarked upon. The hulking blond kept his attention fixed on the gingham-lined basket of baked goods he'd brought along for the trip. Ivan selected a snickerdoodle, then pointed it at Everett for emphasis. "Marybelle and Edina told us so, and they would know." At his mention of the ranch house cook, Ivan appeared momentarily distracted. Then downright dreamy. Then he recalled himself. "This time of year, no man for miles can resist getting hitched. It's springtime wedding fever. That's what Edina said. All you need is a willing bride."

"Which *we* have found for you!" Oscar boasted in his jovial and precise German-accented speech. Keeping a finger hooked in his latest philosophy text—just one in a never-ending series of books that accompanied the dark-haired recent immigrant to roundups, roll calls and every meal the aforementioned Edina served up—Oscar nodded sagely. "A new woman can change things for you, *patrón*. A new woman can cure your broken heart."

Everett didn't want to talk about his "broken heart." Especially not with a ranch hand who'd once quoted poetry to him as an excuse not to tame the latest prize mustang he'd wrangled. Pointedly Everett cast a warning glower in his men's direction.

"The next man who says 'broken heart' will find himself mucking out horse stalls—alone—for a solid month. Understand?"

His *vaqueros* saluted. "Yes, *patrón*. We understand."

They *sounded* suitably contrite. But given the lasting (and incongruous) expressions of schoolgirlish eagerness on their (mostly) grizzled and beard-stip-pled faces, Everett didn't feel he'd sufficiently im-pressed on them the importance of never pulling such a ludicrous stunt again. He crossed his arms for good measure. Then he deepened his frown to a fearsome degree.

"I don't want any more of this matchmaking non-sense. What if I'd already promised myself to some other woman?"

They all sobered. "What other woman?" Ivan de-manded, warily clutching his basket of goodies to his midsection. "Not Edina!"

"No, not Edina, *mi amigo.*" Pedro shook his head at Ivan's protective feelings toward the cook. "We were very careful about picking out Señorita Trent," he told Everett in a self-assured tone. "No one else will be such a perfect lady for you."

"Auch wenn." Carelessly Oscar shrugged. "That may be true. But our *patrón* does not agree. Perhaps he is too inconsolable to agree." The German gave Everett a long-suffering look. He closed his book—something Oscar rarely did—demonstrating the gravity of their situation. "The agency guaranteed satisfaction. Once you have rejected Fräulein Trent, *patrón*, we can request another—"

"No one is going to *reject* Miss Trent!" Everett blurted.

He couldn't help it. Put that way, it sounded hor-rible. While he did not consider himself to be especially softhearted *or* softheaded—and he would have had to have been both to agree to this "wedding"— there were lines that even the strongest, toughest, most uncompromising *hacendado* refused to cross.

What he proposed doing with Miss Trent was not a rejection of *her*. It was merely...changing their supposed deal. Unless she refused to accept a return ticket, of course. That was still possible. Then what in tarnation would he do with her?

Why in blazes had his men stuck him in this position?

Aggrieved all over again by their preposterous plan, Everett paced some more. His battered boots clunked along the platform; his plain work shirt and britches kept him respectably—if not stylishly— clad. He wished he'd uncovered his men's cockamamie scheme earlier. By the time he'd learned of it, it had been too late. His "fiancée" had already been on her way.

"I'm simply going to...return Miss Trent to the city. That's where she belongs. She'll be happier there." *With a citified man like Astair Prestell.* Defensively Everett lifted his chin. "I'm going to thank her for coming, then pay her to leave."

They all gawked at him. "*Pay her?* She's not a prostitute!" Casper sounded indignant. Two bright red spots bloomed on his cheeks, betraying the fact that he'd visited Miss Adelaide's place only once—

and then merely to "chat" with one of the girls. "You can't give her money outright like that. It ain't proper."

"A ticket, I mean. I'll pay for a return train ticket." Everett had explained this to them already. "It's the least I can do," he said. "How else am I supposed to get rid of her?"

"Get *rid* of her?" At that, Ivan and Pedro gasped. They traded fretful glances. "*Patrón*, you don't *deserve* her!"

Damnation. Now he'd been judged and found wanting by his men, too! "How do you know that? None of you have met her."

Oscar raised his eyebrows. "We've corresponded," he reminded Everett archly. "Miss Trent has lovely penmanship and exemplary grammar, two fine qualities for a potential wife."

"Lovely penmanship *and* good grammar?" Everett gave them a sardonic, helpless grin. "Well then. I just changed my mind!"

His *vaqueros* weren't amused by his joke.

But that probably didn't matter anyway. At this rate, Everett reckoned the argument was moot— especially after he swept the assembled travelers with another decisive glance. "She's not here," he announced. "I don't think she's coming."

"She's coming. She paid a fee," Oscar said dourly,

"just like we did. I only hope she was not as idealistic as we were."

Everett swiveled. "There was a *fee* involved?"

His *vaqueros* shrugged. A chorus of yeses in a variety of languages rang out. Oscar's was last. "*Ja.* We all contributed." He raised his mournful gaze to Everett's face. "If it brings back your soul to you, *patrón*…then it will be money well spent."

Doubly troubled now, Everett shook his head at them. This was typical of his longtime *vaqueros*. His ranch hands were commendably dedicated and hardworking. They were also much too willing to come together for a "cause" they believed in.

Last year, they'd pooled their salaries to buy new featherbeds for the girls at Miss Adelaide's place. A few months ago, they'd joined forces to run a roughhousing regular from that same cathouse out of town. Weeks ago, they'd decided their lonesome *hacendado* needed a wife…so they'd ordered up one.

Against all reason, Everett didn't want to disappoint them. These men would likely never have wives or weddings themselves; they had already given their hearts to the solitary *vaquero's* life. He understood the loneliness of that life. He understood its compromises. He'd accepted them for himself. But that didn't mean Everett intended to go along with this nonsense.

He didn't have to. He had blue skies, spirited

horses, plenty of mescal and all the faro-playing, joke-telling, smoke-a-cigar-in-peace breathing room a man could ever want. He didn't need anything else. No matter what his ranch hands said.

"Well, Miss Trent doesn't rate highly in punctuality," Everett groused, on the verge of abandoning this fool's quest in favor of enjoying a lager at Jack Murphy's saloon. "You say she's 'pretty' and 'perfect,' but all I see is 'unreliable.'"

Overhearing his words, a female passerby stopped. Smartly she glanced at Everett.

"That's too bad," she said cheerfully. "Because there are also 'intelligent,' 'intrepid' and 'irresistible' to consider. I have it on very good authority that those attributes apply to Miss Trent as well." Warmheartedly she smiled at him. "Fortunately she's also 'easygoing.' She might be willing to prove it by giving you another try at your description."

Her impish grin called to mind secrets and surprises and unknown wishes granted. It called to mind a woman who was reputedly pretty, perfect and proficient at penmanship and syntax. It called to mind other hasty character assessments that Everett had made...and had lately been proven wrong about.

After all, at one time, he'd believed Miss Abbey O'Neill truly cared about him—and was capable of fidelity, besides. He couldn't have been more wrong.

If he were wise, he'd be more careful this time.

Looking at the woman who'd so boldly approached him, Everett had a jumbled impression of blue eyes, freckled skin and tawny hair. He registered her soot-smudged dress, dark gloves and crumpled red hat. Beneath its blue-ribbon-bedecked crown and woefully bent brim, her face appeared singularly pert and vivacious. Her lips pursed. Her cheeks bloomed. Everett had the unmistakable sense that she had not been exaggerating when she'd called herself intelligent, intrepid...and irresistible.

Was *this* Miss Nellie Trent at last?

His mind whirled. Studying her more closely, Everett no longer heard the metallic squeal of train wheels or the hubbub of conversation. He no longer felt the platform beneath his boots. He no longer sensed his *vaqueros* nearby. He *did* hear his own heart pounding double-time in his chest. And he *did* feel his body tingle with a curious sense of... anticipation? Eagerness?

Oddly enough, it felt like...recognition. It felt the same as when Everett rode across the foothills after a long time away and spied his hard-won *hacienda* in the distance. It felt *good*.

That made no sense whatsoever. This woman *could* be Miss Nellie Trent. She could also be an impossibly nosy bystander.

Either way, she gazed at him interestedly, oblivious to his bafflement, as though genuinely expecting him to reconsider the various qualities he'd attributed to his unknown "fiancée."

"No? All right, then. Maybe later." Her lively smile dazzled him. "When it comes to hearing my finer qualities enumerated, I am willing to wait just as long as it takes."

Belatedly Everett regained the use of his addled brain. "I see. I don't guess those qualities will include modesty?"

She laughed. "Touché, Mr. Bannon!" Her gaze dropped to the grubby blue band on his arm. "It *is* Mr. Bannon, isn't it?"

"It was when I woke up this morning."

Another peal of laughter. "You *are* delightful!" Shaking her head in apparent wonderment at that, the woman lightly touched his arm. "And here *I* was worried you'd be some fusty old coot."

As she lifted her hand, Everett experienced an inexplicable fondness for the tied-on blue armband that had identified him to her. He never wanted to remove it. "If I was, I reckon you'd be the type of woman to tell me so. Immediately upon meeting me."

"Ah. You mean I'm too forward, don't you?" She tilted her head as though the idea had newly occurred to her. "I see. I'll list that attribute right next to 'unpunctual' in my personal ledger." A brief smile. "Although I'm not usually late. Today I was unavoidably delayed in meeting you. It won't happen again."

She did not elaborate, and he couldn't ask her to. Despite her blithe tone and merry eyes, Everett couldn't help feeling his comment had bothered her. He wanted urgently to recall it. "It's no trouble. You're probably just tired and hungry," he assured her gruffly. "Train travel can take its toll on anyone."

"All the same...I'll try to do better. I'm *very* interested in this marriage we've arranged, you see." With a winsome smile that would have tempted any man into unwanted matrimony, she extended her gloved hand. "I'm very pleased to meet you, Mr. Bannon. I, of course, am Miss Nellie Trent. Your bride-to-be."

Hopelessly charmed by the bustle-wearing, blue-ribbon-sporting, outspoken force of nature that was his potential "fiancée," Everett took her hand in his. Warmth passed between them, leaving him surprised and shaken. And just like that, Everett realized that his *vaqueros* were right.

He *did* need something more. He needed Nellie Trent.

Chapter Two

"Are my lodgings very far from here?" Nellie asked.

Interestedly she examined the town of Morrow Creek, nestled in the valley beyond the train depot. It was full of lumber-framed buildings and false-fronted shops and at least one two-story hotel. It bustled with people and wagons and the usual horse traffic. To her ever-curious mind, the admittedly minor and fairly typical town of Morrow Creek looked...*thrilling.*

But then, most unexplored situations seemed thrilling to Nellie. That was part of her nature. She loved new places, new things, and new opportunities. She loved challenges and risks. She loved throwing herself into life with zeal and open-mindedness. That was part of what made her *her.*

It was also part of what made her good at her job with the San Francisco *Weekly Leader* newspaper...part of what had brought her here to the

Arizona Territory—and to Everett Bannon—in the first place.

"Are your lodgings far from here?" Everett Bannon repeated her question in his rumbling, shiver-inducing deep voice. "Well, about that—" He broke off. He took off his flat-brimmed hat. He squinted into the distance. He raked his hand through his hair, then sighed. "I'm afraid there's something I need to tell you."

"Yes?" Pertly Nellie waited. "What is it?"

He hesitated anew, still frowning at the hat he held in his capable-looking hands. "You see, the trouble is, I didn't—"

"Don't say it, *patrón*!" blurted one of the men who stood behind her groom-to-be. The patrician *Mexicano* gave Nellie an apologetic look. *"Por favor,"* he begged Everett, "don't do it!"

There was a fraught moment, during which everyone stilled. Passersby glanced at the man who'd spoken; the other men all watched Everett Bannon. Clearly he was in charge here.

Just as clearly, Nellie reasoned privately, he'd meant what he'd said about sending her away the moment she arrived.

She'd overheard that much of their conversation, of course, shortly after she'd stepped off the train. Her first order of business had been to locate her blue-armband-wearing "fiancé." Her second had been—sensibly enough—to begin surreptitiously eavesdropping on his conversation with his cadre of ragamuffinish men before making her presence known to them.

A woman who'd offered herself up for a mail-order marriage couldn't just waltz into such an arrangement willy-nilly. She had to prepare. She had to gather as many details as she could.

So far, she'd sussed out that Everett Bannon did *not* want her here—but his men did. From the charming man with the silver rings to the curly-haired, book-toting poet and the shy, fair-haired young man standing next to him, to the giant with the enormous appetite and the gingham-lined basket of goodies, they all appeared deeply interested in making sure their "*patrón's*" engagement went off without a hitch.

Nellie didn't want to let on her awareness of those facts, however. She still hoped she could salvage this opportunity. She couldn't do *that* if Everett Bannon put her back on the return train, lickety-split. So, with no other option immediately presenting itself, she waited to see what would happen next.

"Pedro, you and the others head back to the ranch," Mr. Bannon finally said, delivering a quelling look to the dark-haired man with the Spanish accent. "You have work to do."

"But *patrón*! You can't possibly still mean to—"

"*Work like mucking out stalls.* Don't make me ask again."

For a heartbeat, they all quieted. Then the bashful-looking young blond man gestured toward Nellie, his expression adorably hopeful and inquisitive. "But…wait. What about…?"

"I said I'd handle this." Mr. Bannon put on his hat with a decisive yank, casting his square-jawed face in shadows. "All of you say goodbye to Miss Trent now, and get on down the road. I don't want to find any work left undone when I get back."

Incredibly they still wavered. Even beneath the stern, hazel-eyed gaze that Everett Bannon gave each of them in turn, they held fast to their positions. Did his marriage mean so much to them that they would risk his ill temper for it? Evidently, it did. Despite everything, Nellie felt impressed by their loyalty. To have earned that, Mr. Bannon must be quite a man.

"Will you be *alone* when you get back?" asked the largest man, his tone mistrustful as he cradled his basket of baked goods. "Or will you be accompanied by…*someone*?"

His not-at-all-subtle head tilt indicated Nellie—who was dying, by then, to intervene on her own behalf. The passivity of just standing there was making her feel downright itchy.

It would have been more in her nature to argue

her case—to offer a rebuttal or try a negotiation or propose some sort of blandishment. All those tactics had gotten her quite far in her journalism work. Two of them had gotten her *here*, in fact.

But Nellie doubted such aggressive strategies would endear her to an old-fashioned rancher who lived in a tiny territorial settlement like Morrow Creek. So instead, as an alternative to asserting herself, she settled on shifting in place in the travel-dusted, boy-size work boots she wore under her skirts, hoping she could outlast Mr. Bannon's current bout of reticence.

Unfortunately it appeared to be of the abiding variety, and Nellie's store of patience was definitely *not* infinite.

Perhaps, neither was Mr. Bannon's. Because next he crossed his arms over his broad chest, making his muscles flex with impressive amplitude beneath his plain white shirt. "Ivan, do you want me to quit buying cone sugar for Edina's baked goods?"

The big man, Ivan, went pale. "*Nyet.* I do not want that."

"Then quit pestering me. All of you, get going."

Nellie felt almost positive this standoff was concluded.

"Your soul, *patrón!*" the poetic one cried in a German accent. He waved his book. "*Bitte!* Think of your soul!"

Then again, perhaps she was wrong. Mustering up a soupçon more patience, Nellie rocked up on her boot heels. She vastly preferred wearing useful footwear rather than sporting typical high-buttoned, fashionable but *impractical* ladies' shoes. She preferred, overall, being nimble to being prim or well-behaved. If that made her a bit unconventional, well…Nellie didn't mind.

"My 'soul,' Oscar?" Mr. Bannon asked in an amused voice. For an instant, his gaze touched Nellie's directly, then roved over her face and personage in turn. "Have you seen Miss Trent? Next to her, a soul feels about as meaningless as a handful of penny candy. A man would give up heaven itself to have her."

Shocked by his lyrical turn of phrase, Nellie gawked at him. Maybe there *was* hope she could stay on in Morrow Creek.

Maybe there was hope Everett Bannon would truly like her.

Nellie certainly liked *him*. Now more than ever—now that he'd come up with such a quixotic notion about his soul…and her own supposedly irresistible claim upon it. This was by far the most unusual group of rough-riding Western males she'd ever encountered, and she'd only been here a short while so far!

The men of Bannon's ranch seemed similarly

taken aback by his statement. One of them jostled another. They all grinned.

"But I doubt a mail-order contract is the way to accomplish such a miracle," Mr. Bannon went on. "And the longer you no-goods hang around, the unlikelier my chances get. So skedaddle."

"Wirklich?" Oscar exclaimed. "Then you're *not* going to—"

"I'm going to speak with Miss Trent *alone*," Mr. Bannon interrupted firmly. "I believe I owe her that much, at least."

At that, all his men blanched. But Nellie was too busy daydreaming about her handsome "fiancé's" unexpectedly starry-eyed nature to let their obvious consternation discourage her. Because, in a single statement, Everett Bannon had just made her mission in Morrow Creek a personal one—a very personal one.

In that moment, Nellie didn't want Everett Bannon to simply accept her as his mail-order bride; she wanted him to accept *her*. She wanted him to say more sweet words. She wanted him to liken her blue eyes to the springtime bluebonnets sprouting between the railroad ties. She wanted him to hold her hand.

She wanted...*him*. She wanted to know everything about him.

Because even while aggrieved, as he was now,

Everett Bannon was…*wonderful*. His features were even, his eyes kind, his dark hair as long as his collar and as shiny as silk. She wanted to touch it—to sift her fingers through it—and felt shocked by that untoward impulse. She didn't know where it had come from. She'd never been intimate with a man; she'd never even come close. For all her bravado and all the inroads she'd made into what was largely a man's world back in San Francisco, she was still a good woman with all her morals and personal strictures intact.

But oh…how Everett Bannon tempted her to abandon them!

Especially *this* Everett Bannon—the one who spouted romanticisms and watched her blush… however inexpertly she did so. Her own feminine wiles were certainly rusty, but his masculine appeal seemed more than intact. Most likely, he could have had his choice of marriageable women in town. For the umpteenth time since she'd stepped off the train, Nellie wondered why a man like him required a mail-order bride.

He was neither asocial nor ugly. He was not infirm or indigent. He appeared respectable. He owned property. He gave every impression of intelligence and good humor. So why—

"It's been a pleasure meeting you, ma'am." The reticent young man stopped in front of her, apparently having been ordered to do so—again—while Nellie had been woolgathering. He gulped, nodded, then shook her hand. "Goodbye, ma'am."

"Wait!" Nellie lay her hand on his forearm. With concern, she gazed into his face. "I don't even know your name."

He shrugged. "I reckon that ain't gonna be necessary."

Then he screwed up his face in almost comical determination and strode away toward town, his posture ramrod straight.

Pedro smiled at her. "Do not worry," the *Mexicano* said with a gallant sweep of his arm. "He is always as skittery as a preacher in a whorehouse. He will be fine. I'll make sure of it myself." With elaborate gentility, he held her gloved hand in his, then bowed over it. "*Encantado*, Señorita Trent. *Adiós*."

The somber-eyed poet, Oscar, followed him. "I will treasure your letters always," he confessed, tenderly squeezing her hand.

Nellie blinked. *Oscar* had her letters? But why? How?

She could not pursue the question. The bearish Russian, Ivan, approached her next. "Give him this," he advised with another significant nod toward Mr. Bannon. With elaborate care, Ivan pressed something in her hand. "It will work magic for you. It always has for me." With his covert mission accomplished, Ivan tipped his hat to her. "*Ycnex*. That means good luck."

Unaccountably touched by their kindness, Nellie held on to whatever he'd given her. "Thank you. Thank you all so much!"

Curtly Ivan nodded. Oscar bowed. Pedro blew her a kiss.

Mr. Bannon looked on in disgruntlement. "Quit it. Next you'll all be caterwauling, and I didn't bring my handkerchief."

Glancing at him, Nellie grinned. His gruff demeanor didn't fool her. He clearly felt a great deal of affection toward his men. "Hmm. You must have left it in your other suit."

At that, Mr. Bannon glanced down at himself. He regarded his plain, button-placket shirt, brown canvas trousers, braces and scratched-up boots, then frowned. "I only own one suit."

"Well, then. If that's true, you'd better quit looking at that ensemble as though you'd like to start a bonfire with it."

He started. "Are you...*teasing* me?"

"It certainly sounds as though I am."

"But no one teases me." His frown seemed proof of it.

"Then I think *I* will be the necessary exception. While I am here, I've decided to tease you as often and as mercilessly as possible, Mr. Bannon," Nellie declared, alluding for the first time to the possibility that he might make her leave, "until you either give me a genuine smile or— Nope. No, that's all I want. A genuine smile from you. *Then* I will be satisfied."

He seemed on the verge of giving her a genuine smile just then, merely at her mention of her just-discovered plan. But with what must have been a mighty effort, he resisted. Mostly. A corner of his mouth still quirked. Satisfyingly so. She loved having an effect on him, however meager it was. For now.

"I'll wager you do not always get your way, Miss Trent."

"Ah. Now that's where you'd be wrong. Because I *do* traditionally persist *until* I get my way. Indefatigability is the secret, you see." She picked up her two slim satchels—all her baggage—from the spot where she'd set them at her feet, ready to have this settled once and for all. "Also, you simply *must* call me Nellie. And I will call you Everett! If we're to be married, we may as well begin as we intend to go on—informally."

It was a bluff, plain and simple. Nellie reasoned that he would not turn her away—not now. Not after he'd said all those lovely things. She rarely misjudged a bluff, but this time…

Worryingly Everett gazed at her satchels. He glanced over his shoulder at his men, most of whom were already at the hitching posts where they'd left their horses. He took off his hat again, turned it in his hands, then put it back on.

It was, she'd learned, a signifying gesture. He'd decided something. Now he was going to tell her what it was.

"We're not going to be married," Everett said flatly. "I didn't order you from the mail-order marriage bureau. My men did it for me. They wrote all those letters to you, too."

"Mmm." Nellie thought about that. Yes, that answered several niggling questions she'd had about this whole process. "That explains their peculiar emphasis on the rangeland, the bunkhouse furnishings and the variety of livestock present."

He winced. "I believe they took turns writing to you."

"Then Oscar must have sent me the poetry. And Pedro the pressed flowers. And Ivan the stale cake crumbs, and—"

"I didn't even know you were arriving until an hour ago," Everett confessed, seeming unwilling to indulge her attempts at humor. "I didn't want to turn you away outright—"

"Because I'm better than penny candy."

At that, he briefly closed his eyes. Almost imperceptibly, he nodded. So did Nellie. When Everett opened his eyes again and looked at her, something indefinable passed between them. Something laden with possibilities, risks…and potential success, too. Nellie had never experienced anything like it.

It moved her in a way nothing ever had. It made her want to linger near Everett by whatever means possible—a bold idea, perhaps, but Nellie had never been a woman who'd shied away from *those*. Given the stirring and unexpected way he made her feel, staying near Everett Bannon might be the boldest idea of all.

"But I didn't want to lie to you, either," Everett went on doggedly. "So here it is—I will gladly buy you a return train ticket. And I will happily invite you to stay at my ranch house—with my cook and housekeeper in attendance as chaperones, of course—until you feel strong enough to travel." His gaze swerved to hers, full of indomitable honesty and integrity. "But I'm very sorry to say that I cannot promise to marry you."

Evidently on tenterhooks, he waited for her response.

Doubtless, he expected her to be crushed—to have no other options for marriage. But there were things that Nellie knew about herself that he did not—beginning with the fact that she'd always expected to end up a spinster…and ending with the fact that, with one reckless touch of his hand, Everett Bannon had made her hope for something more. Now, she hoped for *him*.

"I see." Attentively Nellie nodded at him, fighting a powerful urge to dismiss his wrongheaded notion that she might be too fragile to travel again immediately. No one had *ever* suggested that Nellie Trent was anything but sturdy, tomboyish and inconveniently ambitious—especially for a woman. No one had ever tried to cherish or protect her. She was "unusual" and occasionally "unruly"—especially to the men in her life—and that was that. It could not be helped. "Why did your men believe you might not only promise to marry me but actually do it?"

"I don't know."

"You *must* know."

"I can't begin to guess." Everett blew out a breath, seeming overwhelmed. "You've met them. You must understand."

"I thought they were very kind," Nellie insisted. "You're fortunate to work with men who are so devoted to you."

"Yes. I am." Mulishly Everett said nothing more.

"They seem to believe marriage would be good for you," she prompted leadingly. "There must be a reason for that."

He refused to speculate—at least for now. But the jut of his jaw suggested there *was* a reason. Innate curiosity demanded that Nellie uncover what that reason was. She simply had to.

"All right, then. That's fine. You can tell me later."

Brightly Nellie unwrapped the item Ivan had given her. She saw that it was an unfamiliar cookie-shaped thing and wrinkled her nose in confusion. *This* could be magical?

"Why does Ivan believe this cookie is magical?"

"Because he believes everything Edina touches turns to gold," Everett grumbled. Then added, "Is that all you have to say?"

"Er..." Nellie thought about it. She raised her cookie. "Would you like half? I'll share with you. Frankly I'm famished. The stops along the way left much to be desired."

When he did not answer, she transferred her gaze from the cookie to his face—and received an unwelcome surprise.

Why was Everett gawking at her? Confusedly Nellie waggled the cookie at him in an enticing manner. "Please. Take some."

He did not. Perhaps he thought she was being too forward again. He'd accused her of that once already. She didn't want to irk him needlessly now. Stymied, Nellie considered what her most ladylike female friends might do in this situation. Aha!

"It's *far* too much for me to eat all by myself," she fibbed demurely, knowing full well she could have gobbled that cookie and another one besides. But she wanted to impress Everett Bannon somehow. She wanted to make him *see* her. She wanted to learn more about him, too. Attempting to fulfill his stated vision of her as a dainty flower of womanhood seemed a good way to do those things. Regrettably Nellie preferred being brash and—occasionally—groundbreaking. Being decorous was hardly her forte.

She did, however, try her best. "You must have some of it," she urged with her most winning smile. "Please do."

Her offer did not have the desired result. Everett only put his hands on his hips. "Do I not suit you?" he demanded roughly.

"What?"

"I've just said I won't marry you. You traveled hundreds of miles to hear me say it." Appearing markedly confounded, he shook his head. "And now all you want to talk about is cookies?"

Oh. Nellie blinked. "I'm sorry, Everett," she told him cheerfully. "I thought you'd already guessed. *I* don't want a wedding, either! And I certainly can't promise to marry you." She chuckled. "That was never my intention at all."

He seemed put out. "It wasn't?"

"Well, I *did* intend to proceed a bit further with the engagement shenanigans and all the wedding to-dos before saying this," Nellie declared, "but frankly, your not wanting to be married comes as something of a relief to me! I was concerned about hurting your feelings with *my* not wanting to be married. But since you're being so straightforward, I think I can be, too." She examined the rapidly emptying depot platform around them, then looked up at him. "I'll tell you all about it on the way to your ranch, Everett. I accept your offer to stay."

Chapter Three

Never in a thousand springtimes had Everett expected to find himself driving along the rutted road between the town of Morrow Creek and his *hacienda* with a fetching woman by his side. Not today. Not ever. He'd thought that Miss Abbey O'Neill's desertion had stolen that possibility from him forever. He'd thought she'd made him give up. Forever. But now, today…

Now, Everett had a new beginning to look forward to.

At least it felt that way. Despite Miss Trent's much-too-nonchalant acceptance of his refusal to marry her, Everett felt things were different somehow. Things were different inside him.

I don't want a wedding, either! he recalled her saying an instant later. *And I certainly can't promise to marry you.*

Well, there was *that* to contend with. Nellie didn't want him—at least not for a husband. But Everett reckoned he might be able to change her mind. He could be damn persuasive when he wanted to be. However contrarily, right now he wanted to be.

He wanted to persuade Nellie to smile at him. He wanted to hear her say his name, to feel her touch his arm again, to watch her crinkle her nose in amusement when she teased him.

Everett didn't know how it had happened, but he was smitten. If he'd guessed right, Nellie was smitten, too.

Why else would she have accepted his offer of lodgings?

Gratified, Everett returned his attention to the road, his team's tracings held lightly in his hands. Beside him, Nellie jounced on the hard plank seat with her skirts spread around her, gazing with interest at the landscape they passed. Her curiosity entranced him; her evident appreciation of the sometimes hardscrabble territory he lived in made him feel that perhaps—if he was lucky—they had something in common.

"I thought springtime would never come," Everett surprised himself by admitting. "Around here, it's been...bleak lately."

"Really?" With her usual high-spiritedness, Nellie looked around. "I can't believe it's ever less than beautiful here. The hills, the grass, all the trees with their tiny, green, newly unfurling leaves, all those wildflowers…they're stunning!"

"They're temporary," he felt compelled to say. He set his jaw in a harsh line. "Eventually the grass will wither. Those leaves will turn brown. The wildflowers will die away."

"All the more reason to enjoy them now! Oh! Listen."

At her urging, he did, prompted by the cute way Nellie cupped her ear. Birdsong floated to him, barely audible above the wagon's creaking and the clomping of his horses' hooves, carried on the same breeze that had threatened his hat earlier.

Nellie sighed. "I certainly don't hear *that* at home."

"At home? In San Francisco?" Reminded of the life she'd left behind to come here, Everett glanced at her perky profile. She nodded, making him worry anew. "Do you like it there?"

"Of course! It's a very exciting place to live."

Exciting. Everett acknowledged that with a grumble.

Undoubtedly, he reasoned unhappily, Nellie already missed the highfalutin life she'd carried on in the city. She probably viewed her time in the territory as a lark. She probably considered him a yokel who wasn't worth marrying. After all, she'd already looked askance at his homespun clothing.

Frowning at his britches, Everett shifted in his

seat. If he wanted to impress Nellie Trent, it occurred to him, he would have to be more like the men who appealed to her—the men who appealed to *all* women: citified men. Men who wore suits.

Men like Astair Prestell, who were cultured and erudite.

Everett was neither of those things. He was…ordinary. He read newspapers, not literature. He didn't know any sonnets. He could not have identified a fine wine or doled out a gossipy tidbit to save his skin. Although he was clean and neat and possessed a strong, healthy body, he did not normally adorn that body with any of the concoctions urbane people favored.

He didn't own a drop of cologne. He didn't gussy up his hair with shiny pomade. In fact, for the first time in his recollection, Everett had cause to regret the slapdash way he'd combed his hair that very morning. And his shaving job…Stealthily he raised his hand to his jaw to gauge the effects of his typically casual appointment with his straight razor.

Hellfire. The stubble there could have kindled a fire.

He had to do something to remedy that. Straightaway.

"So you're probably wondering why I registered with a mail-order marriage bureau and came all this way," Nellie said, "only to reveal that I don't intend to get married at all."

Everett had been wondering about little else since she'd announced her nonintention to marry him. Miraculously, given this chance now to find out more, he managed not to leap on it with both big, booted feet. He held his response to a brief nod.

It damn well nearly killed him.

"The truth is, Everett, that I'm not an ordinary woman."

He couldn't help nodding. "I could have told you that."

He sweetened his statement with a mischievous sidelong glance, caught Nellie blushing, and found himself surprised by that. She didn't seem the timid, tittering, rosy-cheeked kind of woman he was used to. She seemed different. He liked that.

"Well. Thank you." Nellie clasped her hands in her lap, her posture graceful and her demeanor refreshingly direct. He liked that, too. She inhaled deeply—and affectingly. "I will assume, of course, that you meant that in a complimentary manner."

How else could he have meant it? "Of course I did."

"Good. Anyway, as I was saying, I'm not an ordinary woman. I'm..." Here, Nellie faltered. She cast him a helpless glance.

Hmm. The more she hesitated, the more Everett

rethought his original assessment of her candor. It seemed such a natural part of her, as inherent as her freckles or the curve of her waist. Yet there were those odd moments—like when she'd tried to forcibly feed him her cookie, claiming she couldn't possibly finish one of Edina's wee *bizcochitos*—that made Everett wonder if Nellie Trent was truly the woman she appeared to be.

Then, finally, Nellie rallied. "I'm a journalist!"

"A journalist?" Everett experienced a sinking sensation. He gripped the weathered leather tracings harder, his mind filled with the disheartening realization that—most likely—a female journalist would doubly insist on having a sophisticated man.

But he was Everett Bannon, damn it! He would not go down without a fight. He liked Nellie. She liked him. They could—

"Yes. But only for the ladies' society pages!" she assured him hastily, her cheeks growing pink again. "Only to write about parties and art and recipes! And only until I'm married!"

Her rusty-sounding giggle didn't suit her. Plagued by a feeling he was missing something crucial here, Everett pointed out the obvious. "I thought you didn't want to get married."

"I didn't." She flashed him an alluring smile. "I'm becoming more amenable to the idea by the moment, though. In fact, if you could provide me with more of those delicious cookies, I might even be persuaded to consider—"

"You're teasing me again. I warned you about that."

"I am. But only a little." Nellie grinned. "It made you quit frowning about my work at the *Weekly Leader*, didn't it?"

He'd been frowning? If he had been, Everett knew, it had only been because he was planning how to become appropriately sophisticated. But he would have sooner died than admit it.

"Yes, you were frowning. You looked fit to spit nails. But I'll have you know I'm not so very unusual. These days, many women perform clerical work or take factory jobs in the city—"

Everett had had enough of "the city." "What's your newspaper got to do with me? With mail-order marriages?"

With your irksome lack of interest in marrying me?

"I'm writing a story for the newspaper about them."

He was glad to see her directness had returned. He enjoyed that side of her. "A story about mail-order marriages?"

"Yes." Warming to her revelation, Nellie nodded. "The mail-order marriage bureaus claim that anyone can fetch themselves a 'perfect match' for the cost of a few fancifully written letters and a postage stamp. I believe that's misleading—and maybe even fraudulent! So I set out to discover the truth about things."

"By positing yourself as a potential bride," he guessed.

"Yes!" She brightened. "That's how all the best investigative journalism is done these days. Not that I get much chance at that. I'm mostly relegated to—" Abruptly she stopped. Then added, "Let's just say I had to lobby very stringently with my editor to be allowed to go forward with this story."

"But you believe in it."

"Absolutely!" Her expression shone with true zeal. "Who knows how many people are pinning their hopes—and their hard-earned money—on these marriage bureaus? If they're as damaging as I think they are, the bureaus' dealings ought to be exposed before more vulnerable women and men become tangled up in them."

Her dauntless expression endeared her to him all the more. It required a courageous woman, Everett thought, to take on a challenge the way she had. He admired that about her.

As for the rest, though… "Then you don't believe in love?"

"Of *course*, I believe in love! Especially—" Nellie broke off, seeming on the verge of saying more. She gave him a brave, warmhearted look. Quietly she added, "Especially today, I do."

Her gaze met his, full of hopefulness and inquisitiveness—and budding fondness, too. Everett was sure that's what it was.

"Today has been…a good day," he agreed roughly.

She nodded…and in that moment, their new-found camaraderie grew a little bit more. Like the wildflowers that bloomed along the roadside, their mutual interest seemed to be both hardy and fast growing. It sounded fanciful—but Everett knew that those pricklepoppies, brown-eyed Susans and pink primroses were weedy fighters at heart. They might look delicate, but they were inherently unstoppable. They *belonged* in that grass. If they were squashed or uprooted, they rallied like tumbleweeds.

"Also," Nellie said enthusiastically, "if my articles about this issue are successful, it could mean a promotion at the *Weekly Leader*! I've worked very hard at my job, Everett. It would mean a lot to me if I could be assigned more of the—"

"Most interesting ladies' luncheons and parties?" he asked, sensing again that there was something she was withholding.

"Well, of course." Nellie gave a vigorous nod. "Parties! That's what I meant to say." She gave another unpracticed titter. "Only the most radical career-minded woman would want to write about anything other than crudités and ball gowns!"

"Humph. Writing about parties sounds like a punishment, not a job."

Nellie bit her lip. "To *you*, it might. But you're a man!"

Illustratively she gestured at him. To Everett, her motion seemed to paint him as some sort of hairy, hulking, ham-handed brute with all the common sense and usefulness of a horsefly.

"I *do* know how to use a pen and paper," he informed her.

"And I *adore* writing about bustles and fruit punch!" With a sort of wounded dignity, Nellie shot him an inquisitive look. "Don't I appear to be the sort of woman who likes those things?"

"Since the moment I met you at the depot this morning," Everett told her truthfully, "you've seemed to be the sort of woman who isn't sure what sort of woman she is."

Nellie crossed her arms. "You could not be more wrong."

"No, I'm right," he insisted. As proof, he added, "One minute you're traveling hundreds of miles on your own, the next you're insisting you can't eat an entire cookie by yourself. You say you don't want to be married, then you say you might." Everett fixed her with an assessing look, allowing the horses to move at their own pace. "You tell me you like writing about female fripperies for your newspaper... but it's the possibility of writing a real exposé that makes you sit up straighter and wave your arms and look lively. It's the chance of stopping people being taken advantage of by mail-order marriage bureaus that sets your hair afire. A man would have to be blind not to see it."

"Then perhaps you are not as ably sighted as you think." Decorously Nellie folded her hands in her lap. "Because I am *very* dainty and ladylike, and I cherish writing about hats."

Somehow, Everett strongly doubted it. Also, she wasn't the only one who knew how to tease someone. Piqued by her seeming assertion that he was wrong about the observations he'd made about her—observations he *knew* damn well were correct, because his attentiveness had never failed him before, and neither had his intuition—he delivered a ludicrous statement of his own.

"Yes. And I, like every man, want a compliant, trusting, wishy-washy, swooning female straight from *Godey's* magazine to call my own," Everett deadpanned. "It's all I dream about while baling hay and building fences and rounding up wild mustangs."

Her blue eyes brightened—and not at his wit, either.

"You round up wild mustangs?" Fervently Nellie

clutched his arm. "Can I go with you next time? That sounds *fascinating!*"

If she would continue touching him, Everett knew, he would allow her to go anywhere with him. He was definitely in over his head. "It's not very dainty," he warned. "It will be noisy and dusty and dangerous." Then, belatedly reminded of his quest to impress Nellie with his supposed sophistication, he added, "Besides, we could have ourselves a poetry reading instead."

Nellie made a face. Then she caught him watching her.

"Oh! Outstanding! Poetry!" she enthused. "Only… perhaps we could have a tiny excursion to see your horses first? I promise I'll try to bear up under the noise and dust and danger."

At the valiant tilt she gave her chin, Everett guffawed.

"You know, I believe you will." Full of wonder at this contradictorily fascinating woman he'd found, he urged his team of horses onward at full chisel. He wanted to get on with discovering Nellie's secrets—and that was something best done at home. "I'll promise to try not to scare you too much with my swaggering virile ways and coarse language and clumsy shave."

Her eyes sparkled at him. "We have ourselves a challenge."

"Pshaw," Everett scoffed, rubbing his chin. "I'm not that bearded yet. It isn't even noontime. The truly notable stubble won't emerge until supper. And as far as my swagger goes—"

"No, I mean with our 'marriage,'" Nellie said, smiling. "I still want to write my story for the *Leader*, Everett, and since I'm already here anyway…" She bit her lip again, inciting in him an unholy urge to do the same to her mouth himself… very, very gently. "Would you mind very much *pretending* to be engaged to me for a while longer yet?" Nellie asked. "I know your men believe you were going to hurl me back onto the train a while ago—"

"I was never going to *hurl* you anyplace. I'm not a beast."

Why did she persist in believing he was ungentlemanly?

Gaily she overlooked his disgruntled tone and continued.

"—so they might require convincing of our newfound and immediate rapport." With a decisive air, Nellie slid across the wagon's bench seat. She looped her arm in his, then snuggled up to him until their bodies touched full-length along one side. Engagingly she gazed upward. "Do you think this will do?"

It was doing plenty for Everett already. At her nearness, his whole body tightened. Her warmth touched him. Her bosom pressed against his arm. Her softness felt evident, even through all the layers of her dress and petticoats and corset and whatever else she had on. Imagining it, his wits went walking.

With effort, Everett managed not to drop the tracings and pull her into his arms right then. "Do I think this will convince my *vaqueros* we're going through with our 'engagement'?"

"Yes." She seemed concerned. "Are you all right? You seem…distracted. If this is too much for you to take on, I—"

"No." He cleared his throat. "Let's do it. I feel confident I can take on everything at hand and make you feel glad I did."

His head swam with visions of doing exactly that. Lustily Everett pictured himself holding Nellie closer, bringing his mouth to hers, making her open herself to him, so sweet and hot and ready to share herself with him as he kissed her and kissed her, both of them shedding their clothes and losing their minds. Their coming together would be sensual, of course, but also—

"Excellent!" Nellie blinked at him, innocent and pure.

Innocent. And pure. Recognizing those qualities in her, Everett tardily remembered where he was and what he was doing—which was *not*, he reminded himself strictly, taking advantage of a woman who might or might not aspire to great heights of journalistic excellence…but who definitely trusted him to help her carry off the mission that had brought her to Morrow Creek.

He would *earn* her trust, Everett promised himself then. He would help Nellie research that investigative story of hers, he would pretend to be her fiancé, and he would convince anyone who looked at them that he was boots over hat in love with her.

Not that doing so would be much of a stretch. He felt half spoony already, and that was only the effect of meeting her. Who knew how much more besotted he'd become if given a few days?

No, the difficult part would be doing all of those things *sophisticatedly*, Everett knew. The difficult part would be impressing Nellie with his intellect, style and essential refinement without accidentally letting slip his too-manly ways—the aspects of him that had already cost him love once before.

With Nellie, things would be different, Everett swore. With Nellie, *he* would be different. For her. And if he was lucky, he thought as they rounded the next turn and his *hacienda* and its pastures and outbuildings came into view, maybe she would even agree to stay after her story for the *Weekly Leader* was written.

Chapter Four

"...The tricky thing about it," Edina said as she puttered around the kitchen of Everett's ranch house on the morning after Nellie's arrival, "is that the bride doesn't know beforehand that it's her *groom* who's kidnapping her. All she knows is that she has to make a choice—and if she chooses wrong, the glorious wedding she's been dreaming about will go up in smoke. Poof!"

The jolly, apron-wearing cook threw up her floury hands in demonstration, making sure that Nellie understood the significance of the prewedding tradition she'd been describing. It was only one of many head-spinning old-world customs that Edina had insisted everyone in the territory—especially the *vaqueros*—held very close at heart. According to Edina, the ranch hands were hoping Nellie and Everett would include several of their most beloved traditions in their upcoming nuptials.

"It's a test, really," Edina went on, going back to

her stoneware bowl of biscuit dough. "You probably ken that much. But it's certainly not fair to the poor bride! She hasn't even had a chance to sew that last lucky stitch on her wedding dress."

"Zut alors!" Marybelle, the housekeeper, shook her head. "The bride must not sew her own wedding dress! It is bad luck."

"No, it is bad luck to wear a green wedding dress."

"Or a red dress." Marybelle shuddered. "That is almost as bad as seeing a nun on the way to the church and being struck barren. *Non*, Nellie must let *us* sew her wedding dress for her."

"Oh! That would be lovely!" Feeling almost as though the dress in question would truly be hers— and not just a footnote in her story for the *Weekly Leader*—Nellie took an enlivening sip of coffee. "Honestly I hadn't given much thought to what I might wear. I'm not good with fashion. I'm a truly awful seamstress."

Edina and Marybelle stared at her in patent disbelief.

Oh. Fashion and sewing skills were essential for ladies, Nellie recalled too late. "I mean, I don't enjoy sewing."

The two women blinked, still seeming not to comprehend her.

Perhaps some diversion would be best. "What about the wedding itself?" Nellie asked brightly.

"You've told me about several prewedding traditions, but what about the wedding?"

"At the last wedding I went to, I got a daisy pin for a favor," Edina shared. "The unmarried ladies wear theirs upside down, you know. *I* lost mine before the end of the night!"

Mystified by the significance of that, Nellie raised her brows in confusion. Seeing her, Marybelle rushed to explain.

"She thinks that means *she's* next to be married," Marybelle said in her enchanting French-accented speech. "But I put more stock in catching the bouquet, myself. At the last wedding I attended, *I* did that. So I believe *I'm* the next to be married."

Edina disagreed. Their conversation had the tenor of a longstanding rivalry—leavened with affection, to be sure, but a rivalry, all the same. Propping her booted feet on the rungs of the nearest ladder-back chair, Nellie listened with interest.

Idly she reached down to pet the tabby cat that had padded into the kitchen and taken up residence underneath her seat. Nellie didn't know its name, but like everything and everyone else in Everett's home, the cat had welcomed her unstintingly.

"I will have a traditional ceremony, the way we do in Brittany," Marybelle was saying. "Children will block the road with wedding ribbons, and I will cut them with fancy shears. To reach me, my groom will have to remove briars from the road—"

Edina snorted. "Likely they'll be tumbleweeds, you mean."

"—and I will toss my garter and have a *chiverie*!"

"Oh, I do love me a good shivaree!" Edina agreed with Marybelle readily for once. "Staying up till all hours, having a wee nip of whiskey, crowding around the hapless married couple while they try to have it off in their wedding-night bed—"

Appalled at the very notion, Nellie gawked at her. She couldn't help picturing herself and Everett, clad in nightwear with blankets pulled up to their chins, surrounded by boisterous Westerners wielding cowbells and hard liquor at midnight.

While the idea of Everett in bed with her held a certain undeniable…*intrigue*—making her wonder exactly what he *did* wear to sleep—the rest of that scenario left Nellie feeling aghast.

Catching her horrified expression, Edina placidly went back to patting out her biscuit dough. "Not that we'll do anything like that to you and Everett, dearie," she promised.

"Oh, *non*," Marybelle agreed coolly—and not entirely convincingly. "We and the *vaqueros* will leave you alone for your wedding night's *l'amour*. All we ask is that you indulge us with a few harmless *les traditions* in the days before the wedding."

"And during the wedding ceremony itself," Edina put in.

"Bien sûr." Marybelle nodded. "During the wedding, too. You will have your maids of honor, to confuse the evil spirits. You'll need to distract them from making mischief for the true bride."

"I could think of no one nicer than the two of you," Nellie opined, beginning to feel guilty that she couldn't *promise* the positions of honor to Marybelle and Edina, "to stand with me."

At that, both women gave girlish smiles. Their pleasure only added to Nellie's burgeoning sense that she was unavoidably hoodwinking these kind people. Everyone at Everett's ranch had greeted her with open arms. And she was repaying them by being only half truthful about the real reason she'd come there.

But she couldn't write an accurate story for the *Leader* if she didn't experience an authentic mail-order marriage—at least in part—could she? That meant Nellie had to carry on as she was.

"You'll need hearty groomsmen, too," Edina added, filling her pan with several more biscuits. She'd already made at least three dozen of them. "To be sure you're not stolen away by rival cowboys."

"Rival cowboys?" Nellie laughed. "I don't think that will be a problem. For one thing, they won't want me. For another—"

"Won't want you?" Her two new friends regarded her owlishly. "Why not?"

"Well, because I'm not strictly marriageable," Nellie said. "I never have been." That's what had made her ideally suited for her story on the mail-order marriage bureaus. That's what had finally convinced her editor, in fact, to let her write it.

When Nellie had come to him with her "groom's" written request for her, via the mail-order marriage bureau, he'd taken one look at "Everett's" letter and offered a blunt reply.

Well, if those people at the marriage bureau have found someone who wants to marry you, Miss Trent, then I guess they are a bunch of shysters, just like you said they might be, he'd told her, applauding her instincts. *Go ahead and prove it!*

Thus emboldened, Nellie had set out to do exactly that.

Marybelle gave a musical laugh. "Monsieur Bannon would disagree with you about that. He seems to find you eminently marriageable. We all noticed it yesterday, when you arrived."

"Well, he's...*contracted* to marry me. That's different."

"*Non*. You don't understand," Marybelle insisted. "You have made Monsieur Bannon a changed man! He was so gloomy in the days following Miss O'Neill's traitorous departure, but now—"

At her mention of the mysterious Miss O'Neill, Edina slapped down a biscuit with extra vigor. She muttered a curse.

"—now he is like himself again," Marybelle said happily, "only better! And that is only because *you* are here at last."

Nellie sincerely doubted that. Although… "He *did* have the vitality to argue with me on the drive here yesterday."

"You see?" Edina gave a nod. "He is restored! By you!"

"And he *did* have the vitality to tell me," Nellie went on, troubled anew by the recollection, "that he wanted a 'compliant, trusting, wishy-washy, swooning female straight from *Godey's* magazine' to call his own." Worriedly she clenched her coffee cup. Miserably she stared into it. "I'll never measure up."

Marybelle and Edina laughed. "He said *what*?"

Too mortified to repeat it, Nellie adjusted her boys' boots instead. She should have cleaned them last night; they still bore a layer of caked-on mud, earned when she'd sojourned along the railway track during the train's stops, exploring things.

"Never mind." Nellie sipped more coffee, feeling herself growing a tiny bit…jealous? Casually she poked at her boot heels, striving to seem nonchalant. "Who is Miss O'Neill?"

At that, both women began talking to beat the

band. It was as though they'd been *dying* to tell the story of their beloved *hacendado* and the duplicitous woman who'd cruelly wronged him.

In short order, Nellie learned all she cared to know about Abbey O'Neill. She learned how Miss O'Neill had "pretended" to care about Everett, how she had strung him along ("And several other men, too!" a scandalized Edina confided) all through their courtship, and how she had heartlessly abandoned Everett to elope with a man who she'd decided offered better prospects.

Hearing the name of Miss O'Neill's paramour, Nellie gasped. She knew of Astair Prestell; everyone did! His writings were legendary and varied. His speaking engagements were said to be even more memorable. Astair Prestell was witty, sophisticated...

Well, he was altogether dissimilar to Everett Bannon, that was for certain. Astair Prestell was a person of importance in society. Everett was...a man of good character in Morrow Creek.

"Our *patrón* was devastated by Miss O'Neill's betrayal," Edina said in an outraged tone. "She made a laughingstock of him, running off like that!"

Marybelle shook her head. "He is better off without her. In time, his heart will heal. I believe that." She gave Nellie a warm look. "Especially now that *you* are here to love him."

"Yes." Swamped with empathy for what Everett must have gone through, Nellie nodded unthinkingly. "Poor Everett."

Edina and Marybelle traded meaningful glances, as though Nellie's gesture signified her intentions to save their *patrón* from heartbreak. But as much as she wanted to, Nellie wasn't sure she could carry it through.

After all, her own editor at the *Weekly Leader*—a man who knew her thoroughly, had hired her himself, and often professed his esteem of her writing talent—had believed she would not find herself a single potential groom from among the entire catalog offered by the mail-order marriage bureau. He'd believed she was simply *that* lacking in feminine appeal and suitability to become a bride. Worse, this man—whom she trusted—had believed that her apparently glaring deficiency would even come through *on paper*!

Nellie knew she was a good person. She didn't believe she needed to be silly, superficial, or overly concerned with petticoats to be a "real woman." When it came down to it, she didn't believe *any* woman needed to behave in a particular way.

She'd always been happy breaking down barriers, proving herself the equal of men in her workday life, and forging her own way with things. She'd always been happy…period.

But she'd never before been smitten with a man the way she was with Everett Bannon: instantly, giddily and overwhelmingly. And she'd never before been filled with such longing to impress anyone—not the way she yearned to impress Everett right now.

Without a doubt, Nellie was out of her depth. What if Everett truly *did* want a swooning, simpering, idiotic girl, like the "ideal woman" personified by *Godey's Lady's Book*?

Nellie couldn't possibly manage *that*.

Unfortunately the only alternative was revealing her true self to Everett *now*, then trying to bear his inevitable disdain.

Everett would try to hide it, of course. He was honorable that way. He was chivalrous and kind and engagingly down-to-earth. He wasn't like the popinjays and braggarts who filled San Francisco society; he was real and true. Nellie had seen that in dozens of ways already, beginning with the way Everett had sat down to his usual shared evening meal with all his ranch hands, Marybelle, Edina and her last night, and continuing with the way he'd treated Nellie so far—respectfully and generously.

She couldn't afford to lose his positive regard already…not when things between them felt so very new and captivating. Not when she'd only begun to daydream of kissing him—just a peck!—and finding out if his beard stubble felt soft or scratchy.

When she was around Everett, Nellie reflected dreamily, she felt...*overwarm,* all the time. With a single glance, he could pull August heat out of a springtime day and leave her sweltering.

"*Regarde.* Look!" Marybelle nudged Edina, pointing her chin at Nellie. "She is daydreaming about her wedding. Sweet, *non?*"

"Very sweet!" Both older women fairly cooed with delight.

Nellie only frowned, struck by a new thought. "Are you *sure* it was Astair Prestell whom Miss O'Neill ran away with?"

Marybelle gave a languorous Gallic shrug. *"Oui. Bien sûr."*

Edina narrowed her eyes menacingly. "I will never forget his name. I will never buy one of his blasted books, either!"

"Of course not. Me, either." Nellie soothed, stifling a smile. She liked these two women already. Under different circumstances, they might have become close friends. "It's just that he is so *very* sophisticated and witty and well-mannered—"

"I suppose," Marybelle allowed grudgingly. Edina only gave a dismissive wave of her floury hand, urging Nellie to go on.

"Well, that's not quite the sort of person I'd expect to find here in the territory, that's all," Nellie said. "I'd—"

She broke off, startled by a noise around the corner.

She didn't want to be caught gossiping by one of the *vaqueros*. She didn't want anyone to tell Everett that she knew about his ordeal with Miss O'Neill. It was bad enough it had happened; for Everett, having the whole imbroglio spoken about would undoubtedly only be worse. It would only be painful.

Contrary to her fears, a noticeably buoyant Everett sauntered in an instant later, all broad shoulders, neatly combed dark hair and clean-shaven jaw. The noise she'd heard, she realized, had been his boot heels ringing against the floorboards. Now, he offered up a bright morning smile.

It was, it occurred to her, exactly the "genuine smile" she'd sought from him—under threat of further teasing—at the train depot. She hadn't expected it to be quite so…*heartwarming*, though. Everett was *charming*.

"Don't listen to their bad-mouthing me, Nellie," he said breezily, obviously having overheard part of what she'd said. He cast his housekeeper and cook a chiding glance. "Folks around here wouldn't know sophistication if it plumb fell on them."

"Youch! Maybe it already has!" Squinting at her precious *patrón*, Edina shielded her eyes with her hand. She guffawed. "Leastwise, *something's* assaulting my poor eyeballs right now. My money's on that hideous necktie of yours. But if you say it's 'sophistication,' I reckon I'll have to take your word for it."

"Yes. You will," Everett said with a satisfied grin. "Nellie already has. Maybe you should follow her lead, Edina."

Still smiling, he gave Nellie a meaningful, solidarity-filled look. Belatedly she realized that he'd overheard her describing the "sophisticated, witty and well-mannered" Astair Prestell—and had mistakenly decided she'd been describing *him*.

Well, there was no sense disillusioning him now. Especially not since he appeared—endearingly—to have gussied himself up specifically for the occasion of spending the day with her.

"Mon Dieu!" Looking at Everett, Marybelle shied away, too. "You will spook the horses with that ensemble."

Everett chuckled. "Very funny." He strode confidently across the room, poured himself a cup of coffee from the speckled enamelware pot on the cooktop, then sipped. "I have it on good authority that a four-in-hand necktie is very stylish."

"Since when do *you* care about what's stylish? You must've had to drag that suit outta mothballs." Edina squinted again. *"Patrón,* are those *spectacles* on your face, too? Humph. Maybe if you took them off, you'd be able to see how funny you look."

At that, Everett's expression changed. A tiny hint of vulnerability softened his mouth, making him appear...*kissable.*

No! Nellie scolded herself. *No.* Not kissable!

Everett clearly had gone out of his way to look nice for their first full day of being "engaged," and his housekeeper and cook simply weren't used to his newly dapper appearance. Or to his until-now undetected need to wear eyeglasses.

Everett required a show of camaraderie right now, not more teasing, Nellie decided. She had to think of *his* needs—not her own selfish, sinful urgings to cup his face in her palms, touch her lips to his lips, inhale that leather-and-tobacco scent that clung to his skin and clothes, rub her body all over his— similar to the way she had in his wagon yesterday, when she'd brazenly cuddled up to him to "pretend" to be attracted to him—and make herself all breathless and needful and...and... Well, she didn't know what else. But she felt quite certain, just then, that Everett did. She wanted very much for him to share that knowledge with her. She truly, breathlessly did. But first...

"*I* think you look *very* handsome today," Nellie told him loudly. To prove it, she reached for his hand. He took it.

He tossed her another gratified smile, wholly ignorant of the thrills that chased through her body at his touch. His hand felt warm and strong and faintly callused, Nellie observed, and when Everett looked at her again, his eyes were... They were...

They were partly *hidden* by those silly spectacles he had on! An offense like that should have been a crime of some sort.

Displeased with that realization, Nellie did her best to rally. She could hardly begrudge Everett the ability to see clearly. Especially if—as likely was the case—he needed those eyeglasses to read the thick book he held in his opposite hand.

Although on further reflection...Nellie could have sworn she'd glimpsed that very same book in Oscar's hand yesterday.

Truly. And she *still* felt resentful that those eyeglasses had stolen her view of Everett's stirringly warm and intense hazel eyes. And to be one hundred percent honest, she didn't entirely approve of the necktie that had so nettled Edina, either.

But she *did* wholeheartedly approve of the man who wore it, Nellie reflected anew, and that was all that really mattered.

Gently Everett rubbed his thumb over the back of her hand, making another series of thrills rush through her. Bereft of the ability to speak under such heady circumstances, Nellie only gazed, undoubtedly wide-eyed, at her supposed "fiancé."

"Yep. They're adorable together," Edina judged brusquely.

"*Ah oui.* They are *enchanteur.*" Marybelle pressed together her hands in a prayerful position. "Everything will be fine now." She signaled Edina. "Come! Hurry up with those biscuits. We must begin sewing, or Nellie's dress won't be ready."

At that, Nellie started. She couldn't allow Marybelle and Edina to slave away on a dress she would never wear. She had to stop them somehow, without rousing suspicion. She had to—

Abruptly Nellie followed Everett's glance toward her feet. She realized, to her dismay, what he must be looking at.

Her boots. Her muddy, disreputable, *boys'* boots.

Reflexively she yanked them under her skirts again. She'd thought she'd been doing so well in her quest to appear ladylike and demure. Evidently making herself over into Everett's dream woman would be more challenging than she'd expected—and more necessary than ever, as well. She'd noticed, at dinner last night, that Everett had flawless table manners and rarely made a misstep himself. She would simply have to do better than this!

Distraught, Nellie opened her mouth to formulate an excuse for her hoydenish ways. But before she could even begin, Everett squeezed her hand. All her self-chastising thoughts fled.

"Come with me." Cheerfully he pulled Nellie to her feet. "We have a month's worth of wedding fripperies to get to and only a week to do it in. So we'd better get started."

Chapter Five

Striding toward the paddock at his easternmost pasture with Nellie by his side, Everett felt as giddy as a schoolboy. Until that moment, he hadn't realized exactly how fraught with tension his arrival in the kitchen had felt to him. But now…

Now he knew Nellie liked him. She truly did.

His plan was working! He had successfully impersonated a sophisticated man. For her sake. And maybe, possibly, his own.

When he'd arrived in the kitchen, Everett had half expected Nellie to laugh at him. He'd expected her to tease him the way Edina and Marybelle had. Or to reject him outright the way Miss O'Neill had. Instead Nellie had gazed at him with respect and admiration. She'd complimented him on the outfit it had taken him thirty-six vexatious, swearword-filled minutes to assemble. She'd taken his hand in hers and she'd smiled, and in that moment, Everett had known everything would be all right.

He should have known it would be, he chided himself now as they continued alongside the grassy area where his tamest horses grazed. He'd heard Nellie's opinion of him with his own ears.

It's just that he is so very *sophisticated and witty and well-mannered,* she'd been telling Marybelle and Edina in an awestruck tone when he'd come downstairs, and Everett saw no reliable reason not to believe her. Everyone knew that overheard statements were the most honest. Nellie's remark had certainly seemed to be authentic. Especially since she'd followed up by admitting with typical forthrightness that Everett was *not quite the sort of person* she'd expected to find in the territory.

He could tell, by now, that she was changing her mind.

Silently congratulating himself on having carried off his plan so far—despite a few subtle missteps while navigating the multiple forks he'd uncharacteristically insisted Marybelle set for dinner last night—Everett smiled at Nellie. Her strides were steady and sure, purposeful enough to make her skirts swish, and he couldn't help remembering the appealingly self-assured way she'd been perched at his kitchen table when he'd arrived, with her feet propped on the chair rungs and her posture alert.

Nellie Trent was no coy, helpless damsel, he reckoned approvingly as he watched her tramp across the windswept landscape. She was energetic and interesting. She was fascinating and smart and alluring. She was…capable, it seemed, of enchanting all the creatures, big and small, on his ranch.

Even now, he saw, his old dog trotted at her heels, tongue lolling in canine adoration. And when he'd come downstairs, his tabby mouser had been curled up beneath her chair. And every one of his *vaqueros* had quit work to tip his hat at her, grinning from ear to ear. Pedro, of course, had offered a courtly bow.

Glancing again at her doggy companion, Everett grinned. He knew exactly how that helpless mutt felt—entranced and ensnared.

"All right. That's it!" Stopping abruptly, Nellie yanked her hand from his. "You're staring at my feet again, aren't you?" Accusingly she frowned at him. "You can just quit wondering, because I'll admit it—I'm wearing boots." She lifted her skirts a few inches to confirm it, offering a tantalizing glimpse of her stocking-clad legs in the process. Knitted cotton hosiery had never looked better. "Boys' boots. I like them. They're comfortable. They fit me. This pair is a little muddy at the moment, but that's remedied easily enough. It doesn't make me any less ladylike!" She jutted out her chin. A pause. "Well?"

Confused by her beleaguered tone, Everett looked down. "Well…" He searched for a proper reply. "You have nice knees."

She yelped in surprise. Her skirts dropped. *"Knees?"*

"Before, in the kitchen, I could only *wish* I could catch a glimpse of your knees. But now…it's kind of you to oblige."

"I wasn't showing you my knees!" Nellie informed him with another lift of her chin. "I was showing you my boots. Since you were so all-encompassingly curious about them, and all."

"Nope. You were showing me your knees." Everett grinned, recalling the moment with fond remembrance. He'd distinctly glimpsed her shapely calves, exposed knees…and the most elusive, most *haunting* hint of a curvy inner thigh adorned in dark stockings. But perhaps that last had been his overactive imagination. "Whatever your intentions were, I've seen boots before. I don't need a refresher on what they look like."

"I see. So your eyes just naturally wandered upward?"

"Naturally." He took her hand again. "You have a surpassingly fine figure. I couldn't help myself." He remembered his newfound gentlemanly persona and added, "Of course, I'm very sorry if that offends your ladylike sensibilities."

Nellie didn't even appear to be listening. Instead she was gazing at his shoulders in a preoccupied fashion. "My what?"

"Your ladylike sensibilities."

She blinked. "Oh! Yes. *Those*." Her mouth formed a delectable moue of distress. "You're correct. Formally I am offended by that comment, of course. It was impertinent and overfamiliar."

"And yet," Everett pointed out, "you're smiling."

"Posh." Nellie tried to suppress her grin. "I am not. It would not be at all ladylike if I were, say, *thrilled* to hear you remark favorably on my figure. That would be unthinkable."

"Your eyes are lovely, too. And I like your lips."

Appearing mesmerized, she touched them. "My lips?"

Damnation. He was probably not supposed to mention them in polite company. It was just like him, a rough-and-tumble Western man, to forget that. "I'm sure," Everett hedged, searching for a courteous alternative, "they have interesting things to say."

"Not without my running them, they don't." Now Nellie's grin turned mischievous. "Exactly whom do you think is in charge of me? Hmm?" Playfully she nudged him. "Does your mouth do things all on its own, without any instructions from you?"

Everett nodded. "It's been trying to subvert my good intentions all day." He lowered his gaze to her lips. "It wants me to kiss you. I keep having to remind it we've only just met."

"Strictly speaking, that's true," she agreed, shifting her gaze to his mouth…and holding it there with another preoccupied look on her face. "It doesn't feel that way, though."

"No, it doesn't." He took a step nearer, still holding her hand. He lifted it to his chest, letting Nellie feel his heart thumping along underneath his shirt and necktie and suit coat. He raised her hand higher. Keeping his gaze pinned on hers, Everett brought her hand to his mouth. Very softly, he kissed it. "There. Maybe that will keep my subversive impulses at bay."

Shakily Nellie exhaled. She nodded, her eyes enormous and blue and affectionate. "It ought to," she pronounced. "After all, I am a demure lady. And you are a bespectacled gentleman. Between the two of us, we ought not want anything more."

"No," Everett agreed. Even *he* wasn't convinced. All of him yearned to pull Nellie still closer…to kiss her properly. "We are both far too sophisticated to give in to our urges."

"Yes," Nellie breathed, moving a hairsbreadth closer. "We are. Far, *far* too sophisticated." She paused. Then, "Only…"

Instantly Everett felt doubly alert. "Only…?"

"Only we *might*, purely for the sake of our 'engagement,' try out a very minor kiss," Nellie proposed. Devilishly, she raised her eyebrows. "It wouldn't have to mean anything."

"It would mean *everything*."

"Or it could mean everything." A nod. "Yes, please."

Everett nearly groaned aloud. "You really *are* a lady. Only a lady would request a kiss in such a well-mannered fashion."

At that, Nellie perked up. "Well, then! Let's do it!"

"Not here." Lacing his fingers in hers, Everett hauled her sideways. Within moments, the shadow of the barn enveloped them, providing a slice of blissful privacy. The springtime coolness mingled with the earthy scent of freshly plowed soil and the perfume of budding flowers. With his back to the sunshine and his front to everything that mattered to him just then, Everett leaned Nellie against the barn wall. Reverently he brought his hand to her face. He stroked her cheek. *"Here,"* he told her.

Another preoccupied look. "Here what?"

"*Here* is where I'm going to kiss you."

She nodded. "If you don't hurry up, I won't be at all convinced of your impassioned response to your fiancée."

"Are you always this bossy?" Grinning with delight at her puckish expression, Everett brought his other hand to her face. Gently he cradled her jaw in his hands. "This can't be rushed."

"Can it be helped along?" Cooperatively Nellie looped her arms around his middle. She levered herself nearer, making her skirts collide riotously with his trouser legs. "How's this?"

Perfect. It was perfect. That was all Everett could think about. Nellie, in all her directness and enthusiasm, could not have been more wonderful, or more ideal for him. He trembled at feeling her body crowded against his, all soft and warm and giving. He wanted to give *her* everything…to let her know how much it meant to him that she was there, with him, just then.

Instead his borrowed spectacles—a remnant of a former *vaquero* who'd forgotten them when he'd moved on—fogged up.

He'd hoped they would make him appear scholarly. They only succeeded in making him appear… damp. Everett whipped them off.

"It's good," he managed to say with a nod. "Very good."

"I like you without your eyeglasses on," Nellie nattered on as he, having stowed his spectacles, returned his hands to her face. She seemed cheered by the notion that she was being useful. "You have magnificent eyes. And it's only fair that I help with our kiss, since this was my idea in the first place."

"*Your* idea?" If she only knew the largely sleepless night he'd just spent thinking of her. "I won't give you credit for this. Not in the slightest. Not after how much I've wanted—"

"You must!" she insisted with a sincere expression—and a twinkle in her eyes. "It's the only gentlemanly thing to do."

"Right now," Everett said honestly, "I'm no gentleman."

Then he tilted Nellie's head upward, lowered his mouth to hers…and gave in to every ungentlemanly impulse he'd ever had.

Her mouth tasted like honey, her lips felt like heaven, and before Everett had so much as begun coaxing her to open herself to him, he knew he could never get enough of this—enough of *her*. Kissing Nellie was like leaping into the sunshine after a long, cold winter. It was like searching for something long lost, then finding it unexpectedly in a half forgotten pocket. It was like being split in half and then becoming whole again. It was…

"Amazing," Nellie said when he'd lifted his head again. She blinked at him, then traced her fingers over his cheek. "I guess the marriage bureau was right—you *are* ideally suited for me."

"I thought you said they are scurrilous fraudsters."

"Potentially," she reminded him, still looking dreamy. *"Potentially,* they are scurrilous fraudsters preying on the hopes of naive men and women. That was my original hypothesis, at least. But the proof of that remains to be found—and the plain fact is, the evidence at hand just can't be ignored."

Everett wanted to kiss her again. Again and again and again. Instead he made himself converse. "It can't?"

"No." With her gaze lingering on his face, Nellie shook her head. She frowned in thought. "It seems to me that we really *are* wonderful together. Surely *all* kisses aren't like that."

Everett squared his shoulders. "Like what?"

"Magical. You must have felt it."

He wanted to jump for joy. Somberly he said, "Yes, I did."

"Well, then! What if we're *meant* to be together?"

He was having trouble thinking clearly. "If you're expecting philosophy from me, *especially* after that kiss—"

"You *did* have the book for it close at hand. Remember?"

Hellfire. The book he'd borrowed from Oscar. Evidently it had been too effective in convincing Nellie of his erudition. Now she expected deep thoughts and contemplation from him.

On the verge of confessing that the book—in German, no less!—had only been for appearance's sake, Everett stopped. His plan was working. He was impressing Nellie. He had to continue.

"The only way to find out about our future is to live it," he said firmly. "Starting with our 'wedding.' Come on."

Chapter Six

When Everett clasped her hand and urged her toward the barn door, Nellie did not think she could move. She felt too languid, too preoccupied with Everett's mighty shoulders and hard-muscled chest and big, nimble hands…too itchy for more things like kissing to concentrate on mundane matters like a mail-order marriage—particularly a *sham* mail-order marriage for a newspaper story for the nearly forgotten *Weekly Leader*. Her original reason for coming to town felt further away with every passing minute.

But then Everett parted the barn doors. He let them roll aside with all the fanfare of a big-city play on opening night, and Nellie glimpsed what was inside, and she livened up quickly.

"Oh, my word!" Awestruck, Nellie stepped inside. She wheeled around, taking in her surroundings. "Everett! This is— This is—"

"It's all my *vaqueros*' doing," he said, pausing to

put on his dratted eye-obscuring spectacles again. Although they made him appear duly bookish and wise, Nellie preferred him without them. He gestured at the barn's interior. "Do you approve?"

"Approve? I'm flabbergasted!" Eagerly she hurried past rows of empty stalls, taking it all in. "It's beautiful!"

Contrary to every expectation she would have had, it *was* beautiful. The ranch hands had cleaned, scrubbed and polished. They'd stacked hay bales, tied ribbons to the beams and draped cottony bunting from the rafters. They'd hung safety lanterns. They'd created a cozy seating area. They'd *decorated*. Somehow, incredibly, they'd managed to turn a barn into…a cathedral.

Or something that felt very much like it.

"Is *this* where we're getting married?" she asked.

Everett seemed too enchanted by her reaction to respond at first. Then, he nodded. "Unless you'd prefer somewhere else."

"Somewhere else? I wouldn't think of it!" Hugging herself, Nellie turned in a circle. She grinned. "It's so…unconventional!"

That meant it was *perfect*. At least it was for her.

"Oh." Everett frowned. "No one wants 'unconventional.' You're being polite and ladylike again."

His words dashed her hopes in a heartbeat. Brought back to earth by his commonsense statement, Nellie remembered how silly she was being. Of *course* no one wanted "unconventional." She'd been hearing that all her adult life—sometimes about herself.

With effort, she rallied. "What I meant was, this appeals to me because I don't have a family to invite to a conventional wedding," Nellie said as matter-of-factly as she could. Through long practice, she was able to shrug. "My friends and coworkers would hardly fill up two pews, much less half a church!"

"I'm sorry. I didn't know that." Everett's sympathetic gaze followed her. "I read all your letters—Oscar gave them to me last night," he went on, "but they didn't mention—"

"No, they wouldn't have." Giving him a smile, Nellie went to him. She took his hands in hers. "It's all right, Everett. I was an only child, and my parents died a long time ago." She offered him a squeeze. "Do you think I'd have turned out this way if I'd had someone watching over me for all these years?"

Contrary to her expectations, he took her joke seriously.

"I like the way you turned out," Everett said.

Nellie wished she could believe that. But Everett didn't know the real her...and if she succeeded, he never would.

"Someone else likes the way you turned out, too," Everett teased. He nodded toward her feet. For an instant, Nellie thought she was going to have to display her "unconventional" boots again. Everett must have been disappointed to have glimpsed them. He'd been polite about them, of course, by pretending to be more interested in her knees than her wardrobe.

"Have you noticed your entourage?" he asked now, gesturing toward the shaggy dog who'd been following her around. By now, the cat from the kitchen had joined the lovable mutt, too. "Counting my dog, my cat and the mare who was nosing around after you outside, you have a veritable menagerie started."

Nellie laughed. "Now you're just being silly. Horses don't follow around people! They're not like dogs and cats."

Everett shrugged. "The evidence at hand, as you say, can't be ignored." His eyes glimmered at her. "Around these parts, Nellie, you are *beloved*. By my livestock, my *vaqueros*—"

"Ha! If only that were true," Nellie joked, unable to hear more talk like that. But, tellingly, her voice cracked on the words. She *did* want to be beloved, if the truth were known. She wanted to lavish affection on Everett—and on his various animals and his ranch hands and Edina and Marybelle, too. She wanted to give away her pent-up love. She wanted to quit holding it close for fear that no one would want it if she offered it.

She hadn't known she'd been doing that until right now.

"You *could be* beloved," Everett assured her, pulling her closer, "if you wanted to be. If you would accept an ordinary man and a barn-bound wedding and a passel of funny traditions."

Nellie was afraid to hope for so much. "Well, I *am* powerfully curious about all those traditions," she allowed.

"We'll be getting to them shortly," Everett promised. "All fifty-nine of them that my ranch hands made me promise to try."

At his wry but accepting grin, she practically fell in love on the spot. Why did Everett have to be so remarkable…and so increasingly out of her reach? The more he revealed his almost flawless, gentlemanly self, the less she measured up to him.

"And I *do* fancy the idea of getting married in a barn," she added insouciantly, trying her very hardest not to envision that selfsame ceremony. But it was no use. In a heartbeat, Nellie pictured Everett standing handsomely and earnestly by her side while she said her vows in a dress handmade by Marybelle and Edina. If only that reverie could be more than just a dream!

"Well, my barn has never looked better," Everett confirmed.

"But I'm afraid I just don't see an *ordinary* man

around here," Nellie told him, playfully pretending to look for one. Smiling, she brought her hands to his suit coat lapels and patted them in demonstration. "All I see is a fine gentleman!"

"A fine gentleman? *That's* what you see?" Everett stalked nearer, seeming displeased by her compliment. He glowered down at her. "Look closer," he said, then he kissed her again.

Swept away beneath his kiss, Nellie clutched his lapels and just held on. Her heartbeat galloped; her breath left her in a single surprised utterance. All she could feel was wanting. All she could do was kiss him back. Because there had never been anything she'd wanted more than to kiss Everett. There had never been anything she'd *needed* more than to feel his mouth on hers, his hands on her waist, his body pressing insistently closer.

Kissing Everett was like finding a lucky penny that never could be lost again. It was like understanding the meaning of poetry and music and art in a single instant. It was like wanting a drop of water and being presented with an ocean.

Nellie had never dreamed of having as much as she felt in Everett's arms. She had never known she could be so passionate, so needful…so wrong. It was wrong to do this to Everett and his ranch hands. It was wrong to pretend, even for a good cause.

But oh, how she wanted to go on doing it!

Surely the Almighty would understand why she needed to do this. Surely He would forgive her this one lapse in a lifetime filled chockablock with efforts to see more, do more, *be* more.

Surely He would give her a few minutes more of this.

Instead the tall, blond *vaquero* rushed inside the barn like an unwanted heavenly timekeeper, putting an awkward end to Nellie's prayers for more time alone with Everett. Guiltily, she and her "fiancé" leaped apart while the ranch hand came nearer.

It took Nellie a solid ten seconds to recollect that, as an officially engaged woman, she was *allowed* to socialize with her fiancé. She was allowed to gaze wistfully at Everett, to indulge her impulse to hold his hand…to satisfy her curiosity about him.

It was the most liberating realization she'd had all week.

"Aha! *There* you are, *patrón*!" The lanky *vaquero* pointed outside, oblivious to the barn's fancifully decorated interior. "Come quick! You're already late for the bunkhouse jamboree."

Everett quirked his dark eyebrow. "You must be mistaken."

"No, I ain't! Last night, at dinner, you said you'd come."

"To a jamboree?" Everett sounded skeptical. "Impossible. I make it a practice never to attend jamborees—*especially* if they're happening in the bunkhouse. A shindig, maybe. A party—"

Nellie didn't believe him. "Why not? It sounds like fun!"

"Fun? This won't be a fancy, *big-city* soirée, like you're used to," Everett warned. "This won't be a ball or a gala—"

"It'll be a jamboree!" the *vaquero* supplied obligingly.

"—or anything like what you're missing from San Francisco."

Nellie frowned. She wasn't missing anything. But this wasn't the time to say so—especially since she, as a *Godey's*-style "wishy-washy, swooning female," ought to have been wanting a fashionable diversion to occupy herself with. So, dutifully, she smiled at the *vaquero.* "We'd be delighted to attend."

"Thank you, ma'am." The youth shot Everett a victorious look, then swept off his hat. Holding it in his hand, he gave Nellie a bow. "I'm Casper Dietson, ma'am, at your service."

"I'm pleased to meet you, Mr. Dietson." Nellie shook his hand. "I was very sorry not to get your name yesterday before you went to town, nor last night in all the hubbub at dinner."

"Shucks, that's all right, ma'am." Casper plunked on his hat. "I didn't reckon it was safe to tell you my name until now. But now that you're here *for good*, I guess it's all right."

At that, Casper delivered a delighted grin to his *patrón*.

Under his glowing approval, Everett bore up stoically.

Then Casper took a second hasty glance. "What's that you've got on yourself, *patrón*? A suit? And specs? Ain't that somethin'? I never known you to tolerate fancyin' up like that."

Stone-faced, Everett blinked. He tugged at his hat, indicating a decision was at hand. "I guess I was wrong about that jamboree, Casper. Miss Trent likes parties. So I do, too."

His acquiescence had a revitalizing effect on the *vaquero*.

"Well, I suppose you oughtta like the jamboree! It's on account of the two of you that we're having it!" Casper chuckled. He beamed at them both. "It's for your engagement!"

"Well, isn't that nice?" Nellie nudged Everett. "Dearest?"

He recognized her cue and smiled. "Perfect, sweetheart."

Casper squinted at them both. Then he shook his head. "If you two don't beat all," he said happily. "You're as cute as a pair of june bugs! I aim to tell all the fellas that right now!"

The *vaquero* hurried off, clearly pleased as punch with his *hacendado's* new love match...and dying to share his excitement.

Everett stiffened. "I've got to stop him."

"What for?" Nellie put her hand on his arm. "We *want* all your men to believe we're crazy about one another, don't we?"

"Of course we do. For your newspaper story." Unmoving, Everett compressed his mouth. He cast her a plaintive look, full of nicked male pride and patent disbelief. "It's just... He said we were *cute* together, Nellie. He called me a june bug!"

She suppressed a grin. "I heard him."

"So—" as though it were obvious "—I have to stop him."

At that, Nellie gave him a long look. "You know what? Even when you're disgruntled and childish, I think you're adorable."

"Childish?" His jaw tightened. *"Adorable?* Impossible."

"You keep saying that," Nellie told him, unable to hold back a grin. "To you, 'impossible' seems to signify agreement."

Before Everett could respond to her banter, Casper halted at the barn door. "Come on, you june bugs!" he shouted with a hurry-up gesture. "Git your feet moving. Time's wastin'!"

Nellie laughed. "Come on, june bug!" She gave

Everett a poke. "We don't want to miss the party in our honor, do we?"

"Heaven forbid." With a chivalrous gesture of his powerful arm, he escorted her ahead of him. "After you, Miss Trent."

A few steps onward, Nellie realized he wasn't alongside her. She stopped. She looked back. "Aren't you coming?"

"Yes. First I'm consoling myself by watching you walk ahead of me. It's the least I deserve." Everett lifted his devilish, dancing-eyed gaze from the vicinity of her bustle to her face. "From where I'm standing, the jamboree's already happening."

She laughed. "You're incorrigible."

"Absolutely." He grinned. "I think you like it."

"Why, Mr. Bannon!" Nellie gave her bustle a coquettish wiggle. "Would you look at that? I think I just might."

Everett's husky laugh was enough to make her day.

For a heartbeat, as they smiled at one another, Nellie felt certain they were in perfect harmony. She took unabashed delight in Everett's scandalous appreciation of her physical charms—even swaddled, as they were, in boys' boots and last year's dress and a halfhearted attempt to style her hair in a fetching fashion—and she imagined that he, for his part, found an equal enjoyment in her teasing and unladylike repartee.

But then Casper hollered for them both again, wanting them to hurry, and Nellie snapped out of her impracticable reverie.

She could not make decisions based on what she *felt* about Everett, she reminded herself. She had to act based on what she knew to be true about him— what she *knew* to be true about herself. Everett had told her he wanted a swooning, compliant lady. However much Nellie tried, she could not be that for him. Not forever, at least. So unless Everett informed her otherwise between the bunkhouse jamboree in their honor and the "wedding day" they'd ostensibly reach in a week or so, Nellie would have to make do with what was real.

If she could *remember* what was real, that was...

She was meant to be using this time to recover from her arduous train journey—not to fall in love with her host. She was supposed to be writing a newspaper story about disingenuous mail-order marriages—not enacting a similar fraud on herself.

If she fell entirely in love with Everett, would that make it all right? Nellie wondered. Or would that only make it hurt more on the inevitable day when Everett delivered the return train ticket he'd promised her...and made it plain he could not love her back?

"Cheer up, my beautiful bride-to-be." Catching up to her, Everett gave her a consoling squeeze of his hand. "If you're dreading having to endure a rustic territorial party, we'll only stay long enough to make the *vaqueros* happy. I promise."

Nellie gazed up at him. "How long will that be?"

Hours, she hoped to hear. *Days. Years and years and years.*

But Everett didn't seem to understand. "Not long," he said brusquely, then he offered her a smile and took her away.

Chapter Seven

When Everett saw Nellie glance up at him and, in her sweet and undeniably sensuous voice, ask him how long they'd have to tolerate the *vaqueros'* engagement party in their honor, he couldn't help being gutted. He'd wanted her to *want* to accompany him there. He'd wanted her to *yearn* to be by his side—the way he increasingly longed to be by hers—no matter where they went.

Instead her dolefully voiced question had let Everett know unequivocally that no matter how sophisticated he tried to be, he could never be the man Nellie wanted. He could never be the man she needed. He could never, ever, be the man she loved.

But that didn't mean Everett intended to quit trying.

Because Everett Bannon, in his heart of hearts, was not a man who quit. When Nellie had arrived, he'd felt reborn. His reaction to her, contradictorily, had proved he could not stop.

There was too much at stake to stop. Everett had thought he could stop caring, stop wanting, stop needing; now, with Nellie nearby, he could do nothing else. He'd thought he was done with living cheerfully and well; with Nellie at his side, every new moment was a celebration. He'd thought there was nothing more for him to discover; with Nellie there to provoke laughter and surprise and contradictory reactions to everything, Everett knew, beyond a doubt, there was *everything* left to discover.

All the world's secrets could be found in Nellie's heart.

Everett knew he could unlock them. All he had to do was try. He knew he could win. All he had to do was throw himself into every manner of mad shenanigans and prewedding hoopla.

So, over the course of his *vaqueros'* rowdy jamboree—and at all of the many events that followed it over the next several days—Everett did exactly that.

He indulged every tradition. He tried every good-luck charm. He got fitted for a wedding suit, wore a "fruitfulness-enhancing" leafy Slavic headpiece, and slumbered with apples, asparagus and gold coins under his pillow to ensure (variably) a happy marriage, a sweet-tongued wife and future prosperity.

He tripped his way through folkloric dances—laughing as Nellie blushed and skipped and showed admirable prowess with the complicated steps—and selected himself some trusted groomsmen. He let a roving medicine showman predict his prospects... and smiled along with Nellie when those prospects were good.

But Everett didn't restrict his efforts to bunkum like springtime flower selecting and itinerant fortune-telling. He also spent every moment he could with Nellie, talking and sharing and laughing and stealing kisses. In hardly any time at all, he could scarcely envision his household without her in it.

Simply put, Nellie *fit* there. She fit with him.

She understood the wildness and vitality and freedom of the West. She seemed to like it, too. In her hands—and with his *vaqueros'* instructions—a lasso became a thing of grace and beauty. Blessed by her smile, Everett's ranch hands and horses and hodgepodge of pets became something more than they'd been.

Thanks to Nellie, his band of miscreants became a family.

Everett didn't want to lose that. But as he sat at a late-night campfire with his entire world surrounding him—however meager it was—watching Nellie be adorned with garlands of woven flowers in some almost-forgotten marital tradition that Ivan had insisted they observe, Everett had no idea how to hold on to it.

It was possible, he knew as he smiled anew at

Nellie, that *he* was the only one who felt the pull between them. It was possible that *she*, as a citified sophisticate with more suitors than shoes, was still merely *pretending* to care about him.

If she was, Everett decided as he got to his feet to go to her, then she was doing a mighty convincing job of it. Because as he took Nellie's hand and led her away from the firelight, he could feel the heat and need between them. He could feel the unusual strength of their bond, as tenacious and surprising as the fast-growing wildflowers along the road to town. He could *know*, in his heart, that providence had brought her to him.

All he had to do now was make her his forever.

And because he was man enough to do so, Everett drew Nellie into the same space near the barn door where he'd first kissed her. He caught hold of her dewy flower garlands, then smiled.

"Pretty," he said. "But not half as beautiful as you."

He kissed her, hungrily, the way he'd dreamed of doing while watching her "prepare" for their wedding. Then Everett delved his hands in her hair and kissed her again. He needed to feel her mouth against his—needed to sweep his tongue against hers and steal the same breath and give her…*everything* he had.

"I guess they work, then," Nellie said when he

raised his head at last. Playfully she dragged her strands of flowers over his chest, his neck, his face. "They're supposed to make me irresistible to you, so that you want to have the wedding."

"Oh, I want to have the wedding." He kissed her again, letting her know with every thrust of his tongue that he spoke the truth. He pinned her against the barn's rough exterior wall, heedless of the raucous celebrating still going on near the campfire. He roved his hands over her sides, her waist, her derriere. "I want to have *you*, Nellie. I want you so much."

"Yes." Breathlessly she caressed him, too. Her hands touched his back, his nape and then his hair with what felt like wickedly seductive intent. "Oh, Everett. If only you knew!" Eagerly she kissed him. "Marybelle told me it would be *'la torture'* to wait for our wedding night. Edina warned me as well. But I never dreamed it would be like this! I wish—"

Gasping, Nellie stopped. She tossed her head while Everett pressed his lips to her neck, her earlobe, her waiting mouth.

"I wish we were getting married tomorrow!" he said roughly.

At the same time, Nellie blurted the very same thing.

In unison, they laughed, the spell of their kisses momentarily broken. This had been happening between them, too—this eerie synchronicity that suggested something more.

"See what just happened there?" Nellie pointed out with an elfin look. "*Now* do you want to discuss whether we're truly meant to be together, the way the marriage bureau claimed?"

"Shysters," Everett judged. "Fraudsters." He kissed her again, lightheartedly this time, but he couldn't help being reminded of her question to him days ago, after they'd shared their first kiss on this very same spot. Knowing she would persist—another quality he loved about Nellie—he shook his head. "I can't rightly say. I don't have my philosophy book."

And she, most likely, would expect erudition from him—scholarship and wisdom he would have stolen from one of Oscar's many books—as patently false as his need for eyeglasses.

Why in tarnation had he hatched this plan at all? Everett wondered. Right now, it was only separating him from Nellie. He couldn't truly be her man, and he wasn't sure he was helping her with her blasted newspaper story, either—despite all the note-taking and writing she'd done so far. That had impressed him, too—her dexterity with words. But for some reason, her fluent ability to describe her thoughts wasn't evident just then.

"Oh. You can't say? All right then," Nellie told

him with her usual sprightliness. "Maybe you'll tell me later."

It was her customary rejoinder—one that, Everett had learned, signified disappointment as much as resignation. He wished the two didn't come so automatically to Nellie.

He wished harder that she wouldn't feel them at all.

He wasn't sure what he'd done to upset her—and the tempting curve of her mouth prevented him, quite reasonably, from delving into the matter any further. Driven by craving and passion and a need to assure Nellie that he *did* care for her, even if he didn't have the fancy authorial words to say so, Everett kissed her again. He held her close. He let his actions speak as best as they could, in the darkness surrounding his barn and his land and his poor woebegone heart, and if gestures had meanings, then his kisses meant everything. They were promises. And entreaties.

"Come away with me, Nellie," he urged in a husky voice. "Just for the night. Come away, right now. No one will know—"

"*Everyone* will know. Your household is overflowing!"

Everett shook his head. "If we slip away now, no one will see. They're busy weaving Russian flower garlands."

"I saw Ivan give one to Edina," she said chattily. "Do you think they'll be next to be engaged?" Then, looking up at him, Nellie seemed to realize how inadequate her attempts to distract him were. "Not that *we're* truly engaged, but you know—"

"Please." He sweetened his request with another kiss. In his arms, Nellie was pliant and warm and breathless, and he knew she was close to agreeing. "We'll be alone all night."

"Alone? Together?" Her gaze looked tremulous. "But I—"

"Say yes, Nellie. I can tell that you want to. I—"

I want to, too! Everett meant to say, but before he could, Nellie sharpened her gaze. She pulled back abruptly.

"You *can't* tell that about me. You can't! Even if I *am* outside a barn kissing you, I'm a good woman, Everett," Nellie insisted. Sudden tears swam in her eyes. Her chin wobbled. "I am! Maybe not *exactly* the kind of woman you said you wanted—"

"Precisely the kind I wanted," he swore, feeling his meager powers of volubility deserting him like dandelion fluff on a seedtime breeze. *"You're* the woman I want, Nellie! Why else—"

Why else would I be wearing spectacles and a suit? Everett wanted to shout. *Why else would I carry around books and sleep with apples under my head?* But again Nellie cut him short.

"If this is a test, I hope I've passed," she said.

He boggled at her. "A test? Of what?"

Nellie crossed her arms over her chest, making him miss the feel of her arms around *him*. A long moment passed. The balmy April breezes lifted her skirt hem and ruffled Everett's shirt. A coyote howled. In the gloom, Nellie's face turned downcast.

"I have a great deal of work to do," she declared. "Our 'wedding' is just days away, and I've scarcely written enough material to fill a single column inch at the *Weekly Leader*."

"You're thinking of work? *Now?*"

"Well." With a single backward step, Nellie seemed to put a mile's worth of distance between them. "That's what I'm here to do, isn't it? Although we ought to discuss how to break off our 'engagement,'" she went on in a reasonable-sounding tone. "I think *you* should be the one to do it, on account of your—"

"I *won't* do it!" This time, it was Everett's turn to fold his arms over his chest. He glowered at Nellie, hoping she could sense the depth of his dislike of that notion. He wasn't ready for this. "Are you saying you don't want to get married?"

"Are you saying you *do*?"

Caught, Everett frowned. He wanted to cast aside his pretenses, show himself for the man he was…

be *loved* for the man he was. If he was honest with himself, that was *all* he wanted.

Despite that, fear held him silent.

Fear held him silent, stubborn…and woefully alone.

No right-thinking woman wants to live on a hard-scrabble ranch with a burly, unrefined oaf for a husband, Everett, he remembered Abbey O'Neill telling him all those months ago.

Honestly. Did you think I would settle for this? For you?

He couldn't ask Nellie to make the sacrifice that Abbey had refused. Nellie was better than Abbey—better than anyone he knew. Everett couldn't ask her to throw away her work, her talent, her dazzling life in the city, all for his sake.

What he *could* do was sacrifice, this night, for her.

"Let's see this through a few more days," he said. "That will be enough time—" *to get a return train ticket, savor our last few hours together, stamp your memory on my heart, where it can never be erased* "—to put things as they should be."

At that, Nellie's wounded gaze swerved to his. She gave him an unsteady smile. She reached for his hand. Her touch felt more necessary than the air Everett breathed…more heartbreaking than all the moments leading up to this had been or ever would be.

"Gentlemanly to the end?" Nellie said with a faint nod of approbation. She inhaled deeply, then nodded. "I understand."

Everett didn't want her to understand. He wanted her to come away with him, to be with him...to love him. But if this was what he got instead, he vowed to make the most of it.

"You won't want this later," Nellie said in a confusingly wry and self-deprecating tone, "so I'll give it to you now."

Still holding his hand, she levered upward. She looked into his eyes, brought her mouth to his, then kissed him. Softly. Slowly. Sweetly. He'd have sworn her heart and soul was in that one point of contact between them...but as soon as Everett had that fanciful thought and opened his eyes to verify it, she was gone. All he could glimpse in the darkness around him were shadows and faraway flickers, too hazy to make out or hold on to.

Then the darkness filled with sound of a strumming guitar. A dozen hoarse male voices raised in song. Everett knew then that fate had recognized Nellie's departure, too. The song on the air was one his *vaqueros* had written specifically for her on the day of her arrival in Morrow Creek. They played it now like a love song. Like an epic ballad. Like one of the sonnets that Everett had tried—and bungled—reading to Nellie himself.

Inhaling a fortifying breath, Everett joined in, too. After all that Nellie had given him, it was the least he could do.

At least it was…for now.

Chapter Eight

From the night of the campfire onward, Nellie's course of action was plain. She couldn't spend any more time laughing with Everett, exploring his ranch hand in hand, or learning about esoteric wedding customs and the quirky traditions of his *vaqueros'* diverse homelands. As much as she'd loved getting to know Everett and his life in the West, she had to move on.

The strain she'd been under—and the way she'd cracked under that strain when Everett had asked her to slip away with him that fateful night—had made that truth more than evident. She wasn't cut out to be a rancher's compliant wife. The effort of pretending she was was devastating, both to her and to Everett.

Nellie knew, in retrospect, that he hadn't been disrespectful of her. Likely *he'd* felt the connection between them, too…and had wanted to deepen it by being alone together.

In her heart of hearts, Nellie had wanted that, too.

But then, as now, she hadn't been able to face that. She hadn't been able to let Everett throw away his future on an impulse fueled by a single tender moment and a moonlit spring night. Everett deserved more than that. He deserved more than a tomboyish wife who loved his ribald jokes more than his sonnet readings, his rolled-sleeve Henley shirts more than his neckties and suits, and his wide-open lands more than his tidy library. He deserved...*everything*. Everything Nellie couldn't give him.

Everett would never be happy with a hoydenish wife like her, Nellie knew. And she couldn't change her ways—not lastingly, at least. It gave her too much pleasure to tramp through the fields, twirl her heavy borrowed lasso and watch the mustangs run. She didn't want to make either of them miserable; that's what staying together would accomplish. Yet, contradictorily, Everett refused to end their engagement.

He *had* to be the one to do so! In the same way that he'd categorically refused to discuss canceling their wedding, Nellie refused to humiliate him the same way Miss O'Neill had. She refused to run. She refused to toss him away heartlessly.

The only thing to do was to make Everett reject *her*. And the only way to do *that* was simple to discern.

Nellie had to let him see *her*. The real her.

The unconventional, boots-wearing, unacceptable *her.*

So, when Everett happened upon her practicing her new lasso-twirling skills with his ranch hands' help, Nellie spun that hank of braided leather with twice her usual vigor. When she accompanied Everett to their next round of engagement parties and traditional soirees and prewedding activities, she strode ahead of him with stamina and enthusiasm. When dining, Nellie shunned delicate pastries and pies in favor of spicy dishes full of chilis; when dancing, she moved with abandon; when relaxing in the evenings, she forewent her earlier attempts at ladylike needlework and substituted pen and paper instead.

"Read to me what you've written," Everett said on one of those nights. And because Nellie was trying to make him see how unsuitable she truly was for him, she went ahead and did so.

When she'd finished, she lowered her paper. "Well?"

"You have a knack for detail and an evocative turn of phrase. You're even more talented than I thought, Nellie."

Flabbergasted, she stared at him. "You're supposed to say, 'Those are silly scribblings,' or 'Describe the dresses more.'"

"Your article is an exposé of mail-order marriage bureaus," Everett said mildly. "It's not about dresses."

"But a tidbit about fashionable reticules could probably be worked in someplace," she retorted. "Isn't that correct?"

With big hazel eyes, Everett gazed at her as though she were mad. "Are those the kinds of things you usually hear?"

Defensively she jutted her chin. "Sometimes. Of course."

"The only 'of course' thing about that is that you've been listening to the wrong people," Everett told her. Then he adjusted his spectacles and went back to reading his book.

"German philosophy isn't usually read upside down," Nellie pointed out huffily. "And your eyeglasses are on crooked."

But Everett only smiled at her and went on reading.

Her other efforts to make him end their engagement were similarly futile. Nellie kissed him in the upstairs hallway, late at night after everyone else had gone to sleep, hoping to prove how horribly unladylike she was…and had nearly succeeded in starting a house fire with her own body heat for her trouble. She took to showing off her muddy boots, loudly proclaiming her ineptness at cookery and boldly feeding the mustangs carrots.

Everett only watched her with an implacable expression and said, variously, "My boots are muddy, too." Then, "Edina would bawl if you tried to take away her biscuit-making bowl." And finally, blithely, "Watch your fingers. That one bites."

In despair, and with only days left until their "wedding," Nellie finally snatched up a bottle of Old Orchard from the hidden stash in the kitchen, marched out to the eastern barn and proceeded to make herself unavoidably, unfemininely drunk.

Unfortunately Everett found her before she got very far.

"You might have invited me here for a drink yourself," he said as he sauntered inside, limned by the afternoon light from the window in the hayloft, looking handsome and broad-shouldered and breathtakingly necessary for her overall happiness, "rather than leading me on this wild-goose chase." He put his hands on his hips. "Marybelle told me you were down by the creek."

"Aha!" Wild-eyed, Nellie pointed the whiskey bottle at him. "That's what I *told* her to tell you! It was a clever diversion."

"Well, I can't say you weren't thorough." With something akin to admiration, Everett came nearer. He sat on a hay bale beside her, close enough that she could smell his intoxicating shaving soap. "Edina claimed you were at the telegraph office in town. Ivan insisted you were hiding *bizcochitos* in the attic. Oscar said you'd gone to become a dance-hall girl at Jack Murphy's saloon." He grinned. "His was the most entertaining."

"I see." After taking another bitter swig from her bottle, Nellie hugged it to her chest. Inside she felt hollow and desperate—but also a tiny bit hopeful, too. Did Everett's continued pursuit of her mean he cared…a little? "Is that all?"

A chuckle. "Not by a long shot." Squinting roguishly at the bunting and ribbons overhead, Everett recalled more details for her. "Several men pointed me toward the mountains, claiming you'd found a gold strike. Pedro challenged me to a duel, simply for asking about you. He said he would fight for your honor."

"That's sweet. And Casper?"

"Casper confessed everything in five seconds flat. Then he spent the next fifteen minutes begging forgiveness for deceiving me in the first place." A sardonic grin. "That boy hasn't got a sneaky bone in his body."

"Humph. I guess that's how you found me in here, then?"

"No." Shaking his head, Everett gazed fondly at her. His face was clean-shaven, his hair unmussed, his suit rigorously tidy. She longed for the Everett Bannon she'd *first* met—rugged, straight-talking and a little bit wild. "I saw you go in here."

"Then why did you question everyone else?"

"I wanted to see how far their loyalties went."

"Oh." Nellie considered that. "How far did they go?"

"All the way to *defying me* and back." Everett seemed put out by that—and a little bit amused, too. "I never thought I'd see the day. I told you—they all love you." Illustratively he angled his head toward the barn door. "I'll have you know, there are six horses, one cat, one dog and a hungry stray bunny outside right now, all waiting for you to come out."

But *Everett* wasn't waiting for her, Nellie couldn't help thinking. And that was all that mattered to her, now and later and all the painful times in between. *Everett* didn't want her.

At least he didn't want the real her. The *wild* her.

Maybe the original Everett she'd met would have…

Banishing the thought, Nellie gave her Old Orchard bottle a rebellious swish, readying herself for more. She didn't really want to drink any more. To her, whiskey tasted like vinegar…only slightly *less* toothsome. But this was her last-ditch effort to do the right thing by Everett, and she didn't want to fail.

"I don't even like bunnies," Nellie lied. Then, screwing up her face, she valiantly took another hefty swallow of whiskey.

Reflexively she shuddered. Everett gave a knowing laugh.

"It's a good thing the bunnies have the sense to like you anyway, despite all your protests," he said. "Just like the rest of us do." Quietly he covered her hand with his. He squeezed. "Before you get too out of hand, give over that bottle."

Defiantly she clasped it harder. "If you're wanting to be paid for it, I can do that. I have my own money, you know."

"I don't want to be paid for it." Everett peered at its sloshy, foul-tasting contents. "Besides, I wouldn't have the first idea how much to charge for two and a half swallows."

"Humph. I have an excellent job at the newspaper," Nellie informed him proudly, beginning to feel the disorienting effects of the whiskey despite Everett's low estimation of her consumption so far. "Did I ever tell you how I got my job?"

"You did not. I'd like to know."

She examined him, decided he meant it sincerely and loved him a little bit more because of it. "I read a horribly offensive and sexist article in the *Leader* and wrote to the editor in protest. He liked my writing well enough to offer me a job."

"I'm impressed."

Not enough to marry me! her poor sorrowful heart cried, but Nellie forged on in spite of it. "When I arrived and he realized I was a woman, he rescinded his offer." She heard Everett's swearword in response to that and smiled in acknowledgment. "It took me all afternoon to persuade him to hire me. But I did it."

"I don't doubt you did." For a moment, all Everett did was gaze at her, proudly, affectionately and—if she wasn't mistaken—sadly, too. "You're an extraordinary woman, Nellie. Truly."

At that, she scoffed. Everett's sad, stoic tone scared her. She didn't understand it. She didn't want to. And yet…

"If *I'm* so extraordinary, why do *you* sound so miserable?"

"Because—" Everett began, then he broke off. He squeezed her hand in his again. "Because I don't want any of this."

That was blunt. The depth of her despair upon hearing his words shocked her. Morosely Nellie stared at the dust motes floating in a beam of sunshine. The barn would never host a wedding now. It looked so lovely, yet it would remain empty.

She'd *so* wanted it to be filled to the rafters with the wedding vows that she and Everett would exchange. Her heart hurt with the effort it required to suppress her longing for that.

"I don't want to hold you back," Everett was saying, "and I don't want the world to be without your newspaper stories."

She had the impression he'd been talking and

she'd missed something. Perhaps, Nellie realized belatedly, she was more susceptible to the effects of demon drink than she'd thought.

"Don't worry," she told him, doing her best not to weep. "Everything in my story will be positive. None of it will reflect poorly on you or your *vaqueros* or your *hacienda*." Drawing in an empowering breath, Nellie squared her shoulders. She even, miraculously, managed to sound composed. "It turns out that I was wrong about mail-order marriage bureaus. They're not frauds. They really can find ideal matches for people. I know that because they found me *you*, and I feel that *we, together*—"

To her dismay, her throat closed up on the words. Nellie could not speak. She couldn't see through the haze of tears filling her eyes, either. Drat! Why was this so difficult?

Doing the right thing was supposed to be, if not easier, then at least heartening. But Nellie didn't feel heartened. Sitting there, close enough to feel Everett's warmth and hear his breath and know his kindness, she only felt...alone.

So alone. And sad. And hopeless and tipsy and bereft.

"You asked me before if I thought we were meant to be together," Everett was saying now, forcing her to recall those times she'd foolishly shared her feelings—her fantasies that somehow, some way, they were *destined* for one another. "I didn't have an answer for you then. But now I do." He drew in a ragged breath. Then, "The answer is no, Nellie. It has to be no."

Stunned, she let his words wash over her. As gently said as they were, they threw into harsh relief her earlier hopes that Everett's pursuit of her, here to the barn, meant he cared.

That her inability to drive him away...meant he cared.

Wordlessly Nellie nodded. The motion made her tears fall on their joined hands. Embarrassed, she pulled away.

But Everett reclaimed her hand. Urgently he pressed something in her grasp. "That's why I got you this," he said, sounding hoarse and angry and bewilderingly formal. "So you can be happy. So you can go back to the city and be happy."

Dazed, Nellie opened her hand. A train ticket lay there.

Everett was sending her away. Here, in the place they were supposed to have been married—if her daydreams had come true—he was giving her the ticket he'd promised. He did not love her.

She'd succeeded.

Victory had never felt more bittersweet.

"I see." With tremendous determination, Nellie

stood. She wobbled a bit, but she did it. She nodded. "Thank you, Everett."

Through her teary vision, she glimpsed his expression. He appeared aghast—probably at having provoked her tears at all. Men, her editor had informed her, did not like emotional women.

Unfortunately he'd also said there was no other kind.

For no good reason other than the fact that she was at a loss for what to do next, Nellie handed Everett the bottle.

"If you'll excuse me," she said, "I think I might be ill."

"Oh! I'll help you." Sounding aggrieved, Everett stood. Gentlemanly to the end, just as she'd suspected, he reached for her. "Let me help you. I'm sorry, Nellie! Let me help. Please."

But Nellie Trent hadn't been an unconventional, inconvenient, tomboyish woman all her life for no reason. The reason was, it turned out, that her sporting ways allowed her to run. So before Everett could touch her—before he could break her heart all over again by pitying her—Nellie turned and ran away.

Forever.

Chapter Nine

With his head in his hands and his unwanted whiskey bottle on the kitchen table in front of him, Everett moaned in agony.

"Why?" he groaned. "Why did it take me so long to see what was happening?" An idea occurred to him. With extreme bias, he wrenched off his stupid borrowed eyeglasses. He hurled the spectacles away from him, letting them *clink* to a stop on the oak tabletop near Marybelle's basket of clean laundry. "It's probably these damn spectacles," Everett groused. "I could hear that Nellie was upset, but I couldn't see what was wrong. I was confused. It was dark. She'd been drinking. Drinking!"

He had actually driven a good woman to drink, Everett realized. He was a monster. However, drinking sounded like a fine idea for the likes of him, Everett realized tardily. He grabbed the Old Orchard. He took a searing, useless glug.

It didn't help. He was still faced with the reality

that he'd sent away Nellie—likely crushing her heart in the process—and he didn't have the first idea how to remedy the problem.

Why hadn't she been *thrilled* to return to San Francisco, the way he'd thought she would be? Why had she *cried* instead?

Could it be that she *hadn't* been pretending to care about him? If it was, he'd been a fool to push her away.

Melancholically Everett looked up. At least a dozen of his *vaqueros* stared back at him—most of them with distinct belligerence, resentment, or some combination of the two.

"If you want sympathy, *patrón*," Pedro announced, crossing his arms sulkily, "you won't get it from us. We miss Nellie."

"Da," Ivan said, apparently too riled up to eat for once. "This is not the way springtime wedding fever is supposed to go. This is not the way Edina said it would be. Right, Edina?"

"Absolutely!" The cook stepped up to the big Russian's side, stalwartly laying her hand on his shoulder. "The boys went to all that trouble to make everything perfect for you and Nellie, and you ruined it."

At her words, Everett flinched. He drank more whiskey.

"I was lying for part of it," he told her brokenly.

"She wanted an answer from me. When it comes to Nellie, the answer is always 'yes!' *Always* 'yes!'" Everett babbled, awash in raw-feeling memories. "But if I'd said that, she'd have stayed."

"Then that's what you should have done," Marybelle said staunchly. "You should have said 'yes' a thousand times."

His housekeeper was right. She was right a thousand times. And yet… "I couldn't let her stay," Everett insisted in his own defense, unable to reconcile his good intentions with the calamity that had just occurred. "I *tried* to help Nellie once I realized she was crying, but she was fast. Too fast for me."

"She was too *perfect* for you, you mean," Oscar accused with his expression unforgivingly flinty. "Nellie was poetry and light and hope and joy! And *you, patrón,* are—"

"Gonna git her back," Casper interrupted gaily. "Right?"

They all stared expectantly at Everett. He frowned.

"Springtime wedding fever is not about misguided sacrifice and broken hearts and cast-off eyeglasses," Marybelle urged him. "It is a time for *l'amour* and kisses and wedding dresses!"

She traded a look with Edina, reminding Everett that his housekeeper and cook had been diligently at work on a gown for Nellie. She'd even tried it on, he knew. The women had all shooed him from the house before he caught an "unlucky" glimpse of her wearing it. Now, Everett wished he'd looked anyway.

It would have been a memory worth keeping close forever.

"I don't have 'springtime wedding fever,'" he grumbled, irked to have his feelings for Nellie reduced to the equivalent of a bout of sniffles. "That's nothing more than a myth."

"*Sí*. What you've got is *nada*," Pedro said fiercely. "No Nellie, no wedding, and no good reason for any of it."

But Everett did have a reason. "She would not have been happy here," he told them stonily. "She is a citified woman. She needs a citified man. A man like Astair Prestell. Someone who—"

"Someone who will bore her to tears with useless jabbering and endless pomposity?" Edina inquired. "That kind of someone?"

Everett slumped. "A gentleman," he stated carefully. "Who—"

"A gentleman who wears suits?" Casper inquired, an oddly comprehending look on his face. "A gentleman who wears specs and neckties? A gentleman who shaves twice a day and totes around a boring ol' inch-thick book everyplace? That kinda 'gentleman'?" Wrinkling his brows, Casper gestured at Everett. "'Cause you already are one of them, *patrón*. You made yourself into one."

Everett shook his head. "It's fakery. It's all fakery. I'm no more a gentleman than my mustangs out there are," he said. "Nellie deserves better. She deserves…*everything*."

His *vaqueros* glared judgmentally at him. So did Edina and Marybelle. Everett fancied that even his cat and dog scowled.

"You are wrong about Nellie," Oscar said, cutting straight to the heart of the matter. "She is not like Miss O'Neill. She does not want a *Schwätzer* like Astair Prestell for a husband."

"*Non.* Indeed, she does not!" Marybelle nodded vehemently.

Everyone else only gawked at her. There was silence.

Then, "You know what *Schwätzer* means?" Edina asked, turning wide-eyed to her friend. "How on earth do you know that? I mean, Oscar said it like it was something awful, so I guess we all agreed with that part, but you seemed to know it for certain."

Coyly Marybelle said, "I may have been studying *Deutsch*."

Oscar brightened. "*Wirklich?* Marybelle, that is *wunderbar!*" He smiled at her. "I am very impressed by you."

The housekeeper smiled serenely. *"Vielen Dank."*

At that, Oscar seemed almost beside himself with

joy. He grinned at Marybelle. She cast him a flirtatious glance back.

"Well, I reckon Edina and Ivan ain't gonna be the only ones gettin' themselves hitched soon," Casper said gleefully. "Do you s'ppose you can line up weddings like whiskeys and do 'em one right after another? 'Cause the barn's already decorated—"

"There aren't going to be any weddings," Everett interrupted harshly. "Not this week. Not in my barn." He didn't think he could stand it. Not after all that had happened. "I made a hash of things with Nellie. She's gone. It's too late."

"Patrón." Pedro tsk-tsked. "It is *never* too late for *amor."*

"That might be true for Edina and Ivan," Everett agreed. "And for Marybelle and Oscar." Although he was still dumbfounded by their budding romances, he was pleased for all four of them. "But it's not true for me. I know what I'm not, and I'm *not* what Nellie needs. No matter how much I want her, I can't—"

"How do you know?" Ivan asked bluntly.

"How do I know what?" Everett gulped more whiskey. It still didn't help. His *vaqueros'* sour moods didn't help, either.

"How do you know you're not what she needs?" Edina clarified, easily seeming to understand what Ivan had meant.

Wistfully Everett remembered when he and Nellie

had shared a similar synchronicity. The recollection made him feel worse.

With the last of his patience, Everett tried explaining *again* about Miss O'Neill—about her judgments about his ranch and his character and what right-thinking women wanted and needed.

He didn't get far.

"That is *absurdité*! You must fight for the woman you love!"

Oscar's outburst earned him a startled gasp from Marybelle. In an aside to her, the gallant *vaquero* confided, "I may have been learning some of *le française*, as well. For you."

In response, the housekeeper swooned. Oscar winked.

That was it, Everett decided. The world had gone crazy.

Oscar did not wink; he was far too solemn for that. His ranch hands did *not* berate him; they were much too deferential to do so. And he did not, it occurred to him, have to stay here and listen to this. Resolutely Everett pushed back his chair.

Unsteadily he rose, bottle in hand. "I'm leaving."

"Yahoo!" Casper leaped to accompany him. "I'm going, too!"

Everett blinked. "Going where?"

"To fetch Nellie, of course."

"I'm not going to fetch Nellie."

But his *vaqueros* and Edina and Marybelle had already assembled themselves to accompany him. Eagerly they waited.

"You must!" Marybelle urged. "Go get her."

Everett scowled. "I wouldn't begin to know how."

"Apologize," Edina said readily. "Sweep her off her feet. Ask her to go away with you! It will be romantic."

"I already tried to get Nellie to go away with me," Everett said, remembering that balmy moonlit night. "She told me no."

Nellie's rejection of him then had solidified all his fears—that she didn't want him, couldn't love him, didn't need him. Everett didn't want a second dose of that hurtful tonic.

"The old ways have a solution for this, *patrón*," Pedro said. "If you are not sure of your lady's affections, you must—"

"No more traditions." Stanchly Everett held up his hand, cutting off Pedro before his *vaquero* could finish. "No more customs. No more wedding fripperies." He scoured them all with a pain-filled look. "Haven't you all done enough?"

For a moment, they lapsed into regretful stillness.

Then, from Ivan: "*We* have done enough, *patrón*. Have you?"

Everett frowned. About to insist that he *had* done enough—because he *had* loved Nellie, and he *had* tried to do what was right by her, and he *had* believed the right thing was sending her away—Everett was forced to reconsider.

He'd accepted this whole imbroglio the way he'd done everything else so far in his life—with curmudgeonly equanimity. He hadn't tried to fight. He hadn't done anything except enjoy Nellie's company...and then send her away. Maybe it was time, Everett decided, to fight for what he wanted—to fight for *Nellie*, no matter what the risk was to him.

She was worth it. Together, *they* were worth it.

With a decisive gesture, Everett set down his whiskey bottle. He reached for his hat, then tugged down the brim.

"This 'old ways' solution," he asked Pedro. "What is it?"

He could scarcely hear the specifics over the din of celebratory whoops and shouts from his improvised family. But before very long, Everett figured he had enough...if he combined it all with love and courage and a little bit of luck, besides.

It should have been her wedding day, Nellie realized as she paused over her satchel with an armful of petticoats. It should have been her time to declare her love for Everett, dance amid the hay bales beneath his barn's ribbon-bedecked timbers, and find out if Edina and Marybelle were right about the fun to be had during a raucous midnight chiverie.

She should have been finding out what Everett really *did* wear to sleep in…how he felt in her arms and how she felt in his. She should have been loving him. Instead, Nellie reckoned morosely, she was packing for a return trip to San Francisco that she did not want. She was preparing to go back to a life that had never felt emptier or—paradoxically—more constricting.

She was giving up before she'd truly gotten started.

If she could have packed away her feelings as readily as she'd packed away her belongings, things might have been different, Nellie knew as she stuffed in her petticoats and snapped shut her satchel's latch. But she couldn't stop thinking about Everett. She couldn't stop wishing things could have been different between them. She couldn't stop wondering *why* he'd finally decided to give her that train ticket and send her away.

In her most fearful moments, Nellie believed it was because Everett had glimpsed the real her… and then disapproved. But—

A banging sound outside her window cut short her thoughts.

Nellie jumped, staring in that direction. She had arranged this hotel room—admittedly hastily— after leaving Everett's ranch yesterday. Everyone had assured her that the Lorndorff Hotel was reputable. She'd been promised she would be safe there until it was time for her train's departure.

The thumping sound came again, louder this time.

Evidently, Nellie realized, she'd been misinformed. Someone—or something—was outside her hotel room window.

But she had not traipsed across several states and territories on her own during her time as a reporter for the *Weekly Leader* to surrender meekly to any threat. With a second glance at her packed satchels, she judged her escape route to the door and then lifted her chin with inherent pugnaciousness.

She'd been through too much to back down now, Nellie decided. Whoever was outside the window of her hotel room had chosen the wrong woman to pester this morning.

It might feel…*invigorating* to confront whatever was happening outside, Nellie thought as she eyed the drawn draperies with her fists tight, and assert herself against it.

Likely it was a squirrel. Or a cat. Or yet another bunny. Everett hadn't been utterly wrong about her erstwhile menagerie.

Just in case, Nellie armed herself. She stood tall.

A shadow crossed her window. More thumping could be heard.

The window sash lifted. Before she could yell for

help or even reconsider her position, a dark-haired man stepped inside.

Nellie gawked at him. "*Everett? Is that you?*"

At her outburst, he turned around fully. He *looked* like Everett. Except he was dressed in rugged canvas pants and a white Henley shirt, not a suit and tie. And he wasn't wearing spectacles. And his hair was all mussed from climbing inside. And she'd have sworn he was sporting three days' growth of beard, even though it had only been yesterday since she'd seen him.

"You look so...wild," Nellie blurted. "And so *manly!*"

The devilish grin he threw her only reinforced that rogue impression. "This is who I am, Nellie," Everett said. "I'm wild and I'm rough and I don't wear eyeglasses. I don't like suits and I've never written poetry and I can't abide wine."

Frozen in place and entirely unsure what to do next, Nellie clutched the makeshift weapon she'd grabbed: a broom left over from a maid's recent hotel room visit. It wobbled in her grasp.

Audaciously Everett eyed it. "What are you going to do with that?" He grinned again. "Clean up my muddy footprints?"

"Better yours than mine." With nothing left to lose, Nellie stuck out her boys' boots proudly. "This is who *I* am, Everett. I'm ambitious and smart and I don't like sewing. I loathe *Godey's Lady's Book* and I've never had a fainting spell. Ever."

He nodded. "Did you finish writing your article?"

"I forwarded it to my editor already, along with a proposal that I be allowed to work on a freelance basis. I know more than ever now that writing about parties and hors d'oeuvres will never make me happy." Still confused by seeing him there, Nellie set aside her broom. "I'm not planning to stay in town, if that's what you're wondering," she assured him. "I'm leaving shortly—"

"I have a better idea." Everett held out his hand. It trembled slightly. "Come with me, Nellie. *Be* with me. Please."

Even more perplexed by that, she wrinkled her brow. "Didn't you hear me? I just told you I *don't* like sewing. I *don't* like ladylike pursuits like reading about fashion and giggling inanely. So I can't imagine why in the world you would—"

Love me in spite of it all, Nellie finished silently.

"I know. And I love that about you," Everett said.

She blinked. "I must have gotten tipsier than I thought. I thought you just said—" She stopped. "No. I'm imagining you."

At that, he gave a husky chuckle. "Tipsy? Over two and a half swallows of whiskey? Yesterday? I doubt it."

"But I must be!" *Because you're here.* "I must—"

"Come with me, Nellie." Again Everett offered his hand. He wiggled his fingers enticingly. "Springtime is a time for second chances, and I'm asking you for mine, right now. I'm sorry for what happened yesterday. I'll try never to hurt you again. I didn't understand—I should have asked you what you wanted, instead of trying to decide for myself what you wanted."

Nellie frowned anew. "I *like* being outdoors, Everett," she specified with her heart pounding, just so he'd be sure to know the truth. She couldn't move on until she knew he understood. "I like hearing your bawdy jokes, and I like kissing you and I like *you*, so much, in every way, boldly and unstoppably and in no way politely, and I know that makes me less than perfect—"

"You're wrong," Everett told her with evident certainty. This time, he didn't wait for her to take his hand. *He* caught hold of *hers*, then he squeezed her tightly. "You *are* perfect, Nellie. I can't believe you'd think anything else."

"But I don't know how to embroider," Nellie pointed out, quite notably, she thought. "Surely you'll want a wife who—"

"I want *you*," Everett said. "And if you want me, too, then nothing else matters. Not eyeglasses or boots or bustles."

Entirely overwhelmed by that, Nellie gazed at him.

"I didn't like your spectacles," she confessed. "Or your suits. Or your poetry readings. I like you best as you are right now."

"Fine. I'll give away my eyeglasses, hide away my suits and never read a sonnet again. Now can we run away together?"

At that, she laughed. "You can't mean it."

"I just climbed to the second floor of this hotel, opened your window and came inside," Everett pointed out, looking more rascally—and more irresistible—than ever. "I mean it." His grin broadened handsomely. "In case you hadn't noticed, Miss Trent, I'm officially kidnapping you. This is a romantic, unplanned elopement we're having. The least you could do is cooperate."

"If you want cooperation," Nellie said sassily, a little of her verve returning with him, "then you've got the wrong girl."

Then she realized the astonishing thing he'd just told her, and the truth hit her at once. *This* was the kidnapping tradition Edina and Marybelle had told her about! This was… It was…

It was *Everett*, showing her he loved her with a wedding to prove it or without one. And right now, given the way she'd been dithering, he probably believed it would be without one.

Without *her*.

All she knows is that she has to make a choice,

Edina had said about the traditional bride in the scenario she'd been describing days ago. *And if she chooses wrong, the glorious wedding she's been dreaming about will go up in smoke.* Poof!

At the remembrance, Nellie shook her head. She glanced at Everett next, saw the heartrending vulnerability in his face, and knew that this choice was no real choice at all.

"I would rather have *you* than all the fancy weddings in the world," she told Everett truthfully. "I would rather be by your side in a horrible rainstorm than inside, alone by a cozy fire, without you. I would rather take my chances loving you—"

"*Loving me?* Did you just say—"

"—than know I would be blessed by leaving you. If it comes down to you or a beautiful barn wedding...I choose you, Everett. I choose *you* every time, again and again. I choose you. Forever."

Again, he asked, "Did you just say 'loving me'?"

His astounded expression almost broke her heart. "Not yet. Not exactly. But I do." Impulsively Nellie took his face in her hands. She gazed into his eyes and spoke every truth she'd ever tried to hide. "I love you, Everett. I love your strength and your generosity and your way of tugging down your hat when you decide something important. I love your smile. I love your hands. I love your bristly beard stubble—" here, she rubbed her palm delightedly over it and discovered that it felt both soft *and* scratchy "—and I love your gruff ways and your tender heart. I love *you*, Everett! If I ever gave you cause to doubt that, I'm truly sorry. It was only because I was afraid. I was afraid you wouldn't love me back. But now you're here—"

"I'm here because I love you back," he said simply.

"—and everything is all right because of it." Decisively Nellie turned. She snatched up her satchels. With one in each hand, she bit her lip, then gazed inquisitively at Everett. "Do I jump in your arms now? Do you carry me over the threshold? Do we walk away arm in arm? What happens next?"

His intent, loving gaze swept over her. "Next I tell you I love you, Nellie. Because I do." Bravely Everett inhaled. "I love your smile and your vitality and your touch. I love that you can keep up with me. I love that you keep me on my toes!" He delivered a chuckle that warmed her clean through. "I love your kindness and your graciousness. I love your knack for writing and your talent with a lasso. I love…everything about you."

He brought her close, then confirmed his words with a kiss. With her hands still full of her baggage and her heart still full of her newfound second chance at love, Nellie could only hold on…and kiss Everett back with all her soul.

"As far as what comes next goes," Everett continued, wrapping his arms around her middle and smiling, "I guess we'll have to decide that together, just like everything else."

"Well, then," Nellie said. "I have an idea."

"I'm not at all surprised," Everett told her gladly. And not long after that, she shared it with him.

Chapter Ten

Ten minutes later, Everett emerged from the front entrance of the Lorndorff Hotel with Nellie held close in his arms.

Squinting against the bright springtime sunshine, he stepped over the hotel's threshold with exquisite care, making sure there was no chance of tripping or falling. This wasn't the main door of their eventual home together, so the usual superstitions about a hapless bride bringing about bad luck on her wedding day—and hence needing to be carried over the threshold by her groom as a safeguard—didn't strictly apply. But after having been baptized in the mores of at least six different cultures' wedding traditions, Everett was taking no chances. He wanted his future with Nellie to be long and happy.

Right now, he could envision it no other way.

Secure in his arms, Nellie peered toward the street. She clutched her hastily grabbed satchels and squinted, like Everett had, against the glare. "Are they there?" she asked in a low voice, heedless of the curious townspeople who were beginning to stop and gather on the raised sidewalk nearby. "You said they'd all come with you to town. You said they'd all be there."

They're there, Everett was about to say…but then his *vaqueros* did it for him. As they had on that fateful night near the campfire, his ranch hands lifted their voices together to sing their song about Nellie. It was unaccompanied by guitar music. It was off-key and unquestionably rowdy. But it was, this time, a celebration…and to Everett, that's all that mattered.

Because Nellie loved him, and he loved her. In a world full of uncertainty and long odds and hard choices, they'd somehow had the good fortune to find one another, the audacity to fall in love…and the courage to claim that love, no matter what.

If that wasn't a miracle on the order of steam engines and ready-made shirts and good tinned beans, then Everett didn't know what was. He smiled, then set Nellie on her feet.

She set down her satchels. He straightened his shoulders. Then, hands clasped, they raised their arms in the air.

The din that greeted them was overpowering. It was loud and joyous and contained not a whit of ladylike or gentlemanly behavior—but it did contain plenty of hollering and a good deal of whooping. It came from all his ranch hands and Edina and Marybelle and all their friends and neighbors, too. And that was exactly the way Everett and Nellie liked it. Together.

"Aha. They're there," Nellie said, grinning beside him.

"You have no idea," Everett told her. "I heard that later they're planning to 'surprise' us with fireworks and mescal."

His wife-to-be—his *real* wife-to-be this time, and not his sham mail-order bride—squeezed his hand tightly.

"Not much surprises you, dearest," she teased. "Does it?"

"Only how lucky I am to have found you, sweetheart," Everett returned ably, again recognizing what she wanted. "That will surprise me for the rest of my life."

And as Everett delivered Nellie his most genuine smile yet, he knew that it was true. He *was* lucky. Beyond lucky.

"You know," Nellie mused aloud, "I think we *are* adorable."

"Yes," Everett agreed, feeling sappy and overcome, "but I'll still wallop any man who calls me cute as a june bug."

"Hmm. Then I guess, since I'm a woman, that'll just have to be *my* province." After a hug that felt as big and as strong as her generous heart, Nellie nudged Everett to head toward home. "Git your feet movin', june bug!" she said with a nudge and a saucy laugh. "We don't want to miss a minute."

"I'm piling up memories already," Everett told Nellie, picking up her satchels to carry. Then he followed her full-chisel toward their future. Because from where he stood, that future looked to be full of laughter and singing and a whole heap of loving… and, if he didn't miss his guess, a wedding night to remember, too. Reminded of that, he gave her another grin. "I aim to give you a few more memories to cherish later, too."

On the verge of being surrounded by all their *vaqueros* and friends, showered in well wishes, and feted as the savior of the most *formerly* woebegone man in Morrow Creek, Nellie stopped.

"Too late." She kissed Everett full on the mouth. "I've already started in on those happy memories. There's one now!"

Then she wrapped her arms around Everett, lifted her head at a jaunty angle and prepared to give him what he felt certain would be an interesting, invigorating and love-filled life.

Now and forever after…just the way Everett wanted.

* * * * *

Discover Pure Reading Pleasure with

Visit the Mills & Boon website for all the latest in romance

Buy all the latest releases, backlist and eBooks

Find out more about our authors and their books

Join our community and chat to authors and other readers

Free online reads from your favourite authors

Win with our fantastic online competitions

Sign up for our free monthly eNewsletter

Tell us what you think by signing up to our reader panel

Rate and review books with our star system

www.millsandboon.co.uk

 Follow us at twitter.com/millsandboonuk

 Become a fan at facebook.com/romancehq